About the Springfield Writers Group

Established in 2016, the Springfield Writers Group (SWG) is based in Brisbane, Australia. This group of emerging and established writers meet monthly over coffee and too many muffins to support each other's work and efforts toward becoming better writers. There is probably too much time spent laughing and enjoying each other's company, but we do get some work done as well. This anthology represents many months of work, learning, frustration, and joy.

Anyone wishing to contact the SWG can connect through the Queensland Writers Centre, who will forward information.

Rogues' Gallery

2020 Anthology of short stories
By members of the
Springfield Writers Group
Edited by Aiki Flinthart

To all the authors out there – both published and aspiring – don't give up.

The SWG gratefully acknowledge the traditional owners – the Jagera, Yuggera and Ugarapul peoples of Ipswich and Springfield – as the keepers of ancient knowledge and whose cultures and customs continue to nurture this land. The SWG also pays respect to Elders – past, present and future.

Rogues' Gallery edited by Aiki Flinthart

Cover artwork by Pamela Jeffs

Copyright © 2020 The Springfield Writers Group

All stories are original to this collection

A Cataloging-in-Publications entry for this title is available from the National Library of Australia.

ISBN-13: 978-0-6487736-5-8 (Trade Paperback)
ISBN-13: 978-0-6487736-4-1 (e-book)
CAT Press P/L
PO Box 3388, Darra
QLD 4076, Australia

Heartfelt thanks goes to all the authors in the Springfield Writers Group, for their enthusiasm, support, dedication and hard work. Plus their patience with my nit-picky editing (AF).

Also big thanks to our families, for their support of our hiding away for hours on end as we tried desperately to scribble a few thousand words down.

Contents

Three Door Saloon

Palmela Jeffs

JACK

I have one chance in three to secure my heart's desire. But choose wrong and I'll either be frozen in a cryotube or sent to Hell via a swing from the gallows tree.

The Long Sleep or The Long Death.

I go in knowing the odds. Just as my older sister and my father both did before me. One in three and I'm the third.

The outcome has to fall in my favour right?

My father's corpse hangs bloating in the heat. A shoelace, loosened from his boot, dangles limp in the empty space beneath his feet. Bones litter the ground under him. I turn away from the dry breeze that carries the stench of his death to me and ignore the creak of the hanging rope as his body shifts.

A memory from three nights ago—of us both huddled over our campfire—returns to me.

'Now, son,' said my father. 'The demon keeps the colours of the doors a secret. We can only guess at what your sister picked, but either way I'll choose the darkest colour. That'll cut the odds for you' His eyes glitter in the firelight. 'If we both choose wrong—then we go to Plan B.'

'You sure there's no other way to do this, Pa? I ain't got a good feelin' about it.'

'Look, Jack. I made my peace with dyin' a while back. Ever since I found out I was sick. Your sister should never have gone to that place to try an' save me.' He'd pointed to his stomach and the cancerous tumours hidden within it. 'I'm a dead man, anyhow. And I'll be damned if your sister'll be left to rot forever in a cryotube on account of me. Understand? We get her back. No matter the cost.'

No matter the cost.

The recollections of firelight and my father fade, replaced by the reality of a dusty street leading into the even dustier town of Esperance. A two-bit hovel clinging to the edge of the prairie—the arse end of the West. But what I've come for can only be found here.

The Three Door Saloon huddled at the far end of Main Street.

My palm settles on the butt of the pistol holstered at my side— the pistol I use as a lawman to protect people and property. It's tempting to go in all guns blazing, and usually I would, but this time gunpowder won't solve my problems. This time it'll need to be brains over brawn.

And I've got plenty of both to choose from.

I unpin my badge of office and pocket it. I rub my hands down the front of my vest and adjust my hat.

Time to get the job done.

#

The saloon doors hang limp from their hinges, rough and weathered as the posts holding up the sagging porch roof. I hesitate. The reality I've been ignoring suddenly hits me.

It's all distilled to this. The fate of my entire family rides on my father's horse-shit crazy plan.

The doors give way to my hand, swinging open with a squeal. Odours roll past me—whisky and tobacco smoke. It's bright inside, sunlight filtering in through the windowpanes and painting shadows across the worn floor. While not a plush establishment, it's well presented. Somehow, I expected something more sinister. But no. Dolo the Rogue Trader's saloon is full of light.

An unexpected backdrop for a man who deals in souls, wishes, and death.

I step across the threshold and into the room proper. All eyes turn. Except Dolo's. Dressed in a charcoal, pinstriped suit, he sits dealing cards to two others at the poker table—a man and a finely-dressed woman. I suppose it doesn't matter to him who walks through those doors. Only that they do.

Come in, come in, little chickens, he must think. *I love a good game of chance.*

#

DOLO

The man enters, a youngish gunslinger, but built big. At six foot tall he looks more like a bull-rider than a gunman. Pistols hang low on his hips. His eyes, dark as coal, glare from under the brim of his ten-gallon hat. His glance slews across the room falling first on the barman, who continues to polish the whiskey glasses, then past the poker table and the working girls lounging by the staircase. His gaze falls on The Wall.

The Wall. My personal gallery of victories.

The display of cryotubes, stacked vertically twenty wide and ten high, is where I store the catatonic. Well—I let them rest there until I'm desperate and running low on souls to send to Hell.

The man's gaze falls on the young red-headed girl in the highest tube. She came in last month to try her hand at the Three Doors.

The gunslinger's full red beard twitches as he considers the face of the woman. I grin. So he has come for the girl. Just like the old man did yesterday. Could this be another family member, perhaps? A brother?

How delightful. Snaring that one little woman has proven quite profitable. Because of her, I'll have three strong souls tallied this month, alone. I flick another card out onto the table. But my interest in poker has passed. Now I'm intent on a different game.

I nod to Wyatt, the barman. He's one of the lower demons in my employ and has the good fortune to almost look human, except for his slitted pupils.

He places the glass he's polishing down on the countertop. 'Mornin',' he says to the gunslinger. 'You here for the whisky or the doors?'

Red-beard's fingers twitch, like he's uncomfortable without guns in his fist. I've seen his type before. All brawn but no brains.

Red-beard tips his chin toward The Wall. 'I'm here for what those folk all came for.'

Wyatt glances over at me. I smile, long and slow. I tap my unlooked-at cards into a stack and place them neatly onto the table. My heels rock the chair back to rest on its rear legs.

'Well then, shall we be gettin' started?'

Red-Beard's gaze bores into me. Something in that gaze unsettles me. A kind of resolve I've not seen before. Most people come here with hope. But this man?

A chill coils down my spine.

My chairlegs hit the floor again with a crack. I rise, focussing on the theatrics of my game to settle my unease. 'Everyone out,' I say. My gaze shifts to Red-Beard. 'Except you.'

With a grating of chairs and the rustle of fabrics, the patrons in the saloon leave. When all is quiet, I saunter to the wall opposite the cryotube display. A heavy, red velvet curtain, its hem puddling on the floor like new spilled blood, conceals what's behind. Red-Beard's eyes burn as he watches me draw it across.

And the reason why the Three Door Saloon is named such is revealed.

Three doors fitted in the wall.

Red, white, and black.

#

JACK

The room is silent—empty—except for Dolo, his wall of collected souls and me. When the doors in the wall are revealed, those stored in the cryotubes behind me stir. Horrified, I watch them awaken, dazed, from their frozen sleep.

It takes only a moment for them to recall where they are. Their movements grow with sudden urgency. They claw at their glass prisons, screaming silently at me—perhaps telling me the cost is not worth the gain. But I can't hear them through the barrier.

I falter when my gaze falls on my sister. Josie. She kneels in her tube, tears tracking down her cheeks. Desperately, she points to her dress. Over and over. Her lips move. I can't be sure what she's saying, but imagine I know—*Not you, too.*

My father's last words echo in my mind.

No matter the cost.

It's like pulling teeth to turn away from her. But I do it, determined to see this through.

The three doors almost fill the wall. Built from simple timber slats braced across with two rusted iron belts, they seem unassuming. But I don't make the mistake of thinking that doesn't mean deadly. I rub my hand down my face and tug on my beard. The room suddenly feels hot. Sweat drips off my forehead.

I glance at Dolo. 'So how does this work?'

Dolo smiles. His teeth sharp and impossibly white. A glint of red flickers behind his green eyes and the stories I've heard about him suddenly seem like they might be true.

Demon.

Devil.

Murderer.

My hard-won resolve wavers. I re-focus on my father and Josie. I grit my teeth. 'Do I just choose?' I ask.

'First,' says Dolo. 'You need to tell me what you want.'

I glare at him. 'You know damn well why I'm here. I want my sister back.'

Dolo tilts his head. Light splinters off his oiled hair and a diamond stud pressed into his ear lobe. 'What is your name, boy?' he asks. 'You remind me of someone I recently met.'

'I'm Jack,' I growl.

'Jack,' says Dolo as if the word provides illumination. 'You would be Jack Junior then. You look a lot like the man who came to us yesterday.'

'Aye. That man was my father.'

'Such a shame he died.' Dolo frowns but he doesn't truly look sad. 'You know you can't save them both today? If you win, one wish can only buy you one life.'

I'd heard the rules were such from the townsfolk. I shrug and let words, carefully rehearsed, fall from my lying lips.

'I hated my father. He was a bastard. He hurt all manner of folk in his day. If he's in Hell, that's where he deserves to be.'

Dolo's eyes narrow. His fine, long fingers tap a slow tattoo on his chest. 'All right then. It's a deal. Your sister or your soul. Choose your door, Jack Junior. The odds are one in three to win.'

My father chose the darkest.

So only two options remain. I recall my sister pointing to her dress. I glance back at her strained face. Her hand clutches at the sleeve of her blouse. Her favourite white dress. Is she suggesting she chose the white door?

Yes. That must be it.

I make my choice. 'Red for the win.'

Dolo frowns again and my heart surges. I've won—this nightmare is over! But then comes his wicked smile and my heart sinks into my boots.

'Wrong,' he says. 'Red is for Hell. And that is your destination. What a good son you are to follow in your father's footsteps.'

Dolo's hand flicks up. Red electricity trips across his palm. It crackles outward toward the doors, colliding with and shattering them into a thousand splinters.

The doors and the wall of the saloon are gone. A new, ragged-edged hole has opened, looking out over a burning landscape. This isn't the township of Esperance. I'm beholding Hell.

I grit my teeth, grinding back the rage that urges me to the stupidity of pulling my guns. The red door was the right answer. I'm sure of it. Dolo's a liar. His game must be rigged.

Plan B it is.

I only hope my father was right in his assumptions.

The rocky plain of brimstone glows against a stygian infinity. The stench of sulphur catches in my throat. I cough but can't clear it.

A black chain appears, hanging coiled from Dolo's fist. 'Usually, you would be set for the gallows tree,' he says. 'But it has been a busy month for business. The rules say your father's corpse must occupy that spot until his bones fall.' He smiles a smile, a thin, cruel thing filled with malice. 'So,' he says, 'today you receive a special honour. I shall escort you to Hell, myself.'

'Honestly, it's okay,' I say. 'If you're busy an' all, I can be comin' back some other time.'

'Not at all. It will be my pleasure.' He flicks his wrist and the chain, both searing hot and freezing cold, falls to coil around my wrists.

#

DOLO

It's been an age since I was last forced to walk through Hell. It is a decidedly less pleasant place than the human world. The air tastes rank—of bone-smoke and ash. And the cries of the damned are an irritating background litany.

I lead the gunslinger toward the Binding Fields. Past rugged piles of charred rock and the shattered bones of a thousand beings, the fields finally emerge. A wretched stretch of barren soil dotted with the petrified skeletons of long dead trees.

To each of these is tied a hanged soul—souls that I sent here. They are the coin I give to the Burning One in exchange for my freedom to roam Earth. Hundreds swing here, all victims fallen to the promise of my charmed doors.

I tug the gunslinger closer. He stumbles, his boots catching on an edge of old bone peeking out of the dirt. His breaths are irregular; the fumes not suitable to sustain human lungs. No matter. He won't have a need to breathe for much longer.

We pass the first trees. A woman hangs there, her shadowy face filled with anguish.

'My baby,' she sighs in a voice tired and thin. 'I just wanted him back.'

How these pathetic souls disgust me. All wishing and wanting.

The next is an older man, his sightless eyes rolling in their sockets. 'Can I choose another door?' he asks plaintively. 'I just want to see again.'

The gunslinger pulls against the chain and stops walking. His eyes look like bruises in the dim light.

'All these people. What does their pain buy you?' he asks, his voice scuffed raw by the atmosphere.

I jerk on the chain, but the boy pulls back. Even weakened by this place, he is still strong. I decide it's better to answer him. 'What everyone wants,' I say. 'Freedom.'

'No man is truly free,' he mutters.

The mortal dares judge me? What he doesn't understand is that their frail little lives are the currency of the supernatural. They are nothing more than oil to line the cogs of eternity.

I growl and lean closer. 'Then it's lucky I am no man.'

I pull harder on the chain this time and the gunslinger falls to one knee. 'Get up,' I snarl. 'And don't speak again.'

He glares at me, but holds his tongue and pushes upright, awkwardly. I lead him onward, drawing him to the next empty tree. He has annoyed me now, so I'll make sure his eternity is all the harder to bear. I'll hang him next to the father he hates—next to Jack Senior.

To have his soul in despair a little more is not a bad thing, anyway. Any hope in his heart and the armies of Heaven will sense him and descend to take him away. And a lost soul means my freedom could be revoked.

The tree next to Jack's father is a shattered thing. Broken like the souls that surround it. Its skeleton glows scarlet in the light of distant hell-fires. I wrench on the chain again. The gunslinger pulls back again. Irritated, I clench my jaw and turn but his eyes are not on me. They are locked on his father.

The older man is looking at the sky. His eyes are trained on the empty black and his lips move.

'No matter the cost. No matter the cost.'

'Dad?' whispers the gunslinger.

The father stops muttering. His eyes swivel down.

'Hello, Jacky,' he says. 'Plan B then?'

'Aye,' whispers the son.

#

JACK

My heart twists seeing my father on that tree. But it was what we planned—what needed to happen if he didn't win his turn at Dolo's doors.

My father smiles. 'So, the game *is* rigged!' he whispers. 'The game is rigged!'

The other souls on the trees around us start to chant also. 'The game is rigged. The game is rigged.'

Dolo snarls. He tugs me forward and this time I comply. I step up to the tree he has chosen for me. He loops the loose length of the chain around my neck and throws the rest over the closest tree branch. He leans down to pick up the end—

I strike.

With all my force I knee Dolo in the chin. His head snaps back but he doesn't fall. Slowly, steadily he stands up, turns and looks at me. His oiled hair, fallen free, hangs like fat leeches over his forehead. His eyes narrow and his lips press into thin white lines.

'You done now, Jack Junior?'

I flex my fingers, wishing my wrists were free. 'Not even nearly.'

Faster than my eye can follow, Dolo yanks the chain taut and hauls me into the air. The black links bite into the soft flesh of my throat. My spine slams against the iron-hard tree.

But my neck doesn't break.

It's to be a slow death.

Around me, voices rise—angry. 'The game is rigged!' they cry. 'The game is rigged!'

Dolo wrenches the chain again. It tightens further. My vision darkens. I fall limp.

Maybe Plan B won't work after all.

Is the game rigged?

But then the chain loosens and I drop an inch. I swivel my gaze to Dolo. He's pale and struggling to hold my weight. He staggers forward.

I drop another inch.

Then the hanged souls nearby remove their nooses and crawl down from their trees. They move like shadows in the wind, one moment solid, the next just fog.

They gather. They gather. They surround Dolo.

The chain slips from his grip, and I slither down to land on my feet. The Rogue Trader's chest heaves. His eyes glow a dull red. Malicious. Malevolent.

I unwind the chain off my neck and draw in a foul-tasting breath. Breathing never felt so good. Then, of their own accord, the bindings on my wrists fall away. I stand with my hands on my knees for a moment, eyes closed.

A hand squeezes my shoulder.

I look up. My father.

'You did it, son. Look.' He points. 'The Burning One comes.'

A fiery figure stalks the horizon. It draws closer, its shape solidifying into a man with eyes like coals and a body of flame. A darkly burning phoenix rides his shoulder.

The souls surrounding us part, stepping aside. Dolo cringes as he lays eyes on the being.

'My Lord. Why have you come?' he says.

The Burning One tilts his chin. 'These souls have found hope, Dolo.' He raises his arms to encompass the crowd. 'You took three from the same family, and each chose a different door. Now they believe your game is a cheat. They no longer despair.'

Dolo's face twists. He points to the crowd. 'I didn't cheat anyone. You all accepted the odds—one chance in three—and lost.

Back to your trees.'

'No,' says the Burning One. He looks up as the black sky arching overhead fractures into glowing lines of white. 'It is too late. The Heavenly Others already come to claim them.'

Dolo blanches. 'But the game doesn't work like that.'

'Your game was never about the odds, Dolo. It was about giving me despairing souls in return for your freedom,' says the Burning One.

'And now, the belief of your victims, right or wrong, holds power. You took the son, the third of his family-line for you to claim. He believed you cheated him for he was confident he chose the right door. Then you brought him across the threshold with a heart full of hope. That was your mistake, Dolo.'

'This is unfair.'

'No. You played your own game and lost.' The Burning One's chin tilts up. 'And now all the souls you gathered for me are lost. Our deal is broken. You will return to Hell and remain here.'

'Please,' stutters Dolo. 'Wait…'

But the trader's words fall on deaf ears. The dark phoenix rises off the Burning One's shoulders. Where it flies, embers fall from the tips of its wings. It circles Dolo and he begins to change. His human features shift to become monstrous—long-fanged and red-eyed. His arms grow into legs and he becomes dog-like in form. He howls, an inhuman call that echoes off the plain, and runs, disappearing into the distance.

Then the sky tears apart. The Heavenly Others. Sunlight falls on the ruined plains and a gentle breeze starts to blow. I look around. Every soul faces the light, beatific smiles painted on their broken lips.

Next to me, my father sighs. 'I'm proud of you, Jack,' he says.

'You did it.'

'We did it,' I reply.

Heat touches my left side. The Burning One approaches, the phoenix returned to his shoulder. 'I will grant you the one wish Dolo should have given you,' he says. 'Choose, human.'

My father smiles at me. 'It's okay,' he says. 'It's gotta be Josie. It's high time I be movin' on in any case. I'm happy to go.'

I'll miss my father but it's what he really wants. I embrace him then turn to the Burning One.

'I'll take a good life, sir,' I say. 'With my sister in it.'

The Burning One frowns. 'One wish for one soul. You and your sister are both mine. You may save yourself or your sister, but I cannot grant both. Choose again.'

My father stalks past me and stares down the Burning Man. 'The game was rigged. Jack doesn't belong to you.'

'I am truly sorry,' says the Burning One. 'But your son perished the moment he stepped across the door's threshold into my domain. He is mine. The rules are clear.'

My father's face twists. He turns to me. 'I'm so sorry, Jacky. I got it wrong.'

I frown. My father has only ever tried to do his best for us kids. Now it's my turn to step up and do what's best for him. Time to protect my own.

'Nah. It's all right, Pa. We got it right. This is just the cost.' Before my father can say anything else, I lift my chin and stare the Burning One in the eye. 'I choose freedom for my sister.'

The Burning One bows.

The phoenix launches.

Embers rain down.

The last thing I see, framed by the light of the Heavenly Others' arrival, is the main street of Esperance. And my sister on the porch, in her white dress, gaze searching.

#

END

All the Right Things
in All the Right Places

Aiki Flinthart

I'd never been arrested, but today it seemed inevitable. While the exact nature of her crime wasn't clear, Carol's obsessive excitement over the computer and enormous vat of burbling goo in the middle of my toolshed's stained concrete floor worried me. That, combined with the tangle of cables and wire framework dangling into the vat, made me think a permanent vacation might be due.

Carol might not care if she blew out the power grid. But outside, baking in the white-hot haze that passed for early summer in Sydney, were people who did. Right now, there were only two noises: greengrocer cicadas shrilling as they pissed tree-sap on the parched earth, and the distant rattling thrum of airconditioners. But if this went wrong, a torch-bearing posse would bash on the door, screaming for their cold air.

Carol grinned, handed me a circuit board and a screwdriver, and pointed to an empty slot on the side of the vat. I eyed her dubiously.

I had a crappy job to keep and a deep desire to retain the house I'd wrested from my ex-husband's lawyers. To spite him, more than anything. Not because I really gave a shit.

'Carol...' I tried for reason but found only heat-wearied resignation. 'I realise you're a certified genius, but you've flipped into mad scientist mode. What have you got me into? You've been crashing on my couch, using my shed for secret-squirrel stuff, and making me write code for two months. What the hell's going on?'

Her ginger, wire-brush head reappeared from behind the vat, topaz blue eyes sunken and shadowed, gleaming above a knife-edge grin. Her collarbones and cheekbones protruded. She wasn't eating properly; too nauseated to eat most of the time. Or too focussed on this madness, whatever it was.

'You're not well. It's hot. You should be resting.' Flapping my t-shirt did nothing to cool me, only wafted the scent of sweat into my nose.

'No time to rest, Lisa-lu. You know that.' She held an orange male-end power cord in one huge hand and the matching dirty-cream female extension lead in the other. Her prominent Adam's apple bobbed. 'What's something you've always wanted?'

'To be shot of everything. This whole world is fucked.' There was no point in telling her what I really wanted. Our friendship was worth more than a futile declaration.

She pursed her lips and sent me a level look.

I shrugged. 'Failing that, to be filthy, stinking rich?'

'So, if you had the chance to be, would you?'

'No catches?'

She shrugged. 'Not that you know of.'

'Sounds a bit soul-selling-sign-in-blood-ish.' I pointed at the vat. 'What's the connection? Where'd you get the money for all this? Is this some get-rich thing?'

'Maybe, if it works.' Another nervous swallow. 'Sold everything but my bike. Sold my mother's house.' Pain flickered through her eyes. 'About the only good thing she ever did for me was die at the right time.'

I said nothing. Her mother had been a class A bitch.

'So,' Carol said, brightly, 'it seemed appropriate to use her money to get what I always wanted. What she'd never let me have. What millions of people want.'

'A really good latte first thing in the morning?'

Carol accorded that no more than a brief eye-roll.

'Fine,' I replied, humouring her and reciting her favourite quote, 'All the right things in all the right places.'

Her grin turned cheeky. 'You got it!' Her excitement challenged my doubts. Challenged but didn't defeat. She clung to a belief that a righted wrong would make her happy. In my experience, it just made you feel superior for a fleeting moment, before all the other insecurities came crashing in. But my worldview had never been exactly rose-coloured.

'Just hang on a mo.' I held up a hand and peered at the goopy beige mess inside the vat. 'For days you've had me writing software for running servos and hydraulics, while you tinkered in here. Now you've called me out to see...what?' Beige liquid like snotty pancake batter dripped off the end of my finger. I sniffed at it and screwed up my nose. 'This stuff smells like fresh meat. What the hell...?'

'Just wait and see,' Carol trilled in her falsetto range. Her eyes sparkled with a manic glee that stirred ripples in my shallow well of inner calm.

'This'd better not be anything like last time,' I said.

The electrical cables twitched in Carol's hands. Her voice dropped back to its normal, masculine, gravelly depths. 'That did get a little out of hand. Still, no-one died. Well, ok, one cat died, but that was an accident. I made the owner a new one.'

The smile returned, accompanied by a tilt of the head and a coy-innocent look that would have been more convincing on someone ten years younger and a foot shorter. She hitched up the strap of her daisy-printed singlet top over a broad, hairy shoulder and waggled the cables at me.

'This time I know exactly what I'm doing.'

'And what is that, exactly?' I repeated.

'Saving my life and the lives of a crapload of other people.' Carol chortled, low in her throat, and jammed the cables together.

'Wait!' I re-ran our conversation. 'What do you mean you made her a new cat?'

I stared in horror at the vat.

The liquid crackled and stirred as electricity arced through it and played delicately across the visible fragments of wire frame, skipping and dancing. Ozone left a metallic tang in the air. The centre of the liquid bulged. Ripples spread. How far? Beyond my shed and my backyard if my fear was realised.

An amorphous, rounded blob of goo thrust upward. A black hole gaped in it. Slime poured off and vague lumps resolved into vague features. A face. A head. A slender neck. Slim shoulders emerged, followed by a torso, dripping beige goop.

'What the hell have you *done?*' I whispered. An inkling of her intent made my stomach lurch. 'Is this some sort of 3D printer?'

Carol nodded, watching the emerging figure with stark longing in her angular face. 'Sort of. Bit more complicated than that. Called in every favour to get hold of bunch of prototypes.' She leaned over the edge and gripped the figure under the armpits. With a schlorping noise, she hauled the…whatever it was…out. Carol stood the…female, definitely female…on the floor and gave a soft laugh of triumph.

The urge to run from the future pushed me a step back. I tripped over the power cable and collapsed ingloriously to the concrete, smacking my head hard enough to turn the world sepia for a few seconds.

#

'You can't call her Francine,' Carol said, choking on a laugh as she swigged a cold beer.

We stood in my dingy melamine-and-pine kitchen, discussing the immediate future. At least, I was attempting to discuss, while holding a gel ice pack to my head. Carol was mostly grinning at me in a fond way that made my heart jitter. The robot-woman sat on my worn-shiny blue couch, her expression blank as she stared at the tv.

'She needs a name,' I protested. 'I can't keep calling her 'it'.'

Carol's smile shifted, rueful. 'For starters, the monster was named Adam, not Frankenstein. And for finishers, tomorrow her name'll be Carol.'

'How?' I flung out my hands, splashing beer onto the cracked linoleum floor. 'How the hell are you going to transfer your consciousness into another body—an artificial body? I know the chemo means you can't have the gender reassignment op, but it'll be over soon and you can have the surgery next year. This is a pretty extreme alternative. There's got to be another way.'

For a moment her diamond façade slipped, revealing a subterranean flash of stark, fear-filled desperation.

'Don't, Lisa.' Her voice cracked. 'I don't have anyone else to help me. I've tried everything. The latest tests came back. The chemo finished months ago and it hasn't worked. Why do you think my hair's back? I've got maybe three months, max. This is my last shot. And if it works it won't help just me. Think how many other people need new bodies. The *right* body. I watched Dad die this way. I can't...' She turned aside, jaw clenching and fingers white on the bottle.

Sinking horror knotted my stomach. I knew that look. I'd seen it in my reflection the first few weeks after my husband left and a warm bath with a cold razor started to seem attractive. Still did, some days. If Carol hadn't breezed into my house at the right moment, and provided a sounding board for my angry, alcohol-fuelled ravings, I might have acted on my impulse.

Every day I wished she hadn't, even while I was grateful she had. As much as I resented the interference, I owed her. The world owed her. She'd had it far worse, for far longer. Thirty years in the wrong body; a body that was now failing her.

'You know if I could change places with you, I would.' The words came out in a rush.

'I know, Lisa-lu.'

Before I could speak, the glittering smile returned and she lifted her chin.

'As to the mind transfer, leave that up to me,' she added. 'I have a plan. I just need some proprietary coding and a specific cable that I've got to get from—'

'No!' I held up a hand. 'Don't tell me. The less I know the less I can say when they call me into court.'

Carol snorted. 'My favourite pessimist. So what *do* you want to know?' She glanced at her watch. 'Make it quick. I've got to be in

Sydney before the rush hour so I can… Ah, best you don't know that bit.'

'What's she made of?' The robot's skin looked human even down to the tiny pale hairs, pores and creases. The afternoon light gleamed off her autumnal hair and slanted eerily through amber eyes. But she wasn't perfect. Her nose was a little crooked; her eyebrows uneven; her skin lightly freckled. My faded t-shirt and cargo shorts hung limp on her slender form. Her very human-ness unnerved me.

Carol followed my gaze toward the living room. 'A heat-sensitive type of silicone-graphene-polypeptide. Basically, a new type of organic plastic that stays pliable but cohesive between minus-twenty-five and plus sixty-five degrees Celsius.'

All sorts of questions about maintenance and every-day reality danced on my tongue, but I was reluctant to play Devil's advocate and possibly destroy her hope. Carol's achievement staggered…and terrified me. The potential was so vast my head threatened to explode. I glanced at the robot and a frisson slipped down my neck. Yes, it was a good thing we'd destroyed all the evidence in the shed. All that remained was the consciousness-transfer software on her laptop—which sat innocently on my stained melamine dining table.

The world wasn't ready for this. I pressed the cold beer bottle against my hot cheek. I wasn't ready. Part of me wanted to stop her, afraid to lose her. But if she didn't do this, I would definitely lose her.

'Righty-ho.' Carol balanced her bottle on top of the pile overflowing the recycling bin and brushed at her mouth. 'I'll be off. See you tomorrow morning early if all goes well.' She now wore a dark t-shirt and dark long pants. I didn't want to know why.

'What do I do with her in the meantime?' I jerked my head

toward the motionless figure on the couch.

'She doesn't need anything but sunlight occasionally to recharge. Super-efficient photovoltaic fibres. Her hair. One of those prototypes,' she added when I lifted my brows in question. 'She'll power down at ten pm.'

'And between now and then?'

Carol tapped her own temple. 'Nothing up here yet, so don't feel obliged to make conversation. Maybe run her through some of the basic range of motion exercises you programmed. Just to make sure everything's working.'

She kissed my cheek and strode out. The screen door slammed behind her. Seconds later the growl of her Harley rumbled down my long, dirt driveway and dopplered into the distance. I stood for a long time, watching the dust of her passage dissipate in the heavy air.

Shit.

#

Brilliant midday heat melted into afternoon dust-gold outside the kitchen window. Kookaburras warmed up for their dusk chorus of chortling at my shortcomings. The robot's head jerked up. Her eyes flicked to the window before returning to the tv. I frowned. She didn't move again. No. I must have imagined that. Anthropomorphising a blank-minded automaton. Bad idea. The whole thing was a bad idea. I shuddered and turned my back on the living room.

I stomped into my office, closed the door and switched on the airconditioner. It hummed and rattled, comforting background noise as my fingers clickety-clicked over the keyboard for an hour. But my concentration sucked and the net was slow. Treacle and peanut-butter slow. Drumming my fingers on the tabletop did nothing to speed it up. It was only four-thirty pm. Download speeds didn't usually lemming off a cliff until about six.

I snapped a pen by accident and scrubbed at the writers-blood ink staining my fingers black. Fuck. Burying my head in my arms, I clenched my teeth. Who was I kidding? I should have said something. Should have told Carol how important she was to me. If this whole ridiculous charade went wrong, she would die and I'd be left with regrets. But I knew she didn't see me that way. Hell, she didn't see anyone that way

Tears pricked my eyelids and I sucked a deep breath, getting fear under control.

The computer slowed to a worm's racing speed and I swore at it, but felt no better. There were no obvious bottlenecks in my software. The old favourite standby of rebooting didn't even help. In desperation, I reached for the power button on the router. I had actual paid jobs to finish, even if they were just distractions while I waited.

'Please don't.'

I screamed and jumped. My foot caught under the chair and I fell to the cool wood floor in a tangle of plastic wheels and sweaty cushions.

'I'm sorry,' the soft voice said. 'I didn't mean to frighten you. Let me help.' A warm hand grasped my upper arm and hauled me upright.

I gargled as pain lanced up my arm and shoulder bones ground together at a dislocation-prone angle.

'Let go!' The pain reduced to dull throbs. I rubbed at my arm. Five red finger-marks encircled it.

Before me, Caroltoo…robo-girl…whatever…waited with a patient expression on her ordinary face.

I gaped in moronic disbelief. Talking. She was talking. She wasn't supposed to do that. Or anything.

'Did I injure you?' Her arched brows twitched together in a perfect frown. 'I apologise.' She inspected her hand, opening and closing the fingers. Did I imagine the faint whir of servos?

'Why…' My voice cracked like a boy soprano hitting puberty. I tried again. 'Why did you stop me turning off the rout…oh.' The router's net-connection light flickered so fast it was basically solid. 'Are you connected to the net? Did Carol put wifi in you?'

'Carol?' The robot blinked. 'Is that not a female-gender human name? But the person who created me was male gender. Explain?'

I waved a feeble hand. 'Complicated. Er…just go with it. I'm Lisa, by the way.'

'I have no name.' She gazed at me with such simple honesty and guileless innocence I had to look away.

In the long silence that followed my brain produced a dozen scenarios for the next twenty minutes; the next twenty days—none of them good. Carol was going to kill me.

'Francine,' I muttered. 'Your name is Francine.'

'Thank you. Yes,' she said, 'I'm connected to the internet.'

I cringed. 'Well, don't believe everything you see. Most of it's rubbish.'

Francine tilted her head, soft waves of auburn hair sliding over her shoulder. 'Explain?'

'I don't think I can.' I chuckled. 'Tell you what. Go research critical thinking. Then take a fresh look at things.'

Her amber eyes unfocussed for a moment then she nodded. 'I understand. Thankyou. That's useful.'

She stood too close to me and I inched backwards. She followed. I repressed the urge to run. Memories of every sci-fi movie, Asimov story, and horrible nightmare battled with logic. Logic won, eventually, but sweat stained my shirt and my heart raced. Francine watched me, still with that open curiosity, like I was the experiment and she the researcher.

The lounge room seemed safer. Bigger, anyway. I led the way, collapsed on one of the armchairs and gestured toward the other. She sat with enviable grace. At least my software worked.

Silence squirmed uncomfortably between us. No small-talk needed, huh? Liar, Carol.

'So,' I said, 'what else have you learned? Where did you start on the net? There's a lot to digest.'

'I began with your browser history,' she said evenly, 'and links you had followed from your social media.'

Oh, Christ. The last few things I'd procrasti-read. Feminist blogs, cat videos, the latest climate change forecasts, some Star Trek trivia to settle an online argument, more bloody cat videos. What a first impression of our world. Best not to ask what she thought of us. I probably wouldn't like the answer. Definitely.

'How...' I waved a hand vaguely at her. 'How did this happen? Carol said you were...blank.'

Francine tilted her head. 'There was a code. One of the codes running my servos contains a command sequence to learn from mistakes. That merged with another code in my operating software.' She held out her hands, palm up, in perfect imitation of a very human gesture. And then she smiled. 'And here I am.'

Her smile undid me. This wasn't just a well-programmed robot. This was a sentient being. I swore and swiped both hands over my face. It had been a long time since my last decent sleep. I'd done the self-correction servo coding last; copied in haste from a previous job. This was my fault. I should have been more careful.

'My code, dammit,' I muttered. 'Bloody Carol and her bloody secrecy. If I'd seen her OS I might have anticipated this.' I swiped a palm over my face and glanced at the clock. Five-ten. If Carol's estimate was right then I had until maybe ten hours to undo this.

I shifted and pain spasmed in my arm again. The finger-mark bruises were purpling nicely now.

Francine rose and vanished into the kitchen. She returned and offered a gel ice-pack, wrapped neatly in a tea towel. After a moment's hesitation, I accepted and pressed it against my arm.

'How did you know to do that?' I gritted my teeth against the cold-ache.

She sat and shrugged in an exquisitely-smooth motion, distracting me with my own genius for a second. 'I've read a lot of human anatomy and first aid. I wanted to understand how I'm different to you. What it means to be human…or not.'

'What, just in the last few minutes?'

Francine nodded, wide-eyed. 'As you said, there is much to understand and much that conflicts.' She paused and a frown flickered across her face. 'Humans are…contraditory. Both peaceful and violent, wise and blind, selfish and selfless.' Her fists clenched and opened a few times as she studied her hands. Thin slivers of metal extended and retracted from beneath her fingernails. Carol's nod to Wolverine, or maybe the Borg. Typical.

'And…er…' Mathematical formulae of power-to-weight ratios and pressure computations danced in my head. She was far stronger than any human, even with the limitations I'd built into her program.

'Which of those am I?' she finished for me when my throat tightened on the words. She glanced at the tv, its silent screen now a dark mirror. 'I'm not sure. Which is better?'

'For me, or for you?' I laughed weakly.

Her return look was both contemplative and innocent. 'An interesting question. What would you suggest I study to formulate my answer? I've been created to appear human. How do I learn what it means to *be* human?'

'Er…we've been asking the same question for thousands of years so tell me if you find out.' Philosophy wasn't my strong point. In fact, I knew little, which I now regretted. 'Buddhism, Daoism maybe?' If I could steer her away from extremism of any religions maybe I could…crap! What the hell was I thinking? She wasn't my student or child. This robot was meant to be an empty vessel into which my best friend could pour herself and live the life she'd hungered after for years.

I had no right to take away Carol's chance at happiness—and life—because of a dumb coding error or some misplaced Pygmalion complex.

'Look…you,' I said, rising. 'I have…work to do. Power down now and we can talk more when Carol gets back.'

The robot rose as well. 'You are lying,' it said, matter-of-factly. 'I heard you state that Carol intends to transfer his consciousness into this body on his return. What will happen to my consciousness?'

'I…' I sank back to the chair, my legs crumpling under the burden of guilt. 'I don't know. This has never been done! Crazy enough when it was just one mind.' I flailed helplessly. 'Ah, crap!'

'Why does Carol wish to do this? Will it not entail great risk?'

'She's spent her whole life in the wrong body,' I said. 'Hating herself. She can't have the surgery to correct the problem, because she's sick. So this is her only shot, I guess.' I rubbed at my forehead. 'And now I've screwed it up. What the hell am I going to do?'

'And this…artificial body will make her feel more human?' The robot flexed her fingers again and touched her cheek, her eyes mimicking puzzlement. Or perhaps she was puzzled. Who was I to say her feelings were just imitations of ours? Did she even have feelings?

'I think it's about identity, rather than humanity. Carol's always been human—just the wrong gender.'

Francine's eyes blanked again. 'Why cannot she undergo the gender reassignment surgery? The procedure seems straightforward.'

'Did you just research that, too? Well,' I said when she nodded, 'you'd better check out metastasised lung cancer, then, because that's what she's got. Only a few months to live. She's weaker every day and there's no more money. This…' I pointed at her. 'You were her only chance.'

'Ah,' Francine said. 'I see.' She stood and strode to the window, her gaze absent.

I joined her. There was nothing through the grimy glass to warrant her attention. In the eucalypts, the flock of kookaburras imitated an audience at a comedy fest; and I was the lead act. Darkness swept over the dusk-silvered land and Venus glittered above the eastern horizon.

'Tell me about you. And about Carol,' Francine murmured. 'Who is she?'

I shivered as evening chill crept through uninsulated walls. 'Complicated. Driven. Brilliant. Badly hurt. Confused. Human, basically. But one of the good ones.' I smiled bleakly. 'She's worth two of me. If I could swap places with her, I would. She saved my life once, even when I didn't want her to. And look what she's capable of.' I jerked my chin at the robot. 'She can fix the world with this technology. Or she could have. I'm just a coder.'

Francine tilted her head and turned that curious, amber gaze on me. 'But would she be the same person, in this body? And what of me? Is she more worthy of life, simply because she was born human?'

I threw up my hands and moved restlessly away. 'I don't know, ok? I don't know! What do you want me to do? The rest of the world is forty years or more away from this sort of breakthrough. This could change humanity.'

'For better or for worse?'

'I don't know that, either,' I admitted. 'I just know we need people like her to have any hope of surviving as a species. If Carol dies, her knowledge goes as well.'

'No,' Francine replied, cool. 'I would still be here.'

'But Carol's notes are gone. She didn't want anyone to find them if the transfer didn't work. Didn't want them to fall into the wrong hands. All that's left is the transfer software on her laptop.' I sent Francine a bleak look. 'So the only way to duplicate you is to tear you apart and find what makes you tick.'

'Why would they want to do that?'

I shrugged and studied my hands, twisting the hem of my shirt. 'Curiosity?'

'No,' Francine replied. Was that wistfulness in her even voice or was I imagining it? 'Fear. They would fear me. I look human, but I'm not.'

I cleared my throat, unable to deny the truth. 'You're just a little too early, I think. Maybe in fifty years. Oh!' I gripped her wrist. Her skin felt subtly wrong. I released her and wiped my hand on my shorts. Her eyes followed my gesture.

'I can back you up,' I continued hurriedly, picking up Carol's laptop from the table. 'When Carol returns with that cable she needs to connect you, I'll use it to back up your mind. Then Carol can build you a new body.'

Francine stared out the window again. 'You'll have to tell her about me, then.'

'No!' I grabbed her wrist and held it this time, searching her face. 'No. Because I know her. She wouldn't go through with the transfer.'

Francine's brows lifted. 'Explain.'

'It doesn't need explanation,' I said. 'She'd let herself die to save you. It's just who she is. If you were human, you'd understand.'

There followed a long silence. I held my breath, trying to gauge her reactions without seeming to watch. A frown drew her brows close and she sent me a quick, assessing look.

'I have another idea,' she said quietly. She turned to me and gently pulled the laptop from my hand. Laying it on the table, she opened it and plugged in a cable that extruded from a port in her hip.

I opened my mouth to ask what she was doing. She smiled. Her hands shot out and grasped my head.

I jerked back but that implacable grip held firm. Francine leaned in. Her warm lips pressed to my forehead and her fingernails dug into my skull. Agony skewered my brain and flared down my spine. Darkness obliterated thought.

#

I opened heavy eyelids as the grey fingers of dawn crept over my bedroom windowsill. A bone-deep ache weighed down my arms and legs. My body felt too big, too heavy, too full of pain. Pain which pinned me to the bed. Every shallow breath drew fire into my lungs. What the hell was wrong with me? Why couldn't I move? And there was some sort of helmet strapped to my head. A laptop screen glowed, just at the edges of my vision, on the bed next to me. Carol's laptop. With a new, twisted-silver cable leading from it to the helmet on my head.

Carol must be back from Sydney. She would help.

'Lisa-lu? You ready?' that was Francine's voice, but it sounded strange: happy, not calm or curious. And only Carol called me Lisa-lu 'My break-in at the lab's all over the TV. Police'll be here soon.'

Her break-in? Oh. The transfer must have been successful. She was in the right body. She must be so happy. I tried to reply but lethargy and pain held even my tongue still. I rolled my eyes toward the door, willing her to come in.

A female figure pushed the bedroom door open and hurried to the bedside, saying, 'Just have to get your laptop, Carol.'

I managed an incoherent gargle.

My face leaned over me. My grey eyes examined me with distant curiosity. My fingers…whose fingers?… flew over the laptop keyboard. My voice murmured in Francine's flat inflexions, 'I had to transfer you to Carol's old body, as she left it, to free space for her consciousness in the laptop.' She tilted her head…my head. 'Shall I put you back into the laptop? Convince Carol to make you a new body, too?'

The robot appeared at the door and glanced in. 'Don't waste your time on that old shell, Lisa-lu,' it said. 'It's burnt out; dying.' Carol swept a hand over her new hips and flashed a knife-edge smile. 'I have all the right things in all the right places now. C'mon. Leave the laptop. And the headgear and cable. Cops'll be here any minute. That was the plan. They can take that body away, charge the old me for theft, and it won't matter. We'll take your car, go to your mum's and pretend we were never here.' The sheer delight in her voice made my heart ache. She hurried away.

I gazed up at my own face and saw a strange kind of future for myself, there. One of boundless curiosity and vast intelligence. One unfettered by unreturned love or embittered memories. One better than any I could hope for.

I whispered, 'Go. Take care of her. When the police come, I'll confess to the theft. Like Carol said: all the right things are in all the right places, now.'

#

END

A Witch Always Knows Her Own Heart

Lynne Lumsden Green

Libi crouched at the base of the mast, her arms thrown around it, listening to the susurration of the leaves and creaking of the straining rigging. High above, the black flag with its silver embroidery of skull and crossbones snapped too fast to make out the added details of the black bryony and bittersweet growing out of the skull's eyes.

'Wind's still picking up, Captain,' shouted the first mate, fighting the tiller.

'Halyards and hawsers! Like our darling girl isn't acting weatherly enough,' snarled Captain Tea. As she strode past Libi on her way to assist the first mate, she glanced down. 'Stay out of the way, or I'll have you tossed overboard.'

'Yes, ma'am. Of course, ma'am,' answered Libi.

Libi had signed on *The Fancy* as cabin boy at the start this voyage, and had now discovered that storms in the canopy could be just as dangerous as storms at sea; the wind-whipped leaves even sounded like the boom and crash of surf on a beach. Bits of twigs and other windblown flotsam scratched her skin and tangled in her hair 'til she feared getting something sharp in her eyes.

Yet she was still glad she had come. The storm carried her closer to her wyrd. She wasn't going to fail this close to success, so she held on for all she was worth and peered over the gunwale as the ship listed.

Below, from horizon to horizon, stretched the Forest of Mu—the Sea of Leaves. It was a rough and treacherous surf for *The Fancy* as she tacked through the canopy, working to avoid both plunging into the pits or smashing up against the tossing reefs of taller tree trunks. Tops of emergent trees danced like dervishes.

The Fancy's scarlet sails fluttered, valiant as they swelled and luffed in the headwind. But it took all her crew's strength and skill to keep her under control. Most of the sails were close-hauled now the square-rigged ship beat to windward. The captain and first mate stood either side of the tiller, holding the rudder steady between them. Both women looked grim as they fought to control their ship.

Libi wondered if she was the only one whose senses sharpened with the impending danger. Sunset clouds flushed with pink and gold, and the green sea of the leaves took on peculiar tints of blue and purplish-brown.

The air was choked with flying debris, twigs, leaf fragments, pine needles, flower petals. All bruised so that the world smelt like incense or perfume. The canopy looked more like an ocean than ever, to the point Libi half expected a wave to break over the deck and wash her away.

The only thing that gave Libi any comfort was a sure knowledge the high winds pushed *The Fancy* and her crew toward their target: the Talaf. The 'X marks the spot' on her personal treasure map.

It probably helped spur the crew on that she had spread stories about luxury goods hoarded by the fey that lived in the mighty forest giant, the Talaf; exotic fruit and spices, rare orchids and glorious feathers. All worth more than their weight in any currency you cared to name, including fire diamonds. A lure for any scoundrel worthy of the title: pirate.

Libi hadn't lied, but she had emphasized the rewards while downplaying the role of warlike forest fey and fairykin who treasured the goods.

Returning to the Talaf was more important than a few white lies.

With one hand, Libi caressed the necklace of her grandmother's fingerbones around her neck. Until her heart was returned, she was hollow as those bones—a dry, shadow-woman.

'Talaf, ho!' shouted the woman in the crow's nest. The tree loomed, a giant among giants; a rugged island with the forest canopy washing up against its massive trunk. Lights twinkled amongst its foliage, each light representing a fairykin family's home.

'Hey, Libi,' shouted Captain Tea. 'Come help us wrestle with the tiller. We're going to drop anchor.'

Libi scuttled across to the quarterdeck's ladder, her necklace rattling like castanets. But, in the confines of her chest, there was no thudding with excitement; it was a rattle that had lost its bean.

The Fancy was nearly on top of the Talaf. Libi couldn't take her eyes off the the enormous yellow meranti tree, which made her journey across the deck riskier than it needed to be.

She had just crawled up to the captain when a shout echoed down from the crow's nest.

'Bandits!'

'Burning booms and blasted oaks,' cursed the captain. 'All hands to arms. Prepare to be boarded.'

From the high branches of the towering Talaf, small bodies swung out over the canopy, aiming for *The Fancy*. The bandits were small enough to be mistaken for children, except that each brandished a bronze knife. Libi bared her teeth and fingered her steel daggers. She had no knife skills, but the fey didn't like the bitter tang of iron.

A score of the forest kin landed on *The Fancy*, one for each of the crew. Libi huddled at her captain's feet, hoping to appear small and harmless.

Captain Tea bristled like a cat, making herself as big as possible. Not a short woman, and wearing high-heeled boots, she loomed over the trio of fey facing her.

'What do you scunners want?' she roared.

Though they came but to her waist, the forest kin did not quail. One stepped forward and said, 'Your kind is not welcome here.'

'What. Humans?'

'No. Pirates. We know what your flag means.'

Tea clearly saw no point in denying it. 'And you think to stop us?' She gestured to her crew. Apart from Libi, they were all experienced fighters, with the scars to prove it. The women grinned down on the forest kin.

The crew was armed with swords, pikes, muskets, throwing knives, truncheons, and daggers. Each fey warrior wore only armour carved out of bull oak wood and boldly painted with their family's colours. No match for steel.

'You think we are all you face?' The lead fey defender raised his pointed chin. 'In the branches are our archers.'

The pirates glanced up. Above them, a large branch was lined with tree fairies, and they all had bows and quivers.

'Those arrows are tipped with poison and can take down a human in seconds,' said Libi, trying to suppress the mounting horror in her voice. 'And they can hit a hummingbird in flight.'

'Indeed? Libi, m'girl, you left out a lot of important details when talking up this little venture.' Tea sounded more offended than disappointed.

'As the girl says, they won't miss. We can see as well in the dark as any cat.' The warrior gestured toward the sunset. The clouds were barely tinged with red, and the tropical night would soon fall. 'However, if you give up peaceably, we will let you live. We will even take you to the nearest township. But we will keep your ship, to prevent you from returning.'

Captain Tea growled. She grew even larger, though how the captain managed it Libi couldn't imagine. As the windstorm swirled around them, Tea's jaw hardened and her eyes glittered.

'I'd rather die than lose my ship.' She thrust her sword into the air. 'Attack!'

The tiller tore itself out of the first mate's hands as Tea turned to fight. *The Fancy*'s rudder swung the ship around so the scarlet sails caught the full power of the windstorm. The ship listed, dangerously close to capsizing. It looked fair to smash into the Talaf's trunk.

Libi took that as her cue. The pirates and the tree fairies threw themselves into battle.

She dived off the tilting deck of *The Fancy* and into the Sea of Leaves below.

The canopy was less than a metre thick. Underneath lay stygian darkness, but—just like the tree fairies—Libi could see in the dark. The gigantic tree throbbed with life, loud enough to be heard. And, though the force of the windstorm was reduced, a click and buzz of insects thundered.

She managed to slow her dive into a controlled descent by catching at branches as she fell past, scratching and bruising her hands. This wasn't her first time falling through the forest.

Her destination was at the foot of the Talaf.

Libi slid down a hill-sized buttress root. She climbed down to the forest floor. Her feet hit the ground.

The thudding of her heartbeat rose to a crescendo, a deep drumming echoing through the forest.

She looked around and rubbed some feeling back into her stinging hands. Everything looked unchanged. Relentlessly normal.

'I knew you would return,' said a welcoming voice.

A green glow flowed around Libi. She faced its source: the dryad, Talaf. Spirit of the tree. He looked very different from the fairies that lived in his tree; tall and as beautiful as a jacaranda in flower. Around his neck glowed the red jewel that contained Libi's heart.

A witch always knows her own heart.

Libi had to tear her eyes away to look the dryad in the face. 'It's been a long time, Talaf. A decade as humans count time.'.

He took a cautious step closer to her. 'I have missed you. The best days of my life were when I was teaching you the magic of the tree.'

'If I had known the true cost of those lessons, I would never have sought you out,' said Libi, reaching up to clasp her necklace of bones. The weight of them around her neck was both a reassurance and a comfort.

'You were happy to pay the price at the time.' He stepped closer to Libi and held out his hands to her. His were long and shapely, but had too many fingers; more proof of his lack of humanity. 'I offered you my heart in return.'

'What do I need of your heart? But I need my own to come fully into my powers. A witch without her powers is just another ordinary girl.'

'You are no ordinary girl and never could be. You have the love of a tree, and I will remember the sound of your voice and the smell of sunshine on your hair centuries after you have died.'

Libi snorted. 'How very poetical. And yet, here I am, unimpressed with those high-flying words. I want my heart back.'

'But I still have need of it.'

'Gah! No, you don't!' Her hands clenched into fists. 'You aren't human. You don't understand human love. You want to keep me as a pet.'

'Then why do I keep your heart close to my own?' He clasped his necklace. The glow of Libi's heart charm was bright enough to gleam though his flesh, revealing the alien shapes of his bones.

He opened his fingers and looked down upon Libi's heart. 'It's such a rich and passionate red. Surely you can share it with me, and I can share my heart with you?'

'The problem is, I can't feel any love without my heart. And I can't do the job I was born for. So, I must reject your compromise,' snarled Libi, still angry, still savage. 'Why don't we play another game of chance for it?'

'Throw the bones? Like last time? But that's how you lost your heart in the first place.'

'Yes. But this time I will supply the bones,' she said. With a hard tug, the leather thong of her necklace parted. Now her hands were full of the ivory of her grandmother's fingerbones. They were smooth to touch, and dry, dry, dry; dryer than a stone in the middle of a sun-struck desert.

'Only fair, since I supplied them last time we played for high stakes.' The Talaf's bones had been made from his own fingers; he could afford the sacrifice of a dozen or so. He could grow more. Those bones had been silk-smooth and slippery.

Talaf said, 'If you win, you get your heart back. If I win, you must remain here with me. Or would you like my heart in return?'

'The heartwood of the yellow meranti is one of the hardest woods known,' said Libi, with a sneer. 'You can keep your heart.'

'You think me hard-hearted?'

'Very. You left me heartless, without any feelings of love to warm me. You took away the centre of my magical powers and left me hollow, without marrow, without passion. I am only a fraction of the witch I could be.'

'That was never my ambition. All I want is for the two of us to be happy. Together. Like we were before when you came to learn about my magic.' Talaf's green glow was tinged with autumnal shades of yellow and brown.

Libi hesitated, frowning. What did he really want? Not being human, he didn't understand about human hearts. She suspected the Talaf probably believed a human would be more faithful than a fickle fairy. More fool him.

'Play.' She threw the bones down. They fell into a star shape.

'You've been practicing,' remarked Talaf.

'Constantly. But I still don't have the centuries of practice you do.'

She tossed the bones again. This time, they fell into the classic 'tree of life' pattern.

Talaf's eyes narrowed. 'You aren't using any magic, are you?'

'How? You have my heart. And you would know if I cheated.'

Libi gathered up the bones for her final throw. Her hands shook, and she took a steadying breath. She let the bones fall. They formed a crescent moon shape... but with one bone slightly out of alignment.

'Beat that,' she said, though her hands still shook. She brought her fingers to her lips to steady them.

'Easily,' he replied, smiling gently.

Talaf reached down to gather up the bones.

Libi held her breath.

As he touched them, his body jerked and the massive tree behind him groaned. He fell forward onto the bones and lay helpless, writhing, his cries the harsh crack of breaking branches; he appeared powerless to roll aside.

Libi smiled. This was what she had planned for. Prepared her grandmother's bones for. Years it had taken.

Talaf was a being made from thaumaturgy. Now the bones were draining the magic from him.

'Libi!' he gasped. 'What have you done?'

'I am only doing what you did to me…harvesting your magic as you stole mine.'

'I never stole it. You lost it in a game of chance.'

'A game you have been playing for centuries. That's as good as cheating.'

The dryad moaned. 'Not true. Not true.'

Talaf's colour bleached away as he faded. Soon, the red jewel containing Libi's heart was visible through his form. The tree roots beneath him shuddered and leaves started pattering down from above.

'Libi, I'm sorry,' he whispered. 'Even if you can't forgive me, think of all the animals and forest kin dependant on my tree.'

Libi gestured to the treetops. 'Why?' she asked. 'I was too young to know better than to make bets with a mage, and they should have seen that. Did they try to warn me about you? No. They ignored me and so I will ignore them. Being heartless makes that easy.'

'Take pity,' sighed the Talaf.

But it was too late for pity. The dryad gave a final dry creak. The Talaf's luminous eyes closed. His skin withered; a leaf in autumn. Then the body faded away like the shadows of the waning moon. He was gone, and her grandmother's fingerbones now glowed with his green aura. Libi was surprised at how dull the glow was for such a powerful being.

The necklace with Libi's heart lay on the humus, surrounded by the bones. She picked it up. The jewel nestled inside a beautifully carved nut or seedcase, with the red stone its berry. She cracked the little filigree cage between her teeth and spat out the bits. Then she swallowed her heart stone; its beat fluttered all the way down her throat.

For the first time in a decade, the numbness in her chest melted away. Her magic returned, flooding through her veins and arteries. She laughed and flung her arms wide with exhilaration. She flexed her fingertips and foxfire magic crackled between them, dark orange and purple.

'I am the Witch Elizabeth Alecto Delara Hempenstock,' she declared to the wind and shadows.

No more feral forest magic for her! She gathered up her grandmother's bones and put them in a pouch at her waist. The old witch would be pleased to have them back so rich in power.

She paused, frowning. As her own heart took up the tangled reins of her emotions, it began to pluck at her soul.

Something else had changed.

The great wall of the trunk rising into the canopy had fallen silent, while the rain of falling leaves increased in intensity. A vast gap opened to the storm-speckled sky above. Newly-bare branches clawed at the tattered clouds scudding low overhead. The tree would no longer crank a small sea of sap from its roots to its leaves. Nor turn sunlight into fruit and flowers. The great tree that sustained the whole forest and the fey folk, was dead.

Libi had killed it.

She'd killed Talaf. The realisation sent a stabbing pain through her chest, bringing her to her knees. She hadn't felt pain like this since her heart had been taken.

Talaf was dead, by her hand. And by vanquishing him, she had both regained her heart and lost her heart's desire. Every beat of her heart had been for the Talaf, but she'd never tried to understand what that meant.

She wanted to raise her face to the moon and howl. She had spent years planning to take her heart back and now it was a grinding stone of pain in her chest, crushing all hope and happiness. Poor gentle, misguided Talaf had been the originator of his own doom and her heartbreak.

Libi cried until she was weak and drained.

She was tempted to remain in a foetal position on the forest floor—until she remembered *The Fancy* and her crew. She had got them into this mess; she should not desert them to their fate. Things needed to be set right again. She sat up and dried her eyes.

With a mighty groan, the trunk beside her trembled and the ground shook. The patter of leaves became a torrent. She had to protect her head with her arms. The smell of fresh sap began to choke her, as large seams patterned the massive trunk. Creaking and moaning from the tree resonated in her head without going through her ears.

She formed a sphere of protection and that dulled the worst of it.

The trunk cracked open like a cannon shot. Libi was thrown high into the air. Only her witch powers saved her from injury. Her sphere fell back to earth and bounced. She shook her head, battered and dizzy.

Dazed, she looked at the tree. It had split asunder. From the heartwood inside came a bright green glow. More magic? She released the protective spell and clambered through the split in the trunk, getting sticky with sap and pricked by splinters.

There was another filigree box sitting in the ruins of the Talaf.

Small and beautifully carved, Libi recognised the deep golden glow of the wood; the box was made from wood of the Talaf. When she opened the box, it contained a small statuette made from a jade-like green gem, patterned with swirls of a darker colour. Was it petrified sap? The stone lay in her palm, strangely warm to touch. It throbbed, like the tree had once throbbed.

The figurine was a model of Libi, sitting with her arms around her knees, looking up to the sky.

Her restored heart ached for the dryad of the Talaf. She had forgotten a heart was such a heavy burden to bear. Her memories of him were now flavoured bittersweet and sour green, and salted with sorrow.

This stone gave away his deepest secret; his love for a young witch too inexperienced to know true love when she met it.

A witch always knows her own heart.

Libi held it, now, cupped in the bowl of her hands and washed with her tears.

END

Re-ignite the Stars

Annie Bucknall

A fist beat a desperate tempo on Indigo Wild's ancient—and priceless—gothic oak front door. She sighed, breaking off a kiss with Adam, as a muffled yell came from the street below. *This had better be worthwhile.* She untangled herself from his muscular embrace and slipped from her satin aubergine bedsheets.

If one of her students had locked themselves out again…

The voice—angry and female—grew more frantic with each unanswered call.

'Aileen!'

She froze, her hand on the red velvet curtain of her four-poster bed. Was that…? Surely not…

Amongst the indiscriminate shouting, the name came again. Undeniable and in a clear, Irish lilt. There was only one person who still called her that…She gulped.

The game was up.

An icy fist of unease gripped Indie's stomach. Closing her eyes, she took a moment to steel herself for a confrontation two decades in the making. A confrontation, if she was honest, she'd foreseen as soon as her niece rang, begging for help. Family was a pot Indie had outgrown long ago but she'd never fully managed to untangle her roots.

Adam sat up and reached for his satin boxers. She shook her head. Their relationship was easy, uncomplicated. No need for him to get twisted up in this mess. He shrugged and lay back down, his fingers linked behind his head.

Not bothering to dress, she crossed the dusty teak floorboards of her bedroom and flung open the shutters to the street below, baring her breasts to the moonlight. Her elder sister Catriona gasped and averted her gaze, but Indie held the pose—and a cheeky smile— against the bitter chill.

'Put it on ice, Ad,' she called over her shoulder, loud enough to ensure Cat heard. 'We have company.'

#

Catriona pushed through the barely open door and Indie stepped back. She clasped her kimono around her neck to ward off a shot of frigid air that followed her sister in.

'Where is she?' Cat's gaze darted frantically around the shadows of the closed bookstore.

But she wouldn't find the teen. Hell, Indie couldn't find anything here if it didn't want to be found. This deliberately disordered little shop was a place women—and books—came to disappear for a while.

Indie shut the door with a firmer-than-necessary thud.

'Well hello to you too, Kitty Cat.' It was a playful childhood nickname…one Indie and her siblings had been forbidden to use since the first time Cat had brought her now-husband home for tea. *'It's Catriona,'* she'd implored. *'Please, Aileen. Jack prefers it.'*

Cat turned and, for the first time in almost twenty years, Indie saw her sister up close. Time had been kind…almost too kind. The dim light of a nearby electric sconce reflected off Cat's shiny, wrinkle-free forehead and Indie had to suppress a laugh. Cat tried— and failed—to flash her infamous glare. But she'd botoxed the big sister anger right out of her face. Sure, her deep brown eyes still turned black with her mood, but her frozen eyebrows made her look comical. A lifeless mannequin.

She'd finally transformed into the perfect politician's wife.

'She's in one of the nooks, isn't she? Sleeping like one of those *transients* you have here.' Cat started to climb the stairs.

Was she really going to search the shop's alcoves and wake the students in the middle of the night?

'She's gone out,' Indie called, silently cursing the accent that returned whenever she was in the presence of her kin.

Cat paused, her foot between steps, hand clutching her throat. 'Mother Mary.' She crossed herself. 'It's already happened, hasn't it? My grandbaby…'

The pain in her voice almost moved Indie. Or it would have, if Cat weren't intending to strip her own daughter of basic human rights. Tears trickled down her sister's cheeks and Indie rolled her eyes.

'No, she hasn't had an *abortion* yet.' She emphasized the word, letting her sister sit with the discomfort. 'She's at a séance.'

Cat's knees buckled. She paled and clasped at the vines carved into the stair railing. How fortunate that her tendency for hysteria survived their years apart.

Indie pursed her lips. Had Cat even noticed the woodland creatures whittled into every corner? The tiny, mischievous faces peeking from hidden hollows? If she could just get Cat to *stop*, to really look, perhaps they'd somehow slip back in time. Find themselves sitting at their Grandad's feet, listening to fairy stories, thinking anything was possible…back when it still was.

'You let my only daughter go to a s-s-seance?' Cat said, the return of her childhood stutter betraying her distress.

'She's nineteen. I could hardly stop her. Besides, these things aren't exactly scandalous around here. It's not like she's off practicing necromancy.'

Cat covered her mouth, eyes wide.

'Though that would be pretty cool.' Indie grinned.

'Aileen!'

Indie winced at her birth name. A hex with the power to bind her back to a life she'd never fit into. She'd buried that girl—and that name—long ago.

Cat set her jaw. 'I'm not leaving till I've seen her.'

'If Neve wants to see you, she can. But her decision is her own. In the mean time, let's have a cup of tea.'

Indie turned on her heel, trusting her sister to follow into the kitchen. Opening an emerald green overhead cupboard, her hand clutched a decanter of Tullamore Dew. Home in a bottle. Just one sip and the lemony dram would coat her tongue and take the edge off her nerves.

But Cat was a teetotaler. As much as Indie wanted to add a splash to her cup, it wasn't worth the ensuing lecture. Sighing, she slid the whiskey back, retrieving two willow print teacups and her largest tea pot instead.

It was going to be a long night.

Her sister stood in the doorway, arms crossed, leaning on it as though she were holding up the frame. In the harsh kitchen light, Indie saw the cracks in Cat's appearance. Black curls had escaped her French chignon. Tears and an ironed handkerchief had smudged her mascara into smeared-ink shadows beneath red-rimmed eyes. Her navy pants-suit though? Still perfectly pleated, paired with a spotless white shirt. Mother would have been proud.

With a freshly brewed pot, she gestured Cat toward the cluttered round table in the adjacent sunroom. Outside, the moon hung high, its fey light streaming through the glass-paned octagonal walls. Indie often sat here, in the peaceful half-dark, sipping tea under the glittering stars.

Indie threw a glance at her sister. 'You know, they say full moons are a good time for letting go of old hurts, releasing the things you can't control.'

Cat flipped the switch, flooding the room with dazzling light. 'How long will my daughter be?'

'No idea.' Using her forearm, Indie swept aside a pile of papers, disturbing Merlin who gave a mewl of protest and leapt to the floor.

Just before Indie set down the tray, she caught a glimpse of an Arthurian scene in the woodwork on the table below. Guinevere, betraying the faithful Arthur with Lancelot. Indie snorted. Yep. That was appropriate, here and now. According to the tale—and Cat—there were two roles for women in this life—the mother or the whore. Indie'd always preferred the company of whores.

Indie and Cat took their seats, letting the ritual of tea anesthetize atmosphere between them. Pouring, stirring, sipping, chinking. With the warm cup cradled in her hands, and Merlin winding his way through her legs, Indie could almost forget the last time they'd spoken; almost pretend the hurt had disappeared.

Cat broke the silence.

'Working on another novel?' she asked, indicating the papers as she filled her second cup and added three heaped teaspoons of sugar—just like she had as a child.

At the personal enquiry, Indie's heart lifted. She wanted to reach out and squeeze her sister's hand. Maybe the little girl she'd loved was still there...trapped like Rapunzel in the tower her husband, Jack, had built.

But she searched Cat's eyes and the walls showed no signs of crumbling. Ahhh....Of course. Cat must be skilled now in the art of polite conversation with people you barely tolerated. A necessary talent for a trophy wife.

'Someone is.' Indie shrugged. 'I don't write much these days.' With the gesture, her naked shoulder slipped from her dressing gown and the spell of civility between them broke.

'Oh, for Heaven's sakes, Aileen, have you no shame? Put some clothes on.'

'I'm comfortable.'

Cat rolled her eyes. 'Yes, well I'm not.' Annoyance thickened her accent. She looked sharply away, toward the carved stairs. 'Isn't your study up there? If you're not writing, what were you doing? It's late and the light was still on.'

'Well...'

'Wait, never mind. I don't want to know.' She held up a hand as though she could physically stop Indie's words.

But that was one thing Indie had learnt over the years. *No one* could stop her words once she wanted them out. Not her sister. Not their mother. Not an employer. Not even politicians. And she had words that could topple politicians. But she'd held them in to protect her sister; to protect those children who'd never asked for a father like Jack. To protect herself from the lawyers Jack threatened her with if she ever told.

She returned her thoughts to the present. To the comfort of Adam's desire, waiting upstairs. She knew now, what it was supposed to be like. How the right partner used passion to liberate rather than enslave.

Sipping at her tea, Indie raised her eyebrows. 'Oh, I think you do want to know what I was doing up there. We, dear sister, are in our sexual prime.' She took a long, slow drink then winked.

'When have you not been in your prime, huh? I thought you hit that in high school. I shudder to think how many more of these procedures, these *murders* you had done.'

Indie placed her teacup in the saucer soundlessly and bent to fill her arms with Merlin, who purred in delight. She buried her fingers in his soft, grey fur as though the sensation of this moment could keep her mind from slipping to the past. Her sister would never understand…but she'd never wanted to. Cat had always preferred the sugar of spoon-fed lies to the bitterness of truth.

Indie eyed her sister. Was it worth trying to free someone who wanted spend their life living in a prison of denial?

'I believe in a woman's right to choose,' she said.

Cat plonked her cup into its cradle so hard that droplets of tea landed on the pages still littered across the table. 'It's a sin! Neve will go to Hell, Aileen. *Hell.*'

Levelly, Indie replied, 'Some would argue that having a baby you don't want is Hell, *Catriona*. That being treated as no more than a prized breeding mare is Purgatory.'

Merlin kneaded Indie's thigh. His claws hooked her skin and snagged silk threads from her robe. She didn't flinch.

Cat raised her chin. 'That boy is willing to marry her. And we will be there to…help. To supplement their income while they raise our grandchild.'

'And her experience? How will you supplement that? How can you give her back the life this child will take from her? You can't make up for the degree and the career she would have without it.' It was a tired conversation that echoed the one they'd had almost two decades earlier, just after Neve was born. Back when Indie'd still craved her sister's approval.

Cat flung her arms wide and gave a derisive laugh. 'And how warm has that made you, hmm? Has your degree filled your heart, *Professor*? Have you held your novels as they've cried? Don't you dare tell me your book is your baby when you never nursed your own. You can't possibly understand. You don't even write anymore!'

Indie's chair scraped as she stood. 'Get out.'

'I'm waiting for my daughter.' Cat's jaw hardened.

'You're leaving. Now. Adam!'

'You've brainwashed her! She's not doing this, Aileen. Do you hear me?'

Adam's lively footfall reverberated across the upper floor, as though he'd been waiting to be called into action.

Cat stood, her expression stony. 'I will out your little operation and have a picket out the front of your store before you can blink. Think hard, sister. Jack will *ruin* you.'

He's already tried. Indie bit back the words.

Adam—half-naked in blue satin boxer shorts—cleared his throat and Cat guffawed at the sight of him.

'Typical,' she said. 'He's half your age. When will you grow up?' Picking up her purse, she pushed past into the dark belly of the store.

Indie swore she heard whispering as the crowd of mythical creatures spied from the shadows.

When Cat opened the front door, she looked back one last time. 'Who even are you, Aileen?'

'Not. Aileen,' Indie said through clenched teeth.

'No.' Cat's voice held a note of sorrow and she dropped her head. 'No, you're not.'

#

As dawn edged closer, Indie let herself into the guest bedroom and studied her sleeping niece. The girls had scampered in not long after Cat left, at least two of them drunk by their clumsy footsteps and stifled giggles. Her niece, she was sure, had been well-behaved. In the days she'd been here, Neve still epitomized the wholesome Catholic girl...the séance was, perhaps, the first exception.

Neve's blonde curls spiralled loose on her pillow, leaving her looking no more than a child. A memory froze Indie in place and the powdery newborn smell of baby Neve washed over her.

After five sons, Cat's joy had been palpable when she'd placed her daughter, fresh to this world, in her sister's arms. *Isn't she perfect, Aileen? Couldn't you just gobble her up?* Indie had stayed with them a fortnight—cooking, cleaning, and nurturing Cat and the boys. All while Jack—still in the beginning of his political career—went on campaign. At night, she'd collapse into bed, exhausted by the sheer effort of it all, wondering how on Earth her sister found the energy to get through each day looking so perfect, with her husband away so much.

The day before Indie was due to head back home to her teaching position in Dublin, Cat had cried on her shoulder, thanking her;

clinging so tight Indie wasn't sure her sister would ever let go.

Looking at Neve now, Indie wished Cat hadn't.

But they could never go back, never return to that moment, to that bond, to the day before it all changed. If all that had passed between them before hadn't made a reconciliation impossible, Indie's role in what was to come would cement their estrangement.

Jack had won nineteen years ago. But there was no way she'd let him mess her niece up, too.

Neve rolled over, perhaps sensing a presence in the room.

'Aunty?' she said, her voice groggy.

'Get dressed. We're hiking the Tor.'

'I'm tired.'

Indie tugged the duvet back and Neve groaned into her pillow.

'Up, child. The new day waits for no one.' *But your mother'll be waiting for you pretty soon.*

#

They climbed in inky quietude, their flashlights illuminating the path that wound up the hill, toward the ancient monument. Layers of clothing didn't stop their cheeks from pinking or the curl of frosty air from sneaking under their collars, but the exercise heated Indie's blood mercifully against the cold.

Neve attempted her usual chatter but Indie hushed her with a polite smile. The girl needed to learn to commune with her thoughts. She was a young woman on the precipice of discovering agency. But if Neve didn't connect to the power that welled within her, she'd never find the strength to defy Cat.

Strength she'd need today.

Neve wasn't the first girl Indie had taken in from Ireland. This hike was a ritual she followed with each of them—a moment of stillness to ensure they were at peace with their decision. Everyone's reason was different. Everyone's choice was valid. But Indie was damned if she would sit by and watch the faceless men of the Irish government snuff the fire from these girls. Pontificating from their beige offices, they seemed to take pride in upholding these archaic laws; in trying to extinguish these stars.

With the help of some ex-colleagues from one of Dublin's most prestigious universities, she'd been smuggling girls into England for abortions for over a decade, under the ruse of a writer-in-residence scholarship. The scandal, if it broke, would be career-ending for many of them. But they'd all known the risks when they started. And she wouldn't stop now…no matter what Cat—or Jack—did.

This was about the girls. About Neve.

The Tor loomed above them, an ancient tower marking the gateway to Avalon. A sigil of fertility. Of power. Some said, the burial place of King Arthur himself.

They reached the summit just as the sun crested over the horizon and bathed the sleepy, foggy hills in a buttery light. Indie paused, taking it all in, then turned to see her niece doubled over, trying to catch her breath.

'How…did you…get up here…so…fast?' Neve panted, her face flushed.

'Practice. But don't worry yourself. It's the hormones. Makes you lose your breath.'

Neve nodded and unscrewed her water bottle, gulping from the flask.

'This is where I leave you,' Indie said.

A twist of blonde hair had come loose from her niece's ponytail and Indie's hand itched to reach up and tuck it behind her ear. But she wouldn't allow herself the motherly gesture; that wasn't her role here. Neve needed her to hold steady.

'I've made this choice,' Indie said. 'The one you're considering. I had my own reasons and, for me, it wasn't easy. I wrestled with it. And this was the spot.' She outstretched her arm to the sweeping view, trying to ignore the stone that formed in her stomach as she spoke. 'This is where I knew it was right for me. I don't regret it. But there are some who do…just as there are some who regret the children they bear. It's not wrong to do this, Neve. But it has to be right for you.'

Neve nodded, her blue eyes watery. The cold? Sorrow? Probably both. Indie swallowed the cotton-dryness in her mouth. She handed her niece a thermos of tea and a lunchbox of oven-warm scones from her backpack.

'Stay. Think. Come home when you're ready.'

#

The speech on the hill? She'd given it dozens of times before. But this was the first time she wasn't sure of its truth. Dark questions rippled through her mind. Did she regret staying childfree? Would she die alone? Would she have made a good mum? Was this really the life she wanted…or was it the life Jack had forced her into?

She let her feet carry her down the slope, trying to shove his face back under the trapdoor in her mind. But the memories of that night kept springing loose.

His ministerial smile.

She'd trusted that smile, once.

Her sister's sleeping household. *I'm celebrating. Share a drink with me, Aileen.*

Alcohol. Too much alcohol.

His fumbling. Her protests.

His penetration. Her protests.

His climax. Her tears.

Her pregnancy. Her abortion.

Her shame.

Indie reached her car, slid into the driver's seat and banged her hands on the wheel.

Not. Her. Shame. HIS.

He owned it.

And if he wanted a fight, she'd bring it to him.

#

When Indie pulled up, Cat was pacing by the shop entrance. Her hair curled free, wild; her makeup smeared worse than last night. But those bloody pant legs were still impeccable. Indie's heart clenched at the thought of Neve spending all those years trying to live up to Cat's impossible standards. Whatever the cost, she'd free her niece.

Unlocking the door, she let her sister storm inside. A pile of books, waiting to be shelved, stood stacked by the entrance. Cat toppled them like skittles as she bowled through. *The Handmaid's Tale* landed squarely at her feet. Female suppression, a totalitarian government, women as chattel. How fitting.

Indie smirked and handed it to Cat. 'I think this one is for you.'

Cat rolled her eyes. Her arms remained folded.

'Suit yourself.' Indie set it down and shut the door.

'Where is she?'

'On a walk.'

'When's her procedure booked for?'

'That's her business.'

Cat stamped through the shop, heels clacking. She headed toward the register.

'What are you doing?' Indie called.

Cat stepped behind the counter. A carving of Puck leered over her shoulder. Indie tensed and stopped herself from pointing a finger at him. *You stay out of this, you wee devil.* That fairy had a way of amplifying mischief in a person's heart.

'I'm done, Aileen.' Cat said, her voice low and hard. 'Done. When you killed poor Eamon's baby without even telling him, then ran off on your university job to start this…shop, I thought that was the lowest you could go. But to get my own daughter mixed up in this abortion ring you've got going on? We're through.'

Indie's blood flamed. She closed the space between them, leaning over the counter until they were nose-to-nose. 'We were over a long time ago. Your husband saw to that.'

'What's that supposed to mean?'

'You know what it means. You saw me that day, before I left for Dublin. You *know*, don't you? You've always known.'

Cat's cheeks pinked. 'I know you're a liar. I know you'd say anything to justify the devil inside you.'

'Or *you* would, to justify the devil inside *him,*' Indie shot back.

Cat glared then picked up the shop phone and dialled. 'You've brought this on yourself.' She straightened and sent Indie a wintry smile. Then she reported to Jack in sharp, unemotional sentences.

Through the receiver, Indie overheard the baritone of his voice. Knowing he was there, on the other end of the line, was enough to make her jaw squeeze until her teeth ached. She'd felt brave in the car, but now her legs trembled; words strangled in her throat.

And she knew, then, the answer to the question that tortured her on sleepless nights.

Indie braced herself against a nearby shelf, her breath coming in short gasps.

She'd let Jack torment her into this life. From the rape on, her decisions, her choices, had been about not allowing anyone close. She'd never wanted to carry his baby and she had no regrets about that choice. But the fact that she'd never settled down? Never let anyone into her heart? Never started a family?

That was because of him.

No more. She breathed deep. No bloody more. She'd be damned if she let him steal another second from her. *Time to grow some balls, Indie.*

She snatched the phone from her sister, mid-rant.

'Jack. It's me.'

A sharp intake of breath.

'Save it,' she said, pre-empting his reply. 'Save it for your wife. She may have to listen to your lies, but I don't. If you don't leave this alone, Jack, I'll go public. And we all know I'm not the only one with a story to sell. Assholes like you have a pattern…and this is the kind of mud that sticks.' She paused.

'What do you want?' His brogue was thick. She'd gotten to him.

I want the last twenty years of my life back, you pig. Indie inhaled slow. This was about her niece.

'Both of you will stay out of your daughter's decision and her recovery. This is her body, her choice. Understand?'

He was silent, a faint static on the line letting her know he was there. Her heart thrummed. If she spoke first she'd lose.

She wouldn't lose.

He broke, his voice terse. 'Yes. Put my wife on.'

Indie handed the phone back and watched as her sister dried and shrank. Her shoulders rounded and her body sagged, giving her the carriage of a much older woman. A deep lake dammed before she'd ever had time to carve a path through life. Another of Jack's victims.

Indie sighed. Cat might be the formidable, stormy sea but Jack was the sharp rocks she broke herself over time and again.

When Cat hung up, she took a moment to smooth her suit. She turned to Indie, her eyes brimming.

'I will see her before I go.'

'Of course. Cat…I…In 1977, Jack—'

Cat stopped her with a gesture. 'He's my *husband*.'

'But you should know what kind of person he is. Who you married.'

Her face crumpled. 'I know you make things up, Aileen. You have since we were girls.' She pointed at the pixies etched into the wall. 'You're just like Grandad. An over-active imagination.'

'Some of us have imagined entire lives for ourselves,' Indie countered.

The front door opened and shut. Neve's fairy-light footsteps sounded.

'Aunt Indie?' Her charming lilt echoed through the shop. 'I have my answer.'

When Neve appeared, her blonde hair shone against her ruby coat, her face was lightly flushed from the exercise. But, as soon as she saw her mother, the smile dropped from Neve's face and she froze. She wrapped her arms around her belly and hung her head, casting a flickering, fearful glance at Cat from beneath long blonde lashes.

'Mammy? What are you doing here?'

Cat was by her daughter in two paces, pulling her close and scolding at once; reenacting the push and pull of parental love. Indie caught only the occasional word.

Disappointed. Sin. Damnation. The usual bullshit.

Neve met Indie's gaze, a desperate plea in her blue eyes. As much as Indie wanted to step in, she recognised this moment. She couldn't rescue her niece. Instead, Indie jerked her chin, gesturing for Neve to take a stand against her mother. To step into her own womanhood.

Could the girl do it? Would she?

Neve's eyes close momentarily. When they opened they held a sparkle of decision and Indie inwardly cheered. Neve pushed Cat away and moved to stand next to Indie.

'I know what I have to do.' She looked at Indie. 'I'm keeping the baby.'

Cat cried out, one hand smothering a laugh, eyes filled with tears.

Neve lifted her chin. 'But I want to raise it here. With you, Aunt Indie. If that's not too much bother?'

Indie retreated until she was braced against the service counter. A little one. Here. In the shop. It wasn't impossible, but…

'Neve!' Cat cried. 'Conor has rights too. A child *needs* a father.'

Neve scoffed and lowered her hand to protectively cover her belly. 'Conor doesn't want it, Mam. He told me to get rid of it. The only reason he changed his mind was because Dad offered him money.'

'I think you'll find he's come around to the idea—'

'I'm not raising this baby with a man who doesn't want it. And I'm not marrying him either. We weren't even that serious!'

Cat put her hands on her hips. 'Neve, if you do this, you won't get a cent out of us or him. You're on your own.'

Indie straightened and put her arm around her niece, glaring at her sister. No, a true politician's wife. Not a sister. Jack had taken sheers to the fabric of their sisterhood years ago, slicing it clean down the middle. If Cat wanted to, they could stitch together the frayed edges…but not with him still waving the blades about.

She couldn't save Cat, but she could be there for Neve; give the girl a place to breathe and raise this child away from the claustrophobia of her father's house.

'She won't be on her own, Cat. I'll look after them both.'

Cat shook her head. 'You can't take her from me, Aileen.' Her voice became venomous. 'You lost your chance. This is *my* grandchild, *my* daughter.'

'No,' Indie said calmly, glancing at Neve, 'she's—'

'A woman in her own right,' Neve said. She threw her shoulders back. 'I'm of age, Mammy. I'll make my own choices.' Her certainty faltered and tears glittered on her lashes. 'Even if you don't agree with them and even if we never see each other again.' She reached out for her mother.

Cat hesitated, her mouth thinned. She ignored her daughter's hand and looked at Indie.

'I hope you know what you're doing, Neve.' She adjusted the strap of her impossibly-small black handbag, tucked her wild raven curls behind her ears and left the two of them, frozen in place, staring wide-eyed after her.

When Indie heard the front door unlatch something clicked and she ran after her sister. Outside, Glastonbury's main street was beginning to fill as doors opened and signs were turned around. The sun lifted the chill and summoned customers from their cosy homes.

Cat was already a few shops down the road, presumably headed to her accommodation, when Indie caught her.

'Catriona, don't reject your daughter like you rejected me.'

'You give me no choice.' Cat held her bag like a shield. 'Then or now. You did the wrong thing and you're encouraging my daughter to do the wrong thing as well.'

Indie sighed. 'You always had a choice. And I did nothing wrong. You know who the father of my child was, don't you? You know it wasn't Eamon.'

Her sister shook her head, loosening tears from her eyes as she stared at the ground.

'You do, Cat. You know what Jack did. He's done it to others. I'll bet he's done it to you, too.'

She lifted Cat's chin until their gazes met.

'Your children are grown. Stay here, with us. Start again.' Indie's voice cracked. 'Please, Cat?'

Cat locked eyes with her.

Indie waited.

Had she broken the enchantment? Climbed the tower to free Rapunzel from within?

Her sister drew a breath in that steadying way she'd done as a child. The move that signaled the argument was over.

Jack or Indie? Which one of them had won?

Cat's hand trembled. The only sign of a potential fissure in the dam holding back Cat's truths.

But she only said, 'Look after them.'

Indie nodded, choking down a sob. She gave Cat the worn copy of *The Handmaid's Tale*. 'The stamp on the first page has the shop number. Call me, if you ever want to leave, okay?'

Cat swallowed and pressed her palm tenderly to Indie's face. 'I will…Indigo.' She kissed Indie's forehead. 'For what it's worth, you would have been a wonderful mother.'

'For what it's worth, you always were, Kitty Cat.'

#

END

The Jig's Back Door

Reprinted from 2019 SWG Anthology 'Elemental'

DA Kelly

'Are you certain we're heading the right way?' Sneath peered into the darkness. He waved his flaming torch back and forth, illuminating the cave walls. The roof was a jungle of tangled tree roots and low-hanging rock. Not a gem to be seen. Not a vein of gold gleamed in the torchlight. This treasure hunting was harder than he had planned. 'What's the map say?'

'Stupid thing is sulking,' Clutter said.

'Of all the maps in the world.' Sneath cuffed Clutter's pointy green ear. 'You had to steal that one.'

'Of all the goblins in the world, you had to be my brother.'

'Elder brother. Which makes me boss.'

'Then you hold the map.' Clutter thrust the ragged scroll into Sneath's chest. 'See if she likes you any better.'

'PMS,' Sneath said. 'Prissy Map Syndrome, that's what she's got.'

He unfurled the ancient vellum. The sketched landscape had changed since he'd last looked at it. There were no more forests and mountains dotted with towns. Now tunnels, underground streams and caverns sprawled across the map. Trouble was, when he tried to focus on a particular area, it faded and shimmered making it impossible to follow. He tried peering out of the corner of his eye, but the map was smarter than that. All it did was flash the words, *You are uglier than an ogre sucking a wasp!*

Forcing a smile, Sneath turned to Clutter and said, 'You just got to know how to talk to females.'

The map snorted, the sound emanating from the scorched vellum despite it having no mouth. 'Because you have so much experience.'

'If you weren't a scrap of old calf skin, you'd know what a terrific love-maker I am.'

'Thank the Mother Sky for small mercies,' the map said. 'And stop calling me The Map! I do have a name, you know.'

'Lemon-puss?' Clutter elbowed Sneath and grinned, his tiny, sharp teeth glowing gold in the torchlight.

'Amethyst,' the map said, with a haughty sniff. 'Amethyst Diaphany the Fourth.'

'You made that up!' Sneath scoffed.

'Either call me by my name or I stop guiding you.'

'Because you've been so extraordinarily helpful up until now,' Clutter said. 'You don't even have an X-marks-the-spot! I'm tempted to wipe my backside with you next time I—'

'Believe me,' the map said, 'I can make things a lot worse. Now, are you going to show me some respect, or will I roll up and shut up?'

The goblins looked at each other, shrugged and said, 'Amethyst Diaphany the Fourth it is, then.'

'But we're not going to spout that mouthful all the time,' Sneath said.

'Amethyst will do for now. And perhaps a bow here and there for good measure.'

'In your dreams!' Sneath sputtered. 'Why, if you didn't know where that magical Gem was hidden—'

'What was that?' Clutter spun on one boot heel, cocking his head to listen.

'Probably the witch,' Amethyst whispered. 'She's been hunting you since you stole me.'

'And you're just telling us this now?' Sneath said.

'I thought I'd lost her when we forded that river,' Amethyst said.

'You call being swept along by ice-cold rapids, fording a river?' Clutter muttered. 'Crawling out on a slimy finger of rock, shivering, half drowned—'

'Shhh!' Amethyst hissed. 'Douse the torch! Run forward seventeen steps, then turn right, drop to your knees and crawl until I tell you to stop.'

Distant footsteps echoed through the cave. The goblins didn't need further encouragement. Sneath kicked dirt over the flaming torch then shoved it in his backpack, the pitch-smeared end jutting over his shoulder. Never had darkness swooped over them so thick and so fast. Sneath darted through the black, counting as he ran. Clutter was a number behind, but that was typical. He'd probably knock himself out on a low hanging rock because he counted wrong. When Sneath reached seventeen he fell to his knees and scrambled along like a frightened crab. Amazingly, Clutter scuttled along just behind. Freezing, muddy puddles soaked Sneath's woollen trews, squelched between his fingers and splashed his sweaty face.

Amethyst, still grasped in Sneath's hand, coughed and

spluttered. Who knew a map could cough? Sneath flapped Amethyst around, shaking her free of mud and water.

'Yes.' Amethyst wheezed. 'You definitely know how to treat a lady.'

'You get what you give,' Sneath said, puffing. 'How much further?'

'There's a deep ravine to your left, you can go that way if you like. Drop me before you hurtle down to Hell.'

'Oh, you are a rotten joke!'

'Birds of a feather,' Amethyst said.

'Would you both shut up!' Clutter whispered. 'Since when do witches wear hobnailed boots?'

Rhythmic, metal-on-rock steps echoed through the darkness. Stopped. Scraped as though the boot wearer turned on the spot. Probably listening.

'She must mean business!' Sneath scrunched up Amethyst and stuffed her down the front of his trews.

'Please! Kill me now!' Amethyst said, her voice muffled.

'Maybe I'll throw *you* down the ravine,' Sneath said as he crawled forward.

'It stinks in here!' Amethyst groaned. 'Have you never heard of soap?'

Voices drifted through the tunnel.

One deep, raspy and definitely male. 'They gotta be the worst thieves ever.'

The other voice was female, her tone nasty. 'Bright enough to steal from me.'

'Stop!' Amethyst shouted, making Sneath's squashy male bits vibrate. 'Make a slight right. No, your other right. Head into the passageway, but watch it. There's a bit of a drop at the far end, and there could be water at the bottom. The ogre won't fit through the passage. One less to deal with.'

'Ogre!' Sneath and Clutter spluttered together.

'You never said anything about an ogre!' Clutter said.

'My bad.' Amethyst, for once didn't sound glib or insulting, which caused Sneath's heart to flip-flop with fear.

'When we started hunting for the Lost Gem of Nerramai,' Sneath said. 'We never figured ogres would chase us. Still, once we find the Gem, we can level a mountain if we want.' He slithered along on his belly, the map squashing against his male-bits.

Amethyst didn't answer. Probably so impressed she was lost for words.

Sneath stretched his bony, green fingers forward through the mud, feeling for the supposed drop-off. Nothing but rock smoothed by goodness knows what. He felt up and around. The tunnel walls and roof were smooth as polished obsidian. His wiry hair stood on end. Something had worn the rock smooth and there was a good chance they were heading right for it.

Sneath rolled onto his side, tugged his trews open and said, 'You don't have a bit of fine-print stating *This way be monsters,* do you?'

'That will teach you not to read the instructions before you start,' Amethyst said.

'I didn't see any instructions!' Clutter crawled alongside Sneath and, fumbling in the dark, grabbed his brother's trews and whispered down them, 'You hid them from us, didn't you?'

'Do you mind?' Sneath clapped his hand over his crotch.

Amethyst didn't answer.

'Tunnel's not big enough for dragons,' Clutter said. 'So that's something.'

'You want the witch to catch us?' Sneath snapped at the map.

'You want to be locked up in that stinking old trunk again? Squashed among the mouldy boots and socks.'

Amethyst growled. 'She tortured me far worse than that.'

'Why?' both goblins asked.

'To force me to lead her to the Gem.'

'You have a choice?'

'It's complicated,' the map muttered.

'How can *we* be sure you're leading us to the Gem?' Clutter asked.

'You can't. Now come on,' Amethyst said. 'I hear the witch likes goblin flambé. Crawl forward another few feet and you'll be at the drop-off. Hold your breath. Don't complain I didn't warn you.'

Grunting, Sneath patted his trews closed and crawled along the passage, his hands sliding forward so he wouldn't miss the drop-off. The ground vanished, then angled down in a slippery, putrid slide. Normally, Sneath would find the stench and whooshing sensation of careening down a slide of mud fun, but today was a rotten day, and all the excitement of adventuring had vanished in the dark. Clutter squealed and fumbled for Sneath, clutching his jacket with an iron grip.

They both tumbled through the air and plunged into an ice-cold lake. Sneath sucked in a shocked breath and a throat full of freezing water as he thrashed for the surface. Clutter flailed, grabbing for his brother, his nails gouging deep wounds in Sneath's face and neck. Coughing, Sneath fought to stay afloat, clambering onto whatever he could, which happened to be Clutter. Pain shot through his lower arm and he pulled away, his legs still peddling their way up his brother's thrashing body. Clutter disappeared from beneath him, leaving Sneath spluttering and flailing around in an awkward and rather ineffective form of swimming. In the dark, a few feet away, came a great gasp and a lot of splashing.

'Come any closer, Sneath.' Clutter coughed and wheezed. 'And I'll bite you again!'

Sneath sucked on his arm, tasting warm blood and torn flesh. Uncertain which way to swim, he reefed Amethyst from his trews, treading water while he held the map in the air. 'Which way now?'

'I am feeling wonderful, thanks for asking.' Amethyst shivered between Sneath's fingers.

'Come on, Amethyst!' Clutter said through chattering fangs. 'We are freezing here.'

'To your left there's an embankment,' Amethyst said with a sniff. 'It's the easiest way out of the lake. But there is a rather grumpy serpent eyeing you for supper from the shoreline.'

'What!' Both goblins squawked.

'Best you go right. There's a bit of a climb, but at least you won't end up gristle stuck between the serpent's teeth.'

'How do we know you're not leading us astray?' Sneath asked. 'For all we know, the other way will be worse.'

'Because you're my last hope.'

Sneath shoved the map between his fangs and headed right.

A soft splosh, flick and a splash drifted over to the swimming goblins.

The serpent! Sneath swam faster, his arms whirling like bony windmill blades. Clutter thrashed nearby. All smash and kick. Hopefully he was keeping pace.

Something cold and slimy slithered by Sneath, bumping him sideways. He yelped.

A great splash showered Sneath. Clutter howled from somewhere in the darkness above.

Above? Sneath squinted upward but could see nothing. *How did he get up there?*

A colossal splash was followed by a swollen wave that buffeted Sneath as the faintly-glowing serpent dove into the lake. Its sinuous body, ice cold and powerful skimmed past Sneath leaving a slimy trail on his arm. The serpent reared once more, it's snake-like whiskers slapping Sneath as it flicked its head. Clutter hollered high above once again then landed a few feet from Sneath, sinking underwater with the momentum of his fall. He shot to the surface, gasping and, from the speed and chaos of the splashes, Clutter swam like a wild thing.

Gummy lips clamped around Sneath's lower legs. Rubbery, wet whiskers drummed about his body. Sneath kicked and punched the serpent's snout. He reefed the torch from his sodden backpack, beating the serpent's head. Golden, implacable eyes glared at him from just below the surface. It bit the torch and tossed it aside. Sneath drew a small, steel blade from his belt and jabbed furiously in the darkness. The serpent thrashed. Sneath lurched free, surrounded by metallic-tasting water.

The brothers swam until they reached the shore—a greasy landing of rock and pebbles. Sneath crawled forward, groping for the cliff face. Rough stone grazed his hand. He thrust his dagger into its sheath and fumbled around for rock-holds. He began climbing. When he had managed a few feet, he glanced down looking for the orange glow of Clutter's eyes, but there was nothing to see. All he could hear was Clutter's puffing and the scuff of fingers and boots on rock. If only there was a speck of light. Just a chink would be enough to allow the goblins to see.

'Do you have an indilt wight?' Sneath asked Amethyst who was still clamped between his fangs.

'What?' Amethyst grumbled. 'You think I'm a multi-purpose

tool?'

'You're 'agical. I's a logical westion.'

'Stop drooling on me!' Amethyst said. 'It's disgusting, and you're making my ink run.'

'You try talkin' to a shnooty map when i's a'tween your teess.'

'You try being stuffed in a mouth that smells like a sewer. I thought your crotch stunk! By the Sky Mother—'

'Oh, for da luv ov...' Sneath grabbed the map and shoved her back down his trews. 'Happier now?'

A smokey-red light lit the cavern, surging fog-like across the underground lake and up the cliff face where the two goblins clung like a pair of four legged spiders. The magical redfire, though low in power, stung Sneath's skin. He could taste sulphur and ash as though it had been painted on his tongue.

Hope that's all the magic the old crone's got. Sneath shot a look up, then down and across the lake. There knelt the witch and the ogre in the passageway's opening a few yards up the rock-face. The ogre's eyes reflected orange in the rusty light. Damn! He was a night-seer just like the goblins. He stood up and leaned out the hole, scanning the cavern. Though he was fully armoured in boiled leather and steel-plate, he was perhaps five feet tall. Made no sense. Ogre toddlers were taller than that.

'She's summoning redfire!' Clutter moaned. 'How are we going to outrun redfire?'

'From the taste of it, it's no real threat.'

'Hope that's her best trick, then.'

'There they are!' shouted the ogre, his gruff voice bouncing around the massive cavern in hollow echoes. He jumped into the lake and started swimming toward the goblins. With each stroke, the ogre grew, his arms bulging bigger and bigger muscles, his knobby head expanding like a bull's bladder blown full of hot air, his body spreading and lengthening until he was the height of a woolly mammoth.

'So much for redfire being her best trick.' Clutter climbed faster.

Sneath, thankful for the fiery, red light, scrambled upward, Clutter alongside him, his wide eyes glowing orange, his face dripping with sweat.

'Are you sure the gem is this way?' Sneath asked. 'Or are you just making us suffer for your own amusement?'

'Here's hoping, eh!' Amethyst chuckled; there was no mirth in the sound.

Erratic splashing floated up to the goblins. Sneath glanced down, expecting to see the ogre exiting the lake. But the ogre was frantically treading water, searching the darkness behind the him. He ducked beneath the blood-red water, popped to the surface, cursed and swam faster toward the cliff.

Ripples broke the lake's still surface. Slimy humps undulated then disappeared near the ogre. Sneath almost cheered the serpent on. He shot a look at the witch, still kneeling in the passageway. She watched on, her expression lost in the shadows, but Sneath could feel her hatred burning into his back.

The murky, red light she had conjured seared fire-bright, momentarily blinding the goblins before simmering back to a dull glow.

The serpent reared from the lake, its barbed, neck tentacles writhing. Water cascaded down its scaly body. It hissed, flicked its gold, shimmering gaze away from the ogre to focus on the witch. The serpent dived back into the water and swam toward the passageway.

'Good!' Clutter said between puffs. 'Get rid of the dangerous one first.'

'You don't think the ogre is a threat?' Sneath said. 'Because he's out of the water and a good few feet up the cliff.'

'He's heavy and awkward. Hopefully the rock won't hold him and he'll tumble like a turd into a cesspit.'

'You certainly know how to cheer up a goblin,' Sneath said.

'I do try.'

Sneath dragged himself onto the ledge. He fished Amethyst from his trews and lay there on his belly panting. Clutter flopped over the edge, huffing as he rolled onto his back. Sneath struggled up onto his hands and knees and peered over the ledge. The ogre, clinging to the cliff face, glared up at him. Hissing and splashing from the lake drew Sneath's attention.

'On all that's sacred!' He grabbed Clutter's shoulder. 'The witch is riding the serpent across the lake.'

'Crawl, you fools!' Amethyst said. 'To your right there's an overhang. Get under it while I see what lies ahead.'

'I'm more concerned about what lies behind!' Sneath scuttled beneath the overhang. He looked into Clutter's wide eyes. 'She's a Charmer! The witch is a Charmer!'

'She can't be a real powerful one or she would have bespelled us from the other side of the lake.'

'She charmed a serpent!' Sneath said.

'An oversized worm.' Amethyst scoffed. 'Not much of a challenge. Better not let her catch you both, eh?'

Grunting and scraping floated up the cliff, the sounds growing louder.

'Hurry!' Screamed the witch. It wasn't rage filling her voice. It was terror. 'Catch them before they get to the doors!'

'There's a tunnel at the far end of the overhang,' Amethyst said.

'To your right about ten feet away. Crawl along until you can't feel the rock wall. Don't bother feeling about when you get to the tunnel. It's wide enough to fit several mammoths side by side.'

'Where, exactly, are you leading us?' Sneath asked.

'To *The Hangman's Jig.*'

Sneath and Clutter gaped at one another, their eyes fire-gold in the dusky red gloom.

'The *Jig's* just a legend,' Sneath scoffed. 'Magical bloody bar where all the races drink and get along. As if. No such place. No gem is worth all this crud! If you don't stop this farting about and tell us what really lies ahead, we'll take our chances with the witch and that ogre. All we have to do is hand you over and—'

'Please?' Amethyst said. 'No!'

'We might be greedy, but we're not total fools.' Clutter crossed his arms. 'Are you leading us to the Lost Gem of Nerramai, or not?'

'There is a good chance you will find it at the end of that tunnel. In *The Hangman's Jig.* But you must outrun the witch first. She knows she can't go down there.'

'Why?' both brothers asked.

'She'll be tortured and killed.'

'See,' Sneath said to Clutter. 'Told you there was no place where magical folk all got along nice.'

Clutter glanced over his shoulder. 'Don't think we have a lot of choice.'

'And us?' Sneath eyed Amethyst warily. 'Will they torture and kill us? I'm not fond of being killed.'

'Not if you're as wily as I hope you are.'

'You have no idea,' Sneath muttered.

With that, the goblins scrambled beneath the overhang toward the tunnel.

The goblins' rapid footsteps echoed throughout the enormous passageway. Faint, empty things that died somewhere far above. Their whispered conversation lingered in the darkness as though the words flew about on wings.

'We should try and lure the witch down here,' Sneath said. 'Getting her tortured and dead will help us live.'

Clutter nodded. 'I like how you think.'

'How much further?' Sneath held Amethyst up in a futile effort to see directions.

'Not far,' Amethyst said. 'I should warn you. Once the doors open I'll turn into an ordinary map. You must tell Galrash that I am Amethyst Diaphany the Fourth. That you rescued me from Sangyll and that she's in the Serpents' Cavern. He'll know what to do.'

Heavy, iron-shod footfalls pounded along the tunnel behind. Something whistled overhead, thunking into the rock. Shards of stone rained down, scattering across the ground.

Holy Sky Mother! Sneath ran faster. *Rock-iron tipped arrows!*

The goblins hurtled along as fast as their short legs could go, with Amethyst flapping in Sneath's fist. The brothers slid to a halt in a haze of watery grey light at the end of the tunnel. Enormous bronze doors were embedded in the black rock wall before them, the tops lost in shadow. Intertwined floral patterns—green with age and dented and blackened in places—wove their way across the doors. Dim light shone through a lichen-and-tree-root-lashed hole, high in the stone roof, illuminating the platform on which the goblins stood. Deep gouges scored the earthen floor, and the surrounding rocks were scorched and melted into black glass.

The ogre roared. Loosed another arrow. It skimmed Clutter's head and rammed into the door. Clutter shrieked, clapping one hand to the bleeding wound.

Sneath put his shoulder to the great door and pushed, his boots scraping and slipping in the dirt. Clutter planted both hands against the bronze, adding his strength to his brother's. An arrow slammed into the door, barely missing Sneath's shoulder.

The doors swung open with a loud, rusty groan. Both goblins tumbled into a golden, hazy room the size of a small mountain. Sneath landed beside a pair of reindeer hide boots, their length lashed with rough leather thong. He gazed upward. And upward. A gnarly, bearded face stared down at him with amused disbelief.

Troll! Sneath surveyed the cavernous room. Looked like a tavern or maybe a brothel. It was difficult to tell from the view between the troll's legs. He wiggled to one side to get a better look. Smoke, heavy with the sweet smell of the drug, *Golden Brim* clouded *The Hangman's Jig.*

'There are dragons,' Clutter muttered. 'Maybe we should take our chances with the ogre?'

Great, winged serpents lounged here and there breathing plumes of fire into red-hot cauldrons. Spicy vapours rose from the iron kettles like silvery fog. The dragons sucked the drug in through their huge nostrils, their scales glimmering opalescent with pleasure.

'These dragons are flying so high they'll be lucky to see straight for a year,' Sneath said, his mind more on treasure and naked fairies than danger.

From somewhere at the rear of the cavern came warm, lusty laughs and naughty squeals. Cushions in iridescent aqua, blue and forest green scattered the stone-flagged floor, most of them occupied by under-dressed fairies and over-lusty trolls. A rolling bubble noise filled the shadows. From the sharp tang in the air, Sneath knew gurgle-pipes filled with pixie-dust were in high demand.

Could be worse. He offered the troll a weak smile and thrust out one, filthy hand. 'The name is Sneath. Happy to do business with you.'

'Not what I expected.' The troll scratched his warty chin.

'What are they selling?' a voice rumbled from somewhere deep within the brothel. It was a rich, hearty voice, male, and quite possibly the owner of *The Hangman's Jig*.

'From the looks of 'em,' the troll said. 'Nothing we want. Why else would they come in the back door?' He lifted thick brows and patted the huge doors. 'Didn't even know they worked.'

'Back door?' Sneath glared at the map, but she said nothing.

Footsteps clattered in the tunnel outside. Clutter whimpered, gingerly touching the wound on his head and staring at the blood.

The troll ripped an ogre's arrow from one of the bronze doors and looked it over, scowling. 'Rock-iron. Bone shaft.'

'What you got there?' asked a gravelly voice from beside the black-marble slabbed bar. 'That dinner? About time. I ordered ages ago.'

'Anyone feel like ogre for dinner?' the troll waved the arrow about.

'They's too puny to be ogres!' Gravelly Voice said. 'I picks bigger things out my teeths than them.'

Sneath dragged Clutter to his feet and shuffled further inside *The Hangman's Jig*. A shiver vibrated through Amethyst, into Sneath's hand, searing up his arm. He glanced down. She sagged, her images barely visible, her vellum brittle and scorched.

'Best shut the doors,' Sneath said, bowing and fluttering his hand in greeting. 'There is an angry ogre heading this way along with a rather nasty witch.'

'We're looking for someone known as Galrash,' Clutter announced. 'We have an important message.'

'Who's askin?' The troll poked Clutter in the chest, causing him to lurch backward.

Clutter rubbed his chest, wincing. 'As my brother said, before. His name is Sneath. I'm Clutter. Can you direct us to Galrash, please?'

'No one here by that name wants to meet you,' rumbled the voice from the brothel's shadows. A smouldering glow bloomed in the darkness for a moment, revealing one huge, emerald-green eye.

'But,' Sneath spluttered. 'We have a message from Ameth—'

Redfire flooded the darkness, streaming through the open doors, lapping the brothel's stone-flagged floor. The troll grinned, flashing a mouth of perfectly filed teeth. 'Deal with you both shortly.' He dragged Sneath and Clutter up by their soggy tunics and tossed them beneath a huge, ornately-carved table. Long, oak bench seats flanked the table. Luckily no one seemed to be seated on them.

'Ogre hunt! Who's with me?' the troll bellowed and thundered out the doorway. Hooting and hollering, four trolls followed, drawing great, shiny axes from the sheaths strapped to their armoured backs.

Whoops, howls and the clang of weapons rang through the tunnel. The redfire, pooling inside the brothel's doorway, flicked backward, surging toward the skirmish as though it was a living thing. For the first time in what seemed like ages, Sneath sucked in a deep breath.

Safe.

'I think we should live right next door to this place, Sneath,' Clutter said, his voice all sing-song with glee. 'Look, brother. Look at them dancing. All they're wearing are tiny flames and big smiles.'

Sneath turned his attention to a glossy black-stone stage in the centre of *The Hangman's Jig*. 'Ooh! I see what you mean!' Three fairies swayed and wiggled, tumbling through, over and around a vertical, glistening web that stretched the width of the stage. One fairy waved and blew the goblins a kiss that turned into a shower of flaming petals. The magical kiss danced across the smoky haze, seared bright and tinkled into nothing on the stone floor.

On a smaller stage, to the right of the bar, a wyvern the size of a large dog blew smoke rings from her nose and slithered through the hoops, her scaled body like molten gold.

'Why haven't we heard of this place?' Clutter glared at Sneath.

'We did,' Sneath said, 'But everyone made it sound too good to be true. Wonder if they did it on purpose to keep us out?'

Bellowing from the tunnel broke the goblins' dreamy thoughts. Sneath blinked and slapped himself across the cheek.

'Damn!' Sneath shook Clutter. 'Get a grip. The *Brim* is making us all gooey and easy pickings. We have a gem to find.'

'And we have to find Galrash,' Clutter said.

'We have to make sure they get that witch!' Sneath clutched Clutter's shoulder. 'We could distract her so the trolls can smash her one.'

'If there's one thing trolls do well, it's smashing.' Clutter crawled to edge of the table. He grinned, though his skin was sallow instead of his normal dusky-green. 'Oh!'

Sneath looked where Clutter pointed. Tacked upon a wood-panelled wall was a row of Wanted posters. A few depicted ogres, a couple were of fairies and at least half-a-dozen sported the snarling images of witches. One bore a striking resemblance to Sangyll, the witch.

The brothers shared a conspiring look, scrambled out from beneath the table and ran through the doorway.

'Sangyll the witch is down the tunnel!' Sneath shouted, waving his skinny arms, Amethyst flapping limply from one hand. As he pelted toward the fighting, he expected Amethyst to spout a sarcastic remark, or some un-helpful bit of advice. Nothing. She simply hung in his fist. Sneath felt a sharp pang in his gut. Whether it was sadness, fear or wind was debatable. The feeling didn't last long.

Redfire shot toward him, snaking up his body. Now the redfire was localised, it was far more potent. White-hot pain seared Sneath's body and he stumbled. His skin burned, but he didn't let the map go until Clutter snatched her free and darted to the edge of the tunnel. The redfire pounced, engulfing Clutter's wiry, little body. It surged upward, coiling around his arms. Then, just short of the hand that clutched Amethyst, the redfire stopped.

'You see that?' Clutter yelled to Sneath, his voice tight with pain.

'Yep.' Sneath shouted back. 'Seems ol' Sangyll is worried about redfiring Amethyst.'

'You thinking what I'm thinking?' Clutter gasped.

'We need to distract the witch with Amethyst.'

Hopefully the map wouldn't burn to cinders, because that would be unfortunate. The Lost Gem of Nerramai would be lost forever.

'Sangyll, over here!' Sneath screamed, grabbing Amethyst from his brother and waving her around.

'An extra pouch of silver to whoever kills the witch!' Clutter shouted to the trolls battling the gigantic ogre.

Sneath shot him an 'are you mad?' glance.

Three of the trolls grinned, hooted and left the bleeding ogre to their two friends. The ogre might be bigger than the trolls, but he had been no match for five of them.

Sneath flapped Amethyst about like a madman.

In the red light and squirming shadows, it was hard to tell if they were winning or losing.

Clutter ran past Sneath, a ferocious look on his blood-smeared face. He skidded to a stop ten feet from Sangyll and the three, circling trolls, grabbed up a stone and hurled it at her. He threw another, shouting, 'If you want this map, then you gotta go through me!'

Sneath raced up to his brother. 'Yeah! You gotta go through us. Walls of muscle we are. Warriors!' He muttered to Clutter, 'What are we doing? Are you mad?'

'Trying not to get killed.' Clutter pitched another stone, hitting Sangyll hard on the shoulder.

The witch screeched and threw herself between the snarling trolls at the goblins, bony fingers raking across their skin. Redfire oozed from Sangyll's body, engulfing the goblins, searing with magic.

Sneath hurled Amethyst clear.

The goblins howled, their tunics and trews scorched and smouldering. Blisters bubbled on their exposed skin as they rolled to the ground, both clinging to Sangyll like wild animals. As quickly as the fight started, it ended. A troll reefed Sangyll off the goblins and slung her against the tunnel wall. Her body slumped to the ground, unconscious. The redfire retreated into her, sucked away like a falling tide.

Sneath and Clutter collapsed, gasping and groaning. Clutter crawled over and flapped Amethyst triumphantly above his head, smiling weakly.

Two of the trolls stomped past the goblins, hauling a broken and bleeding ogre back to *The Hangman's Jig*. The remaining three trolls stomped down the tunnel. Sangyll sagged over one troll's shoulder, her face smeared in blood.

Sneath and Clutter staggered along behind, through the tavern's gaping doorway. Rich, spicy smoke clouded the fire-lit brothel.

'Give the little warriors an ale on me, Burdack,' called the troll carrying Sangyll.

At once, a bald gnome popped into view behind the bar. Burdack, bedecked in green velvet and frothy lace cuffs and collar, sprang from what must have been a step ladder of some kind onto the bar. He trundled along the black-marble to a huge wooden barrel atop the end, adjusting his spectacles as he went. Burdack pushed the barrel's silver lever, pouring a couple of draughts into two huge pewter tankards.

'Service!' He shouted to no one in particular. One of the web-dancing fairies flew over, collected the drinks, and delivered them to the goblins.

Sneath smiled awkwardly, smoothed down his singed hair, and took a huge drink, the foam dribbling down his chin. Fruity with a bite of fire. Damn good stuff!

'Is it possible to talk to Galrash now?' Clutter leaned against a table leg, his tankard on the floor beside his blackened and burned trews.

A leathery rasping came from the shadows, and the huge emerald eye they had seen earlier fixed on the goblins. The brothel fell silent. As the eye rose higher, tinkling, clanking and jingling filled the hush. Then, a massive, scaled snout thrust toward Sneath and Clutter, swooping down so the dragon's maw was at eye level. More or less. The smell of sulphur, *Golden Brim's* spicy scent, and rotting flesh wafted over them.

'What could two spindly little entrees want so badly they'd go up against Sangyll and an ogre? And, then have the nerve to want an audience with the King of the Dragons.'

'Well, your Most High Royalness.' Sneath bowed, wincing with the pain of his burns.

'You assume I am the King?'

'You have the bearing of a leader.' Clutter bobbed his head, hissing between his teeth with discomfort.

'And of royal blood,' Sneath added with another painful bow.

'And you both have the villainous tongues of goblins.'

'A little harsh, all things considered,' Sneath said. 'But I will give you that one.'

The dragon laughed, a rich rumble that blew the goblins halfway across the brothel's stone-flagged floor. They staggered back to the dragon.

'We are here to deliver a message to Galrash. Either you are he, or you are not.' Clutter wavered on his feet. 'We're tired, injured and we have come a terribly long way.'

'You are brave,' the dragon said. 'I will give you that. Perhaps a tad ignorant but, for goblins, you stack up nicely. I'll tell you what. You tell me your message and I will make sure Galrash receives it.'

'Not good enough,' Sneath said through clenched teeth, his body searing with pain.

The whole brothel erupted with guffaws, hoots and hollers.

'Seems like we'll be getting goblins for supper,' barked a troll. 'Crispy cooked and stuffed with stupid.'

The dragon held up one taloned foreleg for silence. 'All right, I can respect courage. Despite the rude flavour. I am Galrash.'

'How can we be sure?' Sneath eyed the dragon shrewdly.

'Just tell me the information and be done with it,' the dragon growled. 'I weary of this game.' He swivelled his head and blew a gout of flame at the unconscious Sangyll who hung by her wrists from a pair of iron manacles beneath her Wanted poster. The remaining posters blackened, curled and floated to the floor like smouldering moths.

The goblins gazed at Sangyll, her ragged dress alive with flame, her skin charred and crackling. They looked at one another, mouths gaping.

'We have come into possession of a map,' Clutter blurted. 'Not just any map I must add. A magical map that's supposed to lead to the Lost Gem of Nerramai.'

Sneath snatched the limp map from his brother's hand and unfurled it for all to see. Trolls, dragons, fairies and Burdack the barkeep crowded around to see. Sneath had never felt so small and vulnerable.

'And,' Sneath added, 'the map talks.'

'That scrap of skin? You can't even make out the markings!' A troll snorted, grabbing for Amethyst.

Sneath might be small but he was quick despite his injuries. 'She talked until we got in here. She said that we must talk to Galrash and tell him that she is actually Amethyst Diaphany the Fourth. And she was taken by Sangyll.'

'Sangyll tortured her and everything trying to make her reveal the location of the Lost Gem of Nerramai.'

'And did she reveal this information?' Galrash stared at the goblins intently. 'Answer me!'

'No!' Sneath squeaked. He tried his best smile. 'She remained strong.'

'As she would,' Galrash said proudly. He glowered at the crowd. 'Move aside or burn.'

Everyone scrambled back from the dragon leaving the goblins alone in the dragon's shadow. Galrash rose on his haunches and roared. The goblins clamped their hands over their ears, cowering beneath the dragon's mighty bronze body.

'Place the map down and move,' ordered the dragon. 'Long since we have gazed upon Amethyst, the heart, the power of we dragons. Never knowing where she had gone. If she lived.'

Sneath placed Amethyst on the stone-flagged floor, smoothed out her edges and gave a her a little pat of reassurance. The goblins backed away to stand with the trolls pressed against the brothel walls. And waited.

Galrash roared once more. The cavern rumbled. Dust and stones tumbled from the unseen ceiling, crashing into the flagstones. The mighty dragon breathed a soft feather of flame over Amethyst.

'No!' Clutter shouted in shock and stepped forward. A troll grabbed him, dragging him back.

Garash ignored the crowd and sent another tongue of flame across the map. It curled. Writhed. And started to swell, surging upward, outward. The old vellum shimmered in the firelight and burning witch. It changed form, growing legs, wings and a towering body, pushing tables and benches aside as it grew.

'Amethyst!' Sneath said, his eyes wide with awe. 'Look at you!'

There, beside Galrash, where the map had sat, towered a resplendent, golden dragon. Galrash bowed low. 'We have searched for centuries, my queen. For you. And for the Gem of Nerramai.'

'I don't doubt it,' Amethyst placed a taloned fore-leg on Galrash's shoulder.

'What happened, my Queen?' Galrash asked.

'Sangyll's mother found me while I lay brooding. You know how distracted I get. The foolish witch knew nothing—thought I had already laid. She tortured me, but I refused to talk, so she turned me into the map hoping I would lead her to my Nerramai.'

'And you did not, my brave queen.'

Sneath jumped up, arms flapping with excitement. It all made sense! 'You couldn't lead her to the Gem of Nerramai because you hadn't laid it when she cast her spell.'

'The Gem is an egg?' Clutter frowned. 'We went through all this for an egg?'

'An egg from a queen dragon.' Sneath looked pointedly at Amethyst. 'I think, all things considered, that we deserve a handsome reward. A chest of jewels. Or gold? Nothing wrong with gold. Though I do prefer jewels.'

'Don't even think of asking for the Gem of Nerramai!' Amethyst pointed a huge talon at the goblins. 'I'd never entrust my daughter to you pair.'

'How about we allow you to live?' Galrash lowered his head and eyed them shrewdly.

Sneath groaned. 'But after all we suffered. The insults, the pain, the fear, the—'

'What about what you put me through?' Amethyst said with a snort. 'I've seen and felt things that are seared into my memory for all eternity.'

'And it is because of us, Your Highness,' Clutter said. 'You will live out your long years as a dragon and not some mouldy bit of vellum.'

'Well spoken.' Galrash called to the tavern keeper, 'Burdack, tend the wounds of these two rascals.'

'How about the key to your strongroom?' Sneath glanced around, thinking fast. 'A few measly gems, or pearls—'

'No!' Amethyst said.

Galrash chuckled, a deep throaty sound that rumbled through Sneath's chest. 'When you two are healed you may take whatever you can carry out of here in one trip.'

'Er,' Clutter put up his hand, 'do we have to carry it out the way we came in? Could be a bit tricky.'

Sneath glared at Amethyst. 'Why *did* we go that way. I hear there's a front door.'

The huge golden dragon drew herself up and sucked a deep breath, her eyes blazing.

Sneath shuffled a few steps back, dragging Clutter with him. 'Forget it. Doesn't matter. Everyone's happy. We'll just get on with picking out our reward, shall we?'

After a long pause, Amethyst released the breath and her eyes narrowed. 'If you must know, it's because the front door is spelled against goblins. Pesky little creatures you are. Believe me, I'd have preferred that way, too. Especially if it saved me sniffing your crotch!'

Galrash snorted a laugh, which he turned into a cough when his queen glared.

'And,' Amethyst continued, 'once you gather your reward, the back door will be sealed as well. You'll only get one trip to the *Jig*, so make the most of it.'

Sneath elbowed Clutter. 'I'm going to start a rigid exercise regime. Bulk up my muscles and my stamina.'

'I like how you think, brother.'

\#

The End of Another Sneath and Clutter Adventure.

I'll Have a Martini

Sue Stubbs

TONY

Tony held his head in both hands, massaging his thumping brain. Two drinks. He only ever had two drinks.

'How did I get like this?' he mumbled into the pillow. As he let his arms flop, he caught a flash of gold. He raised his left hand. Was that a gold band on his wedding finger?

'What the hell?' He sat up, squinting at the ring.

His guts gurgled and he swallowed saliva. Nope. Not going to work. Tony launched himself off the bed and stumbled to the bathroom just in time to turn his stomach inside out. Then he guzzled water and dragged himself back to bed.

Footsteps tapped on the marble floor. Too loud.

'Ooh, my favourite.' Sheila spun around the bedroom and turned up the radio, blaring the Bee Gees latest number one song until Tony's head ached afresh.

'Not feeling too handsome this morning, are you casanova?' She padded past the rumpled king size bed—wearing nothing but Opium, her signature scent—and tossed a sheet of paracetamol onto Tony's bare chest.

She was loud and often crass but he was a man, after all, and couldn't stop his eyes trailing her curves.

'Be careful Tony,' she said with a coy smile. 'I don't want to refuse my husband on our first day of marriage.'

Tony winced at the word marriage. 'What?' A stabbing pain through his right eyeball forced his head back down onto the bed. The sickly sweet smell of perfume created fresh unease in his stomach.

'You really don't remember, husband dearest?' Sheila's shrill voice echoed in the black marble and mirrored ceiling ensuite.

'You know how this thing between us works,' Tony said. 'Nothing has changed. I'm never getting married.' No-one could replace Carol, especially not Sheila Barocci.

'Oh yes it has, big fella.' Sheila appeared in the doorway in her Dior underclothes and an inch thick layer of foundation. She adjusted her towering nest of blonde hair. 'This thing between us, Tony, it's changed. Big time.'

Tony tried to focus on her face to see if she was as serious as she sounded, but the blaze of lights from the bathroom burned through his pupils into the back of his skull. Nothing made sense.

Sheila finished dressing. 'See you at dinner, darling husband.' She grinned and pressed the private elevator button to take her down to the Black Diamond club. 'Hmmm, will the new Mrs Tony Martini have to work for lousy tips anymore? Don't think so. Because I'm now the boss' wife.' She screeched, waggled the gold band on her wedding finger at him, then vanished into the elevator.

An hour passed before Tony could coordinate his legs to get off the bed. This thing with Sheila had to be a joke. No way would he ever get drunk enough to marry that trollop. He tugged at the wedding band, but it wouldn't budge.

The bathroom stank and yellow splatters dripped down the tiles. His stomach churned so he retreated without trying to remove the ring with soap and water. He made a mental note to apologise to the cleaners and leave a little bonus for them.

#

A short time later, Tony emerged from the elevator into The Black Diamond and tugged at the jacket of his bespoke, ink-blue Sy Devore suit. The set didn't properly hide the Glock under his arm. Imbecile tailor.

Where the hell was Sheila? He needed to sort this out.

She was nowhere in sight, so he began his daily rounds of the gaming room to check in with the pit bosses and floor supervisors. She'd be here, somewhere.

He smiled at the gamblers and leaned in close to the women, quietly enquiring about their luck, pressing a drink voucher into their hand before leaving them breathless.

His manager, Vince, edged up. The pinched expression on his face said there was a problem. A big problem. Great. Just great. Tony threw back his shoulders and forced a smile.

'What is it Vince? You look peaky today.'

Vince jerked his head. 'Not here, Boss. Best you come and see.

On the security videos.'

Tony scowled and headed through the gaming room toward a wide marble staircase that led to the high rollers lounge and to his office. The staircase swept a grand curving line in the centre of the room and was illuminated by a brilliant, six tiered black diamond chandelier. Vince trotted beside Tony, swatting away unsteady gamblers who were already tipsy on shots and good fortune.

'I tried to stop him,' Vince said, half-jogging to keep up with Tony's long stride. 'But he reckons Sheila said it was ok.'

The stabbing returned to Tony's right eye. 'What did Sheila say was ok, Vince?'

'He's here. In the club. With Sheila.'

'You know I don't care for riddles. Who's here, Vince?'

Vince looked like he'd sucked a lemon. 'Oh jeez, Tony. There's no other way to break it. Sheila said Frank Marachino could come into the club. She says…he's her uncle.'

Tony froze. How could he not have known? Frank Marachino, dirty, scumbag owner of the Golden Deck Casino—the only other five-star club in Vegas—was Sheila Barocci's uncle? A cold rage surged through his veins. Fire lashed at his skin and scorched his brain.

Vince took a step back. 'There's something else.'

Tony turned to face Vince, who tried to dissolve into the patterned carpet.

'What?' Tony barked.

'He, ah, he has someone with him,' Vince stammered. 'A woman…his fiancé.'

'So?'

'It's Carol.' Vince jumped back, out of striking range.

Tony raced up the staircase, two steps at a time, heading for the security room. 'Get me eyes. I want every camera on that scumbag. Now!'

Vince gestured the security team out and took over camera operation. The camera's grainy black and white image showed Frank holding court at the main roulette wheel. Carol stood beside him.

Tony zoomed in to focus on the glamorous pair. Carol stood slightly behind Frank, who slid a tower of chips onto black ten and another onto red sixteen. The fact he was out on the floor, not in the premium player lounge, was a stunt designed to stick a needle in Tony's eye. It worked. Tony steadied himself against the chair. His his temples throbbed.

Instantly, he was back in 1965, staring into Carol's beautiful blue eyes over dinner at Gino's Diner in downtown Las Vegas. In love, yet stupidly arrogant. He'd foolishly believed Carol would follow him into the business, leave her study and ambition to become an investment banker and be content to live a life of glamour on his arm. She hadn't. Her determination and independence were part of what attracted Tony to her and, ultimately, what tore them apart.

Tony blinked his eyes back into focus. What an idiot he'd been on that final night ten years ago. Looking at Carol tonight, he knew he had to make amends and prove himself worthy of her love.

How, though?

He surveyed the scene playing out on the cameras. Sheila and Frank played at the eastern side tables. Her in garish sequins, him in a satin trimmed jacket. Carol stood at Frank's side, the image of understated glamour in a sleek, light-coloured suit.

Slowly, Carol glanced up at the camera focussed on her. She gracefully lifted her arm from behind Frank's chair to display the enormous, gaudy engagement rock drooping from her finger.

Tony's heart dropped into his stomach, leaving an ache in his chest. Carol twisted the engagement ring round her finger a few times. On the final turn, she hid the rock under her palm. She raised her other hand and turned it over to reveal a second ring—a princess cut, deep ocean blue sapphire surrounded by diamonds on a white gold band.

Understated. Divine.

Theirs.

Carol looked directly at the camera once more, but this time with a gentle smile. Tony's heart skipped a beat. This was a game changer. Carol had literally shown her hand. She had come back to him.

Now he must figure out how to release her from Frank's controlling grip. His eyes slid from Sheila to Frank to Carol.

A plan began to form.

First he must show Carol he had received her signal. He grabbed the control and moved the camera up and down as if nodding in agreement. Carol's face relaxed and she turned back to the action at the table.

The desk phone nearby buzzed. Tony's thoughts snapped back to business. He snatched up the handset. After all, he still had a club to run, and a wife to get rid of—along with her slimebag uncle.

'What?' With one eye on the floor cameras, he listened to the day's reports.

'What do you mean Lenny can't deliver?' he barked down the line. 'If I don't have enough booze they'll stampede my office. Damn it. Bring the truck in anyway.'

Tony and Vince made their way to the back dock to meet with his stock controllers. Sure enough, the truck had only half the load of booze he'd ordered.

'Lenny, where's the other half of my booze,' Tony demanded. 'You know you don't get paid if I don't get the complete order.'

The driver clambered from the cab, cringing. Damp patches of sweat stained his faded blue uniform and his eyes slid from Tony's. 'Well, ah, they ran out.'

'I thought we had a trustworthy relationship.' Tony kept his tone patient. 'But now, my friend, I question our friendship.' He strolled over to where Lenny stood, slung his arm around the man's neck, and brought his fist close to Lenny's jaw. He squeezed—gently, of course.

'I'm a reasonable man.' Tony squeezed harder and Lenny's face flushed an unhealthy shade of plum. 'So I trust,' Tony continued, 'you will tell me if there is a problem.' He released Lenny, who staggered back, gasping.

'I tell you what.' Tony slid a hand under his jacket, locating his Glock. 'Because I am such an understanding man, I'll only shoot one of your knees.' He fired a shot straight past the man and into the bags of dirty linen lined up against the wall. The explosive *crack* sent Lenny hopping wildly.

'Ok, ok, I'll tell you everything,' Lenny pleaded. 'Frank's getting it all. He paid me double.'

Tony stormed out of the loading dock. Vince trailed behind.

'It's clean up time,' Tony said fiercely. 'Vince, let's go find Frank. I'd like to invite him to dinner.'

Vince's eyebrows nearly shot off his already shiny, sweating head.

'I'm hungry,' Tony said, smiling devilishly. He held up his left hand. 'And get me a PI. I want to know how I got married to Frank's niece without knowing about it. Something is definitely off.'

Frank and Carol had moved to a more private table in one of the exclusive, roped off seating alcoves. Tony smoothed his jacket, strolled up two plush carpeted stairs and stepped through the sheer swirls of fabric draped to create an illusion of privacy.

'Welcome to the Black Diamond,' he said, arms outstretched. 'Frank Marachino, your presence has made it a spectacularly interesting morning.'

Meeting Tony's fierce stare, Frank curled his top lip in a half smirk. Tony turned to face Carol. He studied the sapphire and diamond ring before slowly looking up, to meet her cool gaze. He knew, by the dilated pupils hiding the ocean blue of her eyes, she was struggling to maintain her calm exterior.

'Why Frank,' he said, 'surely you'll be charged with kidnapping the most beautiful woman in this filthy city. Miss, I am at your service.' Tony produced a business card and, as Carol accepted, their fingers brushed, sending sparks zapping.

Frank's arm curled round Carol's shoulders like a python claiming its victim. His fingers pressed a little too firmly into Carol's shoulder, pulling her toward him at an awkward angle.

Tony resisted the urge to punch him. Marachino's time would come. Soon.

#

CAROL

That afternoon, in Frank's apartment, Carol slipped off her shoes but did not undress. How the hell had she ended up here? She sighed. Her original plan of using her casino contacts to build a client base for her financial investment company did not include becoming the object of Frank's obsession. But the situation could finally work in her favour now she had lured Tony back into her life.

She took a shaky breath to calm her nerves and sat on the lounge, turning Tony's card over and over, contemplating her future. Despite her efforts to delay again, Frank wanted to set a date.

A shadow fell across her.

'Oh, Frank,' Carol gasped, 'you frightened the life out of me'.

'Good,' Frank said from behind her, lacing his strong fingers around her throat.

She stiffened but his hands slid down to caress her shoulders.

'You seem on edge, my darling,' Frank said, flopping onto the lounge next to her. He yanked at his bathrobe and covered his bulging gut.

'I guess I'm just tired.'

'Show me that card.' He stuck out a hand.

Carol knew from painful experience it was futile to resist. He snatched the card from her and turned it over.

'Well, well. Seems like we have a slight problem.' A malicious glow burned in his eyes. He held up the card to display the love heart Tony had drawn on the back. 'Something you need to tell me?'

Carol exhaled. 'I've already told you about Tony. It was a very long time ago and I broke it off. He always put the business first. It doesn't mean anything now.' She shifted in the seat. 'Besides, Tony's safely married to Sheila, just like you planned, remember?'

'A long time ago,' Frank echoed. 'Hmm. Time has a funny habit of going in circles. Bringing things back to us.'

She could hear the air coursing in and out of her lungs. She glanced around searching for the closest escape route in case Frank launched toward her.

Finally, Frank said, 'But you're right, he is…married.' He smirked. 'Still, I think we should send a message back to your precious Tony.'

What did that mean? Carol's body was in lock down; unable to move or speak, waiting.

'Mr Marachino?' Yvette walked into the room and Carol could have kissed the woman. Frank liked to be waited on, which meant Yvette, his personal assistant, was around so much she practically lived with them.

'Excuse me, Mr Marachino,' Yvette gushed. 'I'm sorry to interrupt, but I have a message for you.'

'Of course, my sweet. Come.' He patted the lounge next to him. 'What is it?' Frank pretended to straighten the frill on the blouse stretched tightly across her ample breasts. She giggled and blushed.

'You've been invited to a private dinner tonight at the chef's table with the owner of the Black Diamond, Mr Tony Martini,' Yvette said.

Frank slapped his thigh. 'Wonderful! Now we can deliver our message in person.' He looked Carol up and down. 'My darling, why don't you change into something less…demure.'

Carol lifted the corners of her mouth to force a smile and escaped into the bedroom. Her mind buzzed like a fevered hive. This would be her only chance to turn her dream into a reality. She chose the simple lines of her favourite strapless black dress.

When she emerged from the bedroom, she caught Frank's eye and purposefully paused in the doorway, letting her hands glide across her breasts and down to rest on her thighs. She let him gape at her leg peeking through the high split in her gown. Her hips swayed as she walked into the sunken lounge.

Frank's eyes glazed over. He licked his lips and adjusted his position on the lounge. She had him on the end of her line.

'Frankie darling,' she said, taking advantage of his good mood. 'I'm wondering…' She allowed him to wrap his arms around her waist. 'Do you think it might be prudent to bring Yvette with us tonight?'

Frank pulled away from her a little, his gaze wary. 'Why?'

She pressed her body against his and tilted her head. 'Well, I wondered if you need her to distract Tony and maybe she could bring those transfer papers I saw on the table. They looked important. I didn't want to say too much but am I right in thinking you could be the next owner of the Black Diamond?' She ran a finger under his chin.

'Oh Carol, you are not just a pretty face. Yes. Although I had planned for it to be a surprise for you.' He waggled a chubby finger in mock admonishment. 'I know how much Tony hurt you. I hoped if I bought his precious club it would heal your broken heart. Perhaps then we could set a date for our own nuptials.'

She pushed out her lower lip. 'But you still have to deal with that horrible tax department auditor.'

'Pfah!' He waved away the investigation and ran a hand up her leg. 'They won't find nothin'. I'll take care of you. You'll have all the money you want. Your idea of distracting the auditor while my accountant jigged the figures worked a dream, sweetheart. Nothing to worry your pretty head about.'

She looked down demurely, hiding a smile of satisfaction. So he still didn't know about the second set of books. Excellent.

He leaned in, parted his lips and extended his tongue ready to kiss her.

Carol leaned away to avoid his slobbery attempt at passion. Her stomach churned. His arms tightened, pulling her closer.

Once again, as if on cue, Yvette appeared at their side.

'I'm sorry to interrupt again Mr Marachino.' She batted her fake eyelashes.

Carol extricated herself from Frank's grip.

'Mr Martini has called,' Yvette continued, 'and everything is ready. He asked if you'd be kind enough to join him now for dinner.'

Frank smoothed his sparse hair across his scalp and grinned. 'Good, good.'

Carol caught Frank's eye and gestured toward Yvette.

'Oh yes, come here Yvette, let me look at you,' he said.

Yvette's gaze, which had settled admiringly on Carol, shifted back to Frank who slid his arm around her waist.

'Yvette,' he said with exaggerated importance, 'you will accompany us to dinner this evening and make sure you bring all those transfer papers. I have a score to settle.'

#

Carol managed to keep a cool expression, but dinner was excruciating. Sheila would not shut up, leaning over Tony to talk loudly at anyone who looked in her direction, while her boobs struggled to stay confined in her strapless, backless, tasteless bright pink dress.

Carol's breathing came in shallow gulps. She forced herself to slow and regulate. Yvette flirted with Frank and it made Carol queasy to see his pudgy hands rub and squeeze a little too high up her thighs. She felt a pang of guilt but it had to be this way to keep Frank distracted enough for her plan to work.

How easy had it been to encourage Frank to block Tony's supply orders and delivery routes. Even easier to tip off the tax department about Frank's money laundering and hand over the second set of books to the auditor. How satisfying to know part of Frank's downfall was his eagerness to become engaged to her. Too bad he hadn't bothered to find out her investment business commanded a sizeable asset base of her own.

Carol hid a smile and caught Tony's eye He leaned back, one corner of his mouth curled up, visible behind his glass; only for her to see. Carol lifted her martini in a silent toast. He'd bend over backwards to bring down Frank. Especially if it included taking her away from Frank. The two men were like strutting peacocks crowing about who had the most impressive tail spread.

Frank clinked his glass and announced to the table, 'A toast, to Tony, who has generously brought us together tonight.'

Everyone murmured their agreement.

'I am afraid, however,' Frank continued, 'I cannot accept your latest offer.'

The fractured conversations stopped. He held up Tony's business card, turning it to display the love heart. Sheila giggled and let out a snort. Tony scowled.

'We have no secrets, do we?' Frank roughly nudged Carol and jerked his head toward Tony. 'Tell him, my darling.'

Carol met Tony's eyes with a cool stare. 'I must return this card to you, Tony. You have offended me, as I am engaged to be married to Frank.' She took the card and placed it in the centre of the table with the love heart facing up.

A large red cross was drawn, in lipstick, over the top of the heart. Most people, including Frank, would be fooled, but she was certain Tony remembered. It was their secret sign from all those years ago. 'X' marks the spot meant their love was still alive.

Sheila brayed like an old donkey and slapped the table with both hands. 'Golden, oh this is golden. We haven't even been married for one day and you're already cheating on me, Tony Martini. Everyone is my witness.' She waved her arms around wildly. 'I am going to sue your arse for every cent I can get.'

'Would you shut that big mouth of yours,' Tony snarled. 'I will see you in court, Sheila, but it'll be you in the defendant's chair. You're nothing but a fraud. And, while we're all in the sharing mood, it's time we were honest with each other, Frankie.'

Standing, Tony lay his hands on the table, a malicious glint in his eyes. 'We've known each other for a long time and I thought we'd developed a mutual respect.' He paused while Frank grunted and slopped his chops, picking at the leftover steak between his teeth. 'But I seem to have been mistaken,' he continued.

No one moved. Carol held her breath. This could go badly. The Glock Tony carried bulged under his arm. Frank had a similar weapon on his hip. Beneath the table, she slid her high-heeled shoes off.

Finally Frank exhaled loudly. 'You'd be wise to choose your words with great caution.'

'You're right, Frank.' Tony sneered. 'Caution is needed. I have exercised a great deal of caution today after I discovered you're blackmailing my suppliers and delivery drivers. It's hard to run a casino without booze, Frank.'

Frank's lip curled into a satisfied smirk. Carol could barely breathe. Sheila giggled hysterically and Yvette's eyes darted from one side of the table to the other as if watching a match-winning rally.

'Fortunately,' Tony continued, 'a man who is being blackmailed is easily swayed to the other side.'

Frank's smug expression dropped and a frown creased his brow.

'So…' Tony spread his hands '…it's you who's facing an uncertain future. Along with your scamming niece.'

'How dare you?' Sheila jumped to her feet. Her face reddened, her makeup melting, threatening to slip right off her face.

Carol dabbed a napkin to her lips to hide another smile.

'Uncle Frank,' Sheila whined.

Frank raised an indifferent shoulder. 'Your problem, sweetheart.'

'Awh, Tony,' she cawed like a strangled feral cat. 'I love you, can't you see. You know what a lying cheat Frank is. I love you so much!' She clung to Tony's arm.

He brushed her off. 'You know nothing of love or loyalty Sheila. A deficit which appears to run in your family.' He looked down his nose at her. 'I know you spiked my drinks and I have proof you forged our marriage certificate. I also have proof Frank's laundering money. Proof you schemed this fake marriage up with Frank to get your hands on my club. Think you can scam me out of my money? I know you, Frank, stalled my deliveries to send me bankrupt to take control of my club. Thought you had it all planned didn't you, Frankie-boy.'

Tony's eyes glittered. His smile was a shark's.

Carol waited, her heart stuttering. She was so close to success.

'You see, Frank,' Tony said, walking around the table to where Frank sat next to Carol, 'I am the winner.' He took Carol's hand and kissed it lightly. 'My darling Carol, come with me. We can be together. There's nothing left for you here. Let me take you away tonight. We could have our honeymoon and start over again.'

Carol flashed him a blinding smile and shifted away from Frank, just in case.

'And when I take over *your* pathetic club,' Tony said to Frank, 'my first decision will be to demolish it. Then I'll build the largest casino in Las Vegas and it'll be all mine.'

With a sense of clarity and relief, Carol listened to Tony—drunk on the flood of power—outline his grand plan. Frank sat open-mouthed, apparently too stunned to speak. Sheila downed her fifth martini, sobbing, her mascara bleeding down her face.

Tony pointed to the paperwork in Yvette's lap. 'I see you've brought a contract with you. Thought you'd take control of the Black Diamond, huh? Carol, tell Frank's lovely assistant to make the necessary amendments to this document. I want the immediate and complete exchange of Frank's entire holdings to me'.

Carol nodded and Yvette began making notations on the pages.

'Carol?' Frank pleaded.

'I couldn't take it any longer Frank,' she said. 'You don't love me. You were using me. Besides, I had to tell the tax agent everything. They said I'd go to jail if I didn't cooperate. They know all about your money laundering.' She rose, stood beside Tony, and held his hand.

Frank's face turned beetroot. He glared at Tony. 'There's no way you can make this stick. How dare you!'

Tony laughed. 'Don't look so upset. This calls for a celebration. I invited a few friends to join us for after dinner drinks. Champagne all round.' He gestured toward the door.

FBI badges flashed in the hands of the five men waiting in the doorway.

'All you have to do is sign the contract Frank, and it all goes away. Just say you had no idea Sheila was blackmailing me and she was behind all the tax evasion. The laundering evidence will disappear, too.'

'What?' Sheila screeched. 'You can't double cross me, Uncle

Frank. It was all your idea!'

Frank shrugged and grabbed the pen and papers. 'I've got plenty of other deals up my sleeve, sweetheart, but I can't work them if I'm in prison.' He quickly scribbled his name and shoved the papers back to the centre of the table. 'Now call off the dogs, Tony.'

Carol gathered the documents and held them close to her chest. She blew a kiss to Tony. 'I can't wait to get out of here. I'll pack my things and be ready in an hour.'

Tony kissed her, his eyes sparkling. 'We'll be together, as we were meant to be.' He released her and gestured to his staff to escort Frank off the premises. Sheila, he handed over to the FBI.

Carol took Yvette's arm and pulled her toward the exit, saying, 'There is nothing left here for you, either. Perhaps we can find you a new job.'

#

An hour later, Carol sighed and relaxed in front of the crackling fire. She snuggled close against her lover as they lay together on the sofa, fingers laced and legs entwined.

Carol broke the comfortable silence. 'I only have one regret,' she said, looking into the eyes of her true love. 'I regret not seeing his face when he realised I'd substituted all the files for *both* companies. He was so hungry for power he didn't notice the contracts were changed to sign everything over to us.' She chuckled, looking back to the flames licking at the charred logs in the grate.

'Mmm, I'd love to have seen his face too. But I prefer being in your arms, looking at you my love,' Yvette said.

#

END

The World Left Behind

Neen Cohen

The stench of burnt onion, stale beer and old smoke assaulted Lu's senses as she stepped into the small saloon. Not the place she wanted to be, but she had to earn enough money, somehow.

She slipped her sunglasses into her coat's front right pocket. The left barely held together; in need of a few stitches since her last encounter. A monkey, that one had been. Vicious little beast.

The coat was the only item of her Granny's that Asher had allowed her to keep. Lu no longer remembered its original colour. Faded, patched, and stitched, but it still smelt of her Granny. She had been more than a little crazy. Her prophecies, as she called them, made the whole family shun her: plants being smart, animals taking revenge for human destruction of the planet, changelings being more than myth. But she'd been Lu's Granny; always there for her.

And she had been right about the animals.

They'd killed her.

Lu grimaced. Not long, now, and she'd be off this hell-hole planet. Away from the memories. The animals. The pain. The loss. Somewhere new. Just a couple more bounties—a few more dead beasts for Asher—should do it.

She blinked against the darkness, and the sting of old tears, and waited for her eyes to adjust to the saloon's hot darkness. The scarred wooden tables were all occupied. People escaping the worst of the day's heat.

Asher sat at a round table in the corner, dusty leather boots propped on the surface, crossed at the ankles. A dark bandana lay loose around his neck, and a scar from the left corner of his mouth turned his expression into a permanent sneer.

Lu nodded at the bartender. He glared from behind the bar, watching her every step. The whole room radiated fear at Lu's presence. She'd heard it all. The freak, the witch, the crazy and unnatural one who went out willingly into the re-growing forest. And, more frighteningly, the one who returned.

It was amazing how far anger could carry you.

She lowered her faded bandana before approaching Asher.

'You've gotta bounty for me?' Lu said

'Hair's growin' back I see.'

She said nothing—any reply would be seen as a challenge—only nodding as she ran her hand over the stubble on her head, feeling the short soft bristles tickle her palm. Another punishment. She could still feel the raised scartissue from his careless hacking.

'New boots?' Lu asked as she emptied both pockets of her jacket and dumped things on the table for Asher's inspection; a weapons check. He still didn't trust her. The last of her dry fruit, and the heavy worn padlock, and sunglasses.

She pulled out the chair, turning it around to sit on it backward.

'Boots ain't that new,' he said.

'Nice leather. This town don't much like animal defilers, though.' Lu's eyes met Asher's.

'Ya threating me, Lucy?' He glared but pulled his feet off of the table and tucked them beneath the old scarred wood. His eyes were pits that promised pain. But she was so familiar with them now they no longer had the same effect. Not since the beating he and Mark had given her. She resisted the urge to run her fingers over the old scars on her back. Not much worse he could do to her.

'Nope.' She still couldn't hold his gaze. 'I'm a defiler, too. If they go after you, they go after me.'

The retaliation of nature was everywhere. Small outcrops of trees were stretching further along the riverbanks, destroying towns and people alike. Seeming to know who was friend and who was a defiler.

Few towns would let someone who went in search of hurting and harming animals linger in the safety of their shade. But somehow Asher always had luck staying safe.

Him and Mark.

She hadn't seen her older brother since that day. The day he'd betrayed her; run to Asher and told him her plan to get offworld. Since then Asher had made sure she couldn't quite afford it.

But she was so close now. He didn't know how close.

Asher huffed and leaned forward, forearms covering most of the small table.

'I need ya to get a big one for me.'

'Animal?'

Asher flicked a look around the dark room, but no one was giving them any mind, not even the barkeep.

'Elephant's been spotted.'

'An elephant?' Lu baulked at the idea.

Yes, nature was coming back after humans had left the dying world behind to burn in the fierce sunlight. But she had scoured what little nature existed on this lump-of-rock island. Only smaller animals had been left, taking refuge below ground and in caves. How could she have missed something large?

'An actual elephant?' she said. She'd caught dozens of smaller ones as they returned to the light. But bigger animals?

'Trust me, I seen the beast myself,' he said 'It's a baby.'

'Price?'

'20K.'

Lu blinked. And blinked again.

'20K?' He must be desperate. He had to know that would give her enough to get off planet.

'Gotya 'tention now, don't I?' He slipped one hand into the pocket of his dust jacket. Pulling out a small dirty calico bag, he dumped it on the table with a grin that sent a shiver up Lu's spine more than any of his scowls could.

'Quarter advance. I'm bettin' the rest'll finally give ya enough to get off world, yeah?'

Lu nodded slowly and swallowed hard, staring at the calico bag. 'How much of the animal ya need brought back?'

'Alive!'

'Alive?' He hadn't asked for a live one in a while. In fact, Lu pondered, he hadn't put a bounty on any animal for a while. She'd only had human bounties the last few months.

'Alive, or you don't get the rest.'

She reached for the bag. His beefy, scarred hand landed heavily on hers.

Of course this was too good to be true. She took a deep breath and closed her eyes.

'If you're too scared or you don't come back,' Asher said, 'I'll send me boys. All me boys. Mark, too. The rest of the reward'll be enough for them to risk the forests.'

She opened her eyes, staring into the black pits and nodded, liberating the calico bag from his grip. She was one of Asher's only bounty hunters willing to go into the forests. And she had her own special skills with finding the animals. She wasn't scared of nature and its ability to fight back. He knew that. Knew why she went.

He grinned. He always took pleasure in exploiting her desire to exact revenge on the monsters.

'And use this.' The chain Asher placed on the table sparkled strangely in the bar's dim lighting. 'I hear it's one helluva beast. Your usual finesse may not be enough.'

Lu placed her hand on the chain and felt it tingle against her skin. Something about the metal made her skin crawl. But 20k was more than enough to ignore the heavy fist that clenched in the pit of her stomach.

She tucked the padlock,chain, and the rest of her belongings back into her pocket, along with the bag, and left with a small nod to the barkeep. She tried not to run.

Stepping outside, Lu flinched against the light. Almost too late in the day to go out. Heat shimmered off the ground; the sun a pale, hot disc in a dirty-blue sky. Colours bled to nothing in a dusty haze of heat and death. She tugged up the faded bandana and pulled the battered sunglasses from her pocket. Both padlock and payment rested heavily against her thigh.

Once past the town's boundary she paused and looked out over the desolate landscape. Relics of a past long gone stood sentry; hunks of twisted plastic and metal too big to be hauled off for new uses; too toxic to be dissolved back into the earth. But, to the south, a hint of new greenery along the river.

The adrenalin of a new hunt tingled beneath her skin. There

were more animals returning? Not on her watch. She would repay every single one of them for the life they had doomed her to. The life without Granny, and left in the hands of Asher—a whole different breed of monster.

Lu smirked and nodded. It seemed right that an animal hunt would be the last payment she needed to finally get off world.

She began to follow the line of the river.

#

'Hello, my beauty,' Lu mumbled, slipping into the small clearing and sighing with relief. Three days she had spent tracking an animal she hadn't been entirely convinced still existed. But here it was.

Its trunk broke the surface of the water, drinking and breathing and real.

Lu dumped her backpack by the edge of the clearing and drew closer. Time to get to work.

The beast turned and she saw its back—covered in swollen, angry crosshatching. Her own back twitched at the memory of similar whip marks left by Asher's anger. No. She was here to do a job. One of these…things…had killed her grandmother. This was not the time for pity. Not when she was so close to getting off planet.

The animal moved and its skin shimmered with a white outline, calming for some strange reason. Its trunk sprayed a fountain of water that caught the light in a rainbow, hypnotic. Lu pressed her lips tight, refusing to be distracted.

It was a killer.

The corpse of a man dangled from a nearby tree, vines wrapped around his neck and body; almost decorative. A lone wind chime waiting for a companion. His face was swollen, blackened, unrecognisable. Lu shivered.

The trees encircling the river began to rustle loudly in a breeze Lu couldn't feel. The elephant looked up, its eyes startling Lu. They were a black so different to Asher's. Had it seen her? Animals normally didn't even hear her coming. That what made her so good at her job.

So, what had frightened it?

A soft crunch—not soft enough—made Lu freeze. Slowly she turned, keeping the elephant in her periphery.

'What ya doing here, Mark?' Lu relaxed, but only slightly. Her brother's face was older, sunburned into deep creases; his dark hair matted and unwashed.

'Here to get my bounty, lil sis.'

'Your bounty?' Lu laughed as she scowled.

'Turns out Asher don't trust ya after all.'

'Asher don't trust nobody. Ya think I'll just stand aside and let ya take my money?' she said.

Mark shrugged and drew closer, knives in hands. He was prone to overcompensating, ever since Lu had proven she was the stronger of the two.

'So, ya finally overcome ya fear o' the trees and animals didya?' she asked. She pointed over to the line of trees, certain Mark hadn't noticed the corpse, now swaying in the unfelt breeze.

Mark's face paled at the sight. Pulling her own knife from her belt, Lu slashed out and caught his upper arm. Blood stained his faded blue shirt scarlet.

Just a warning, a playful tiff between siblings.

'You bitch!'

'Get outta here, Mark.'

The rustling of the leaves grew. Lu still couldn't feel the wind.

The elephant trumpeted. Mark jumped. Lu dropped her knife, pressing her hands against her ears. The corpse slid limply to the ground.

Vines snaked out from the trees and wrapped themselves around Mark's feet. He screamed and lashed out, knives cutting through branches. His back was turned to Lu.

Heavy feet thundered past her. Something shoved her and she stumbled, falling to her knees. She had no time to cry out a warning to her brother.

The elephant pushed Mark to the ground. He rolled over, knives up.

'No!' Lu tried to get up, but vines snaked around her ankles, tightening when she resisted. Was her escape from the planet going to be ripped out of her hands? Mark was no match for her, but Asher had trained them both and the elephant didn't stand a chance.

Lu searched the ground for her knife, hands blind, her eyes never flicking away from the scene. She couldn't lose the elephant now.

The animal charged Mark again. He rolled out of its way, slashing its ankles as it passed. The elephant's trumpet sounded like a scream. The smell of blood filled the clearing. Lu fought against the vines again, but they held tight. Where was her knife?

Mark was back on his feet, his smile cocky, knife twirling in his fingers.

'Thought you had more than that in you, elephant.' He hacked a chunk of flesh from the elephant's trunk.

Lu watched, unable to move, her breath shallow and fast.

Mark laughed, too arrogant. Hostility flamed in the elephant's big eyes.

The elephant reared up. Its front feet caught Mark in the chest. Stumbling back, he tripped over the fallen corpse, and lost his grip on his knives. They fell to the ground, trampled into the dirt by the huge, heavy feet. Fear flickered in Mark's eyes. The trunk swung, blood drops flicking from the missing flesh, and pushed him back. He fell with a *whoomph.*

Mark's arms rose impotently against feet that came down heavy and hard over and over again. Lu swallowed down vomit. She forced herself to watch as her brother's bone and skin were mashed in to paste.

He died at the hands of an animal, like their Granny.

But he had been an animal, like Asher. One that deserved to die. Mark had betrayed her too often.

A relief that extended beyond her cash prize swept over her.

Until the elephant, feet and legs now covered in her brother's blood, turned back toward her with eyes now much closer to Asher's than they had been. Much blacker. Much more frightening.

The stink of old and new death filled the clearing.

Lu searched again for her knife, a rock, anything to get the upper hand. She was too close to freedom to die now. Last time she had huddled inside her Granny's coat, hiding tears, she had promised herself she would die anywhere but here in the forest.

When it was just a few steps away, the elephant stopped. The burning anger in its eyes dimmed. The light that surrounded it shimmered in the filtered sunlight. The shimmer grew to an eye-watering intensity, giving Lu no choice but to turn her face and close her eyes. Her heart raced.

Light slowly returned to normal. The glow no longer pressed against her eyelids. She kept her eyes closed until she heard weeping, then opened them.

Tears and blood streaked the face of a naked woman standing before her.

'Where's Alice?' the woman said.

'Where's my elephant?' Lu said the words, but she already knew, looking at the gore-covered woman.

The woman let out a harsh, bitter noise before she crumpled to the ground. The vines around Lu's feet loosened. She ripped herself free, moving toward the river—away from trees, the woman, and the mashed paste that was once her brother.

'You're a changelin',' Lu said, flatly.

'Where is Alice?' The woman looked so small and pale, curled up on the ground. If she weren't still covered in Mark's blood, Lu might have even thought her innocent.

'Who's Alice?'

'You smell of her.'

'Me Granny?'

'You have her smell. And you have changeling blood as well.'

'No,' Lu shook her head. 'Granny wasn't changelin' and neither am I.'

The woman glared. 'Just because you don't believe it, doesn't make it a lie. Her blood wasn't as strong as yours, but she only had one parent with changeling blood.'

'You're seriously cracked.' Lu's laugh held no humour. 'Now get up. The sooner I hand ya over, the sooner I get my reward.'

'Please, don't take me back.'

'Back?'

'To his people.' She nodded toward Mark's remains and Lu felt heat rising in her chest.

What was goin on?

No. It didn't matter, she was getting the hell off this planet, no matter the cost.

'My people. He's me brother.' She narrowed her eyes. 'And

you're ma ticket outta here. Ya gonna come quiet? Cause by the looks, the old stories are true. Changelin' loses strength when they shift'

'You shouldn't believe all the old stories.' The woman squinted up at the harsh sun. 'I may be weak but the sun is too strong for either of us to leave yet.'

Lu cursed under her breath. She should have known that. This changeling was rattling her thinking too much. Granny'd always said they were tricksters.

Lu picked up her pack and hauled out the chain. She dragged the woman into the river, steering clear of the trees. The woman didn't have the physical strength to fight, just used more words to plead for help—but Lu ignored her. She hurriedly washed the blood from the changeling's body, gentling her touch slightly when the woman flinched at Lu's fingers on her cut back.

Finally, Lu threw her a spare set of clothes to put on. Lu ignored the bitter look she was given. She didn't want to know what it meant. Nothing had changed. When the woman was clothed, Lu wrapped the chain around her feet and hands, snapping the padlock into place.

'Get some sleep,' Lu said, settling in the shade of a rocky outcrop. 'We'll leave at dusk.'

#

'It's time to get going.' The light had dimmed enough to be bearable.

Lu had dozed through the midday heat in short fits and bursts once she was certain the woman truly slept. Her mind wouldn't stop but she didn't want to know; didn't want to care.

But nothing was making sense. And while she had never much worried if she was thought of as simple, she didn't want any more surprises.

The woman moved to get up but was pulled back, her leg caught, now shackled by the chain clasped in Lu's hands.

'Seriously?'

Lu simply raised her eyebrows and jerked her head toward where Mark's body and the other corpse still lay.

'I'm not going to hurt you,' the changeling said.

'Ha!'

'You are one of us, I wouldn't hurt someone with changeling blood.'

'He's me brother, elephant. And you killed 'im.'

'He was different. And my name's Mial.'

Lu stared at the ground, thoughts moving and churning. In her mind's eye, she again saw her brother being trampled by Mial. It made her ill to think of. Not because of the sight of her brother's mutilated body, but the relief and joy she had felt.

Things had shifted. She had never needed to know before. But if changelings were real, what other crazy shit had her Granny been right about? And what was Asher really up to?

'Did Asher really have ya before?'

'Does it matter?' Mial stood, arms crossed. 'Why do you hunt us?' Mial's voice softened. She cocked her head, trying to catch Lu's eyes.

'Who says I hunt more than just you?'

'You're too good; you shouldn't have been able to find me. So, why do you hunt us?'

'Why do ya kill people?' Lu asked.

'I killed him out of defence.'

'And me Granny?'

'What? She was a changeling. We don't kill our own kind.' Mial's voice cracked.

'Asher told me it was one o' your kind tha' killed her. An *animal*.' Lu spat the last word. 'And she weren't no changelin'.'

'He lied. She told us she was worried about being followed by humans when she came to warn us of planned raids. If she's really dead, then I'm betting it's on Asher's hands.'

'Why would I lie about her being dead? And Asher never lied before, even when I wanted him to.' Lu's voice quivered. Why did this make sense? Why did this sound possible, even familiar?

'He lied about this. *He* killed Alice, not us. Killed her because she was protecting us.' Mial glared. 'He wanted you because he thought you might change, too. She told me.'

'You're lying!' Lu's heart stuttered. 'He took us in after Granny died. We would have starved.'

Mial just stared back, her mouth set thin and her arms folded.

'Gotta get goin'.' Lu gripped the chain tighter and yanked. Her feet pounded on the ground, sounding like a rain turning into a storm, heavier and faster as they drew closer to town.

She can't have had it wrong all this time. All the animals she hated and handed over so willingly. They were the problem, not her.

#

They sat side by side on a small outcrop of rocks, looking down at the town that lay below. Lu had left Mial chained when she went to tell Asher's messenger that she had the animal and set a time for the handover. It wouldn't do to just walk a chained woman or elephant through the town in full view of the folk there.

She had found Mial sobbing on her return. Without a word, Lu had unchained the woman—keeping one leg bound—and dragged her to the spot where they both now sat, waiting for Asher's instructions. Most likely he'd want her to come to his tent on the other side of the town, just before sunset.

She checked the changeling, who sat, shivering. 'You're cold.' Lu was just as surprised as Mial looked when she took off her jacket and draped it over Mial's shoulders.

'Please, can't you just kill me before you take me back?'

'Kill ya?'

'I can't go back. You can't even imagine what is going on in there. You only saw the wounds.'

Lu ran her hand over her own back; her own scars. She knew why they had looked familiar. No. It wasn't her problem.

'Why haven't ya changed?' Lu demanded. 'Why didn't ya just shift and leave while I was in town?' Lu wasn't sure who would win between the two of them, especially if Mial changed during the fight.

Mial's eyebrows drew together. 'The chain.'

'What about it?' Lu remembered the sparkle on the links at the bar.

'It's coated in a specific mixture of herbs. Stops a changeling from being able to shift. It locks us in whichever form we have taken.'

Asher's chain. Asher had known he was sending her to find a changeling. What else did he know?

She hadn't asked about her Granny while she was in town, she was too scared of the answer.

Lu set her mouth. It didn't matter, not when she was so close to freedom.

So why the tightened fist in her chest?

'Are there other animals still alive?' she asked.

'You don't know much do you? Did you never think to ask a single question?'

Lu hated that Mial's judgement hurt.

'You lead us there and you don't know what he's up to?'

'He's killed the other animals I brought him, why should I have thought anything had changed?'

The silence hung around them. Lu bit her tongue against wanting to somehow justify her actions.

'He calls it his circus,' Mial said softly. 'They pay him money to come and see how easy it is to hurt us. He trains them how to torture us. I was one of his test subjects for the herbs that stop us from changing.'

Lu felt the bile rise in the back of her throat.

'Please.' Mial turned huge, dark eyes on Lu. 'Don't take me back. At least, not alive.'

#

They skirted the town in the lengthening shadows. Lu unchained Mial's leg before they came into view of Asher's tent. Knife in hand, she gave her the choice, elephant or human. She would be handed over in her chosen form.

Mial chose the elephant.

The two men standing sentry outside Asher's tent eventually let them inside—once their mouths closed again. Now Lu could still hear the low rumble of their discussion; the words elephant and beast spoken in hushed reverence. Or fear. Probably both. Her smile was bitter, fear always won out.

The tent reeked of musk and sweat. But beneath those smells, Lu smelt others. Softer and sweeter, like fresh leaves and running water. Like a waft of living nature. How had she never noticed before? The scents made her stomach roil. She swallowed and clenched her teeth. She had to stop caring, that was how she had survived.

She could get through this. She just wasn't sure how.

Pressing her lips closed, she held tighter to the chain and took another step inside.

Her skin crawled and she stopped her lip from curling into a scowl when Asher laughed and got up from his chair. The chair was made of bone. Lu knew it wasn't human. It had been her first bounty.

'I always knew you would beat Mark. I only keep the best.' He slapped her shoulder so hard she almost dropped the chain.

'And yet, ya doubted me.'

'Nah, just a way to get rid of him.'

'Money?' Lu struggled to keep her breath even.

'Yes, yes, all business.' He threw her the payment, holding his hand out for the chain.

'I'll lock 'er up,' Lu said. 'She's a bit of a kicker. Can't be letting the main attraction of the circus free again.'

Asher was quick to cover up his surprise, but it was enough to confirm what Mial had told her. She wondered how many of the animals she had hunted for him were still alive, being tortured and wishing for death.

And how many were changelings.

'Oh, she'll be a kicker when I'm finished with her.' He laughed coarsely.

Lu again fought the bile rising in her throat again. She avoided the elephant's eyes as she looped the chain through a ring that had been driven into the ground.

'Sorry,' she murmured. With Asher's eyes on her, Lu slipped the padlock through the chain.

'Locked up tight?' Asher's expression was eager.

'Yep.' Lu turned her face away and shoved her hands deep in her pockets.

Mial pushed forward, her trunk catching Asher across his face. Asher scowled and picked up a whip leaning against the tent wall. Lu didn't want to see what happened next and slipped out of the tent, gulping in the fresh air.

#

She reached the rocky outcrop on the other side of town and stopped, chest heaving. Her pace had been too quick, but soon it wouldn't matter.

She pulled out the payment and weighed it heavily in her hand. In the distance, a shuttle flared into the starry sky. She watched its glow fade. She now had enough. Years of this nightmare, and salvation was at hand.

Instead of heading off, she sat down, staring blankly back at the town—at Asher's tent, outlined in torches that flickered in the dark.

It wasn't long before the screams carried up to her. Floating on the dust. She almost wished she could have seen Asher's face; had the satisfaction of him knowing that she had done it on purpose. Then her thoughts turned again to Mark's mashed body and her stomach gave up its contents, vomit splattering on the dusty ground.

Lu wiped her mouth and the tears, and waited.

An eternity passed before the silhouette emerged from the darkness, shifting from elephant to human.

She watched Mial approach, jerking in response to Mial's

stumble. But the changeling kept on coming. Slowly, she was joined by other detaching shadows, all limping and stumbling.

Mial stopped. She stood, painted in blood and shivering, before Lu.

Their eyes met. Lu didn't need to hear that Asher was dead. It lay in Mial's gaze.

Lu took a deep breath, pulled the closed, unused padlock from her pocket and threw it on the ground. She wouldn't use it again.

She held out the bag of coins.

'Not enough for us both to get offworld,' Lu said. 'But enough for all of us...' she pointed at the other freed changelings '...to get out of this town, find somewhere with less humans and no defilers.'

Mial's fingers curled around the bag. Lu took off her coat and helped Mial put it on over sticky, clumsy limbs. With a sigh, Mial leaned against Lu and they headed toward the forest. The vines opened at their approach and the other changelings followed.

#

END

- 136 -

Old Dogs, New Tricks

Sam Brown

Freddie Snow was measuring out the precise portions of her chihuahua's breakfast, as she did every day, when she noticed the patio light was on at No. 42, opposite.

Not normal.

At her feet, Monique yipped.

'Don't blame me, Monique.' Freddie wagged the teaspoon at her faithful little friend's expectant face. 'It's the gnome lady. Did she come home last night?' She went back to spooning out dog food but stared in consternation at the patio opposite.

'I know I shouldn't call her that. How rude of her though, making me fret like this.' She threw up her hands. 'The curtains are open, too!' She picked Monique up and carried her to the front window for a better view.

Marion Burgess, Freddie's neighbour, was a short, rotund, white-haired English woman who favoured loud clothing and louder laughter. She played the poker machines at the Returned

Servicemen's Club more than she went to church. Freddie did not approve of the woman, but nor did she wish her ill.

And it was clear: her neighbour's patio light was on, and the curtains were open.

Freddie fished her safety alarm out of her blouse and clutched the cool white pendant to in a frail fist.

'It was yesterday she went out, wasn't it, Monique? The days do blur.' She put the Monique on the back of the sofa so the dog could join the surveillance. 'She does come home awfully late sometimes, but she always closes the curtains.' Freddie worried at her safety pendant.

The company of people her own age was one of the reasons her children had urged her to move into Twilight Gardens after Malcolm's death. Marion Burgess had tried to fulfil that promise. She'd invited Freddie to social events in the Village, to go with her to the Servicemen's Club, and on a bus trip to the outlet shopping mall. Freddie had refused all invitations but was nonetheless hurt when they stopped. That was when she started referring to Marion as gnome-lady and complaining that she had no interest in spending time around old people.

'I shouldn't worry, should I?' she asked the little dog. 'Marion's an adult. She knows what she's doing.' But her head filled with the many horrors that could befall an old lady. Her hand once again wrapped itself around the cool plastic of the personal alarm. After all, if she fell and couldn't get up and nobody came for *days*... Freddie shivered and gripped the alarm tighter.

'Oh, Malcolm, what should I do?' she cried heavenward to her husband. 'I don't know how to be old and alone! I don't want to be old!'

Monique snuffled.

What to do, what to do? Freddie went to the sideboard and picked up the phone. Her fingers hovered over the neatly labelled speed dial buttons. Her children would say call Security, but Security would think she was a frightened old lady.

She dithered.

Colleen would get on and *do* something, which would be reassuring, but Colleen could be…impatient. Connor was so much softer than his younger sister, but he'd be at work and he was very clear he was not to be called at work.

'What if it's something serious?' Freddie had once complained to him.

'That's why you've got the panic alarm.' His calm had not soothed her.

'What if it's not a panic but it is serious?' she'd countered

'Then call Security and they'll deal with you.'

Freddie had bristled. 'Deal with me! Like I'm a deck of cards.'

'Muuuummm!'

Oh, how that patronising tone irritated Freddie!

She pressed the CONNOR button anyway. Maybe his wife, Penny, would answer. Penny frequently said what a *strong woman* Freddie was. What a *rebel* she had been: emigrating to Australia on her own in the sixties, insisting on working even when the children were small. All true, but Penny may as well have been describing a stranger. That was another lifetime ago.

As the phone rang on, Freddie got that sinking feeling. Penny probably didn't want to take the call either. Was she just being mocking with the flattery?

When voicemail answered, Freddie vented her fears to the machine. 'Too busy to answer the phone again! My neighbour is missing, not that you care. It could be me!'

As she hung up, she felt a sting of shame. The room swam and she flushed hot, then cold. A tea towel had found its way into her hands and she twisted it into a knot as tight as her stomach.

'For all they know it's me lying dead in an alley,' she said to Monique, and pressed the button labelled COLLEEN. 'She won't answer either, I bet.'

Freddie was wrong.

'Hey, Ma.'

Freddie's heart slowed and she relaxed when she heard her daughter's broad Australian accent.

'Oh, hello, Colleen love. How are you today?'

'I'm good, Ma. I'm at work. Remember, I work Tuesday to Thursday?'

Freddie could hear tapping sounds in the background, and a distracted tone in Colleen's voice.

'I know, Colleen. I wouldn't have rung but I'm very worried. The lady across the way didn't come home last night.'

The tapping sounds stopped. Started again. 'I'm sure she's fine, Ma.'

'What if she's not?' Freddie's voice wobbled.

'I can't do anything from here, Ma. Call Security, that's—'

'—what they're paid for. I know, I know.'

'Ma-a.'

'Never mind, Colleen. You go back to your important job. Don't worry about me.'

'Ma, we've talked about this.'

'Yes, Colleen, yes we have. I shouldn't bother you. I shouldn't bother anybody. I should just hurry up and die so I don't have to be a burden on you all.' In a fit of pique, Freddie did something unthinkable: she ended the call without a further word.

At Freddie's feet, Monique whimpered. Freddie picked her up and cuddled her close.

'They've sent me here to die, Monique. They don't care about me.' Tears fell wetly onto her cheeks. She pressed her face into the dog's chubby warm body and let a sob escape. 'Imagine if it was me, Monique. Who would come to my rescue?'

Monique barked. Freddie sniffled and straightened. A mobility scooter, with a bright orange flag waving high, zipped past. Noel Whittaker! The cavalry!

Freddie put Monique down and hustled to the front door. She knew Noel from church, but he was married and his wife was quite snippy so Freddie usually hid when he made his tours of the Village. What would people say if she entertained gentlemen callers? Still, needs must.

'Noel!' she called, but there was no response. She stepped out further and waved, 'NOEL!'

His small, lined face lit up. He steered the scooter toward her.

'Freddie Snow! Home for once! Good to see you, good to see you!'

Monique trotted to the scooter and investigated it with her nose.

'I'm very worried, Noel,' Freddie blurted. 'That one over there hasn't come home. And no one cares.'

'No one cares about us. We're just taking up space,' said Noel.

'Exactly.' Freddie basked in righteousness. 'Something has to be done. My daughter told me to call Security.'

'Don't call them!' Noel's eyes darted around, as though they might be being watched. He steered his scooter toward the gnome lady's unit. 'You certain she's not home?'

'Ninety percent. She always comes home. Always!'

'Let's go check it out, then!' Noel motored up the ramp so he could see in.

Freddie hesitated, then picked Monique up and followed. They all peered into the unit. The layout was a mirror image of Freddie's, but the space was cluttered with furniture suited for a much bigger house, and every surface lay covered with gewgaws, knick-knacks and dust collectors. The tiny woman was nowhere to be seen.

'Anything could have happened,' said Noel, in dark tones.

'Anything,' Freddie echoed.

'Somebody's got to do something, and it's going to have to be us.' Noel was surprisingly decisive.

They decamped to Freddie's unit to plan. Freddie opened her garage and Noel parked his scooter inside. She tried to help him, but he produced a walking stick and brandished it cheerily.

'I can manage. Bung knees, bad back, and no bloody stamina but hasn't stopped me yet!'

Freddie made them both a cup of tea and they watched the unit across the forecourt while she told him what she knew. Noel interrupted frequently with questions, which made it hard to get up a good head of steam for storytelling. She didn't mind much. His attentiveness was gratifying. Her family mostly nodded and smiled with their phones in their hands.

'Were you a detective?' she asked. He laughed, a lovely sound that made Monique bark.

'Only when my girls were sneaking out their bedroom windows to meet boys. I was a sparky by trade.'

'You're very good at this.'

He brightened and pushed out his skinny chest. 'I do love a good detective series.' For a while they were distracted from their mission by a lively discussion of their favourite shows.

'Morse would know what to do to find your neighbour,' Noel

said eventually.

Freddie stood up abruptly. How could she have forgotten her quest? She got dizzy from the sudden change in blood pressure and sat down again.

'Oh, Noel! What if she *is* dead and no one cares?' Her chest felt as though a snake was constricting it. Panic attacks were familiar now. She no longer thought she was having a heart attack, but the sensation was still frightening.

Noel patted her hand with his small, gnarled one. 'Now don't you get yourself all worked up. I'm here.' He wasn't a very robust hero, but his support was better than none. 'The last known sighting was when she left here yesterday morning, you say?'

'In one of those Uber cars,' said Freddie. 'I saw the sticker.'

'Well, the driver must know where he took her Let's try them.'

Freddie got out the Yellow Pages directory book but there was no listing for Uber. She made them another cup of tea to drink while they considered who else to ask.

'We need a young person,' said Noel. 'What about calling one of your kids?'

Freddie glowered at her sideboard phone. 'They don't listen. It's up to us, Noel.'

Noel scratched at his bristly grey chin. 'There must be someone around here.'

As if by magic, the familiar car of the visiting nurses pulled up in front of Freddie's unit, and a young man climbed out. He was one of Freddie's favourites.

'Usama will help!' she said.

'Oh-sama?' said Noel, looking alarmed. 'Like Osama Bin Laden?'

'No, no, no. He's not a terrorist. He's not even a real foreigner,

- 143 -

he's a Christian!'

She opened the door and Usama smiled warmly at her, his white teeth and dark hair gleaming in the morning sunlight.

'We need your help,' she said, hurrying him inside. She peeked out to make sure no-one saw him come in, just in case.

If Usama was surprised to be hustled into Freddie's front room to be interrogated by amateur detectives, he was too polite to let on. Such politeness was one of the traits that endeared him to Freddie and overcame her fears about both gentlemen callers and Muslims.

'Let me see if I understand, Missus Snow,' Usama said when she finished. 'Your friend went out and didn't come back, and you want to find her?'

Freddie nodded enthusiastically.

'In a Youber,' Noel agreed. Usama scratched his head and looked off into the distance.

'They're like taxis,' Freddie added.

'They don't have a light on top,' said Noel.

Usama held up his hand. They looked at him expectantly.

'I think I can help,' he said. 'I know some people who drive for Uber.' He went outside and made calls, speaking rapidly in a language Freddie couldn't have named. She and Noel watched through the front window as he paced back and forth. To Freddie's dismay, he lit a cigarette.

'Terrible habit.' She tutted.

Noel inhaled deeply. 'I'd kill for one. The fun police won't let me do anything. Bloody rabbit food. No smokes. No full-strength beer.'

'It's good for you.'

'Not you, too,' he grumbled. 'You sound like my kids.' He looked so peeved Freddie feared their mission might be at risk.

She gave a nervous laugh. 'We don't want that!'

'Don't you get sick of being told what to do? Eat this, take that, go here. I ran a successful business and they treat me like I'm a child.' His wizened little face became quite pink. Freddie was surprised by the outburst. At church, he was all smiles, although he never said much when his wife was around.

Before Freddie could muster a response, Usama re-entered the unit and grinned.

'I have good news, Missus Snow. I have found the driver who collected your friend.'

Freddie pressed her fingers to her hot cheeks. She didn't know whether to be excited or afraid.

'Don't hold your waters, son!' said Noel, sitting a little more upright in the deep chair. 'Where did he take her?'

'To Lucky Star Casino,' said Usama.

'The casino?' Freddie stared, puzzled. 'Why would she go there?'

'We shall ask her that.' Noel pushed to his feet. 'When we get there! Will you take us, young man?'

Usama turned to his patient. 'Missus Snow, I am here for you. What can I do to help today?'

It took a moment for the penny to drop. 'I don't know—oh!' Freddie beamed at her own cleverness. 'I think today I'd like an outing!'

Usama smiled. 'If you say so, Missus Snow.'

Thrilled with the conspiracy, Freddie let Usama help Noel, then her and Monique, into his car. He clipped a smartphone into a holder on the dashboard.

'Navigate to the Lucky Star Casino,' he instructed it.

Noel, sitting in the front passenger seat, exclaimed at the marvel.

'You know, when I was a boy people didn't even have telephones.'

Unable to hear Noel's lively questioning properly in the back, Freddie fell asleep.

#

'Missus Snow, we are here.' The voice woke her, and Freddie sat up, blinking at her surrounds. Usama? What was she doing in a car with her nurse?

'Missus Snow, I cannot wait long. I have other patients.'

Monique wriggled inside Freddie's shopping bag and yipped sleepily. Before Freddie could ask her dog what they were doing, another man's voice called out.

'Come on then, Freddie!'

She looked up to see Noel Whittaker from church manfully push his passenger door open.

'Concierge, please!' he called, waving his walking stick about. A uniformed man trotted obediently down shiny marble steps.

The fog of sleep cleared. Freddie remembered their mission. The enormity of what they'd done made her suddenly conscious of her crepey skin and aching bones.

'This was not a good idea,' she muttered. 'The Lucky Star Casino is a dreadful place. Full of gamblers.'

But the uniformed man was helping Noel into a wheelchair, and another was opening her door.

'Noel, maybe we should…'

Too late. He was wheeled away from her through the grand entrance way. Her escort, whose name badge said *Carlos*, helped her from the car. As Freddie looped her shopping tote over her arm, Monique poked her head out.

'Oh, Monique, what have we done?' she whispered as Carlos

lead her inside.

It was her first visit to the Casino. The foyer was an atrium several storeys high that opened out onto rows and rows of poker machines on the casino floor. All shiny and modern and loud. Her heart seemed to beat a little faster. And was she short of breath? Before she could worry about an incipient panic attack, she and Carlos arrived at the concierge station.

She was in time to hear Noel lie, and almost gasped aloud.

'It's my wife,' Noel said, looking worried. 'She left her pills at home and asked me to bring them. Silly duffer that I am I've gone and left behind the piece of paper with her room number.' He shook his head and sighed.

When did he come up with that story? Freddie was impressed and horrified at the same time.

'And what's your wife's name?' the concierge asked.

Noel looked blank; his mouth hung open.

'Marion,' Freddie blurted. 'Marion Burgess.'

The concierge frowned suspiciously at Noel.

'Stroke,' Freddie whispered, with a nod toward Noel. 'Tragic. Forgets his own name sometimes.'

The concierge tapped keys on his computer. He believed her! She felt like Mrs Marple.

'Ah, yes,' the concierge replied. 'One of our big winners. She's in the Galaxy Suite. Top floor, third from left. Big celebration, eh?'

Freddie nodded, then smiled and pushed Noel toward the lifts. As they passed the slot machines, Freddie tut-tutted. It was barely midday and all the machines were full of people throwing away their money. Bells going. Lights flashing. So noisy!

'My Malcolm was never a gambler,' she said. 'His father was. That's why Malcolm was so against it.'

'Same,' Noel said. 'Dad gambled. Horses. I wouldn't touch the stuff. Mug's game.'

Freddie warmed toward Noel anew. They left the lift and found the gold-plated door of the Galaxy Suite.

'Here goes nothing,' said Noel and rapped his walking stick firmly on the door. He'd barely finished when the door was swept energetically open by a paunchy middle-aged man wearing nothing but a white bath towel.

'You're not room service,' he said.

'I'm sorry,' Freddie replied. He was quite handsome in a DCI Banks sort of way, but if DCI Banks rather too much enjoyed his puddings. She tried to look elsewhere, and her cheeks warmed. 'We must have the wrong...' She froze on the spot.

'Wrong?' he prompted, raising thick eyebrows.

Freddie couldn't respond. All her words had vanished when the gnome lady swanned across the room, wrapping a towel around her plump naked body.

'Is that the room service, lover?' Marion said, sliding gnarled hands around his taut barrel belly. She peeked around him. When she saw Freddie standing there, still stunned, she withdrew her hands and clasped the towel tighter.

'Frederica. What are you doing here?' Marion lifted her chin and looked Freddie up and down.

Something in her tone made Freddie snap. 'Looking for you is what I'm doing here! I've been worried sick!'

'Don't talk to me like that!' For a small woman, Marion made a big noise.

'I'll talk to you how I like,' Freddie retorted. 'I'm 84.'

'Do you want a medal or a chest to pin it on? I'm 86.'

Freddie gasped. She'd assumed the energetic woman was much

younger.

'Ladies, ladies, settle down,' said Noel, gesturing for calmness.

'Don't tell me to settle down,' Freddie and Marion snapped in unison. A young couple coming up the hall stopped and stared. Freddie pictured the sight through their eyes: four old people, one shirtless, one wrapped in a towel, one in a wheelchair. All having a barney in the corridor of a fancy hotel.

She was mortified. 'You're making a show of me!'

'Ummm…' interrupted the man who'd answered the door. 'I'm going to…' He backed into the room, his widened eyes avoiding theirs.

'Oh, don't go, Greg, lover,' said Marion, trying to stop him. He muttered about getting home and vanished through sliding gold-mirrored doors into another room.

Marion turned to Freddie. 'Now look what you've done! Can't a woman have some fun once in a while?'

Fun? Freddie glared and gripped her tote bag tighter. This was not fun, it was…it was wrong, that's what it was.

'A woman your age has no business behaving like this.'

'A woman my age can behave any way she bloody well likes!'

'That's the spirit!' chimed in Noel, earning glares from both women. He held up his hands. 'Don't shoot!' His face was alive with mischief.

Down the hall, the lift announced its arrival. They all turned to look. A waiter emerged pushing a room service trolley in their direction.

'You might as well come in,' said Marion. Freddie was torn: dig her heels in and refuse to enter the den of iniquity, or get stuck out in the corridor being judged by the waiter?

'Come on, *Frederica*,' said Noel. 'Let's see how the other half lives.'

She let herself be led into the luxurious suite. While Marion dealt with the waiter, Freddie looked around. They were in a lounge area, with two vast cream leather settees, and a stocked bar. The massive windows provided a spectacular view of white sands and deep blue water that reached away to the far horizon.

'This is a bit of alright, eh Freddie?' said Noel, wheeling himself to the window and peering out.

'Sure beats The Village,' said Marion. 'Help yourself to the food. I'm going to talk to Greg.' She disappeared through the sliding doors.

There was more gold in the lounge room than Freddie had ever seen, other than in a church. She tried hard not to be impressed.

Noel pulled himself out of the wheelchair and took the lid off the trolley. A feast of fresh fruits and pastries was arranged on a platter.

'Second breakfast,' he chortled, tucking in happily.

'How could you?' said Freddie. 'She's a sinner!'

'Ah, Freddie, aren't we all? This is the best time I've had since my stroke. I'm taking advantage!' He popped a pungent piece of papaya in his mouth and closed his eyes to savour the sweet flesh.

'You can at least cook for yourself.' He reached for another piece. 'You should see the pap we get fed.'

Freddie had seen the pap they got fed. Who was she to deny Noel a bit of pleasure?

After a few moments in silence, he twinkled at her. 'Make a man a cuppa, will you?' Despite herself, she agreed.

She was carrying two mugs when the sliding doors re-opened. Marion and Greg emerged, both fully dressed, and walked to the door. He gave Marion a goodbye kiss that made Freddie's eyes pop.

Marion closed the door and sighed. 'Well, I doubt I'll see him again.' She sat next to Noel.

'If I wasn't married and impotent, I'd offer to stand in for him!' he said, around a mouthful of Danish. Marion laughed heartily, and Noel joined in.

'It's not funny!' said Freddie. 'Women our age don't go gallivanting around the countryside. It's dangerous.'

'At our age, going to the toilet's dangerous.' Marion winked at Noel.

'Stop it.' Freddie's voice cracked. 'I thought you were lying dead somewhere!'

Marion's smile faded. 'I'm sorry to worry you. It's very kind of you to care.' She sounded sincere.

Freddie was only partly mollified. 'Nobody cares about old people.'

'You're not wrong about that, love,' said Marion. She tucked into a pastry, and the three sat in silence.

Marion's earlier words echoed in Freddie's head. A *woman my age can behave any way she bloody well likes*. It had been so long since Freddie had done...anything. She absently fed a piece of pastry to Monique and scratched at the small dog's head, thinking hard.

'How did you find me, anyway?' Marion asked. Noel launched into the story, and as he talked, Freddie forgot her anger. Reliving the adventure gave her a thrill, and she enjoyed Marion's loud and appreciative laughter.

'Well done you two!' Marion chuckled. 'Right little detectives. What do you want to do now? Hit the slots?'

Freddie stood abruptly. 'We really must go. People might worry.'

'Wouldn't it be fun to stay here another night?' Marion wheedled, nudging Noel. He gazed around the opulent surrounds but shook his head.

'If I'm not there when my wife gets in, she'll have my guts for garters.'

Outnumbered, Marion gave in. 'Alright. Let's go.' She rose and brushed crumbs off her red-flowered blouse. 'I've got enough money, now. I can come back any time.' She gathered her bag and pushed Noel out the door, chattering cheerfully. Freddie trailed behind, clutching her tote.

#

They travelled back to The Village in a traditional taxi called by the concierge. Freddie offered to pay, but Marion grinned.

'The casino's paying,' she said. 'They want me to come back and spend my winnings.'

'Is this where you go every day?' Freddie asked, working hard to keep judgement out of her voice.

'Not always there,' said Marion. 'Sometimes down over the border. I like the RSL. And a couple of the taverns. But I get bored of poker machines. I like to play the tables.'

'Don't you worry you'll lose all your money?'

'Pffffft. What else am I going to do with it?'

'Leave it for your children.'

Marion rolled her eyes. 'I didn't work my whole life to spend my old age sitting at home watching TV. Besides, they'd just squabble over it. They're a bunch of ungrateful idiots half the time.'

Freddie was taken aback. 'How can you say that?'

'Oh, and you're telling me your kids are saints?'

Freddie was about to leap to their defence, but Marion continued, 'They're alright, really. They have their lives, I know.

But I'm entitled to my life, too. And it'd be all medical appointments and Midsomer Murders if I didn't get out and have a bit of a lark.'

Freddie's cheeks burned. Medical appointments and Midsomer Murders were pretty much her life, except for visitors—who were mostly nurses. Why did it never occur to her to do more? She hadn't always been so fearful.

'I once hitchhiked to Byron Bay.' She blurted the memory as it popped vividly into her brain. 'The kids were in their teens and they were being awful. I asked Malcolm to take me away and he refused, so I took myself away.'

Marion beamed.

'And went to Cairns once,' Freddie added warming to the topic. 'Chained myself to the public bar of the Criterion in a protest, too. Got arrested.' What a day that had been!

'That's the spirit,' Noel said from the front seat. Freddie was about to tell them how she drove without a license for years, but Noel added, 'Allo, allo, what do we 'ave 'here then?'

Marion and Freddie leaned into the gap between the front seats to see what he was talking about. The taxi approached the retirement resort's main entrance. A police car was parked on the street. And another inside. A small crowd of Village residents, police and staff was gathered outside the main building.

'My goodness! What can have happened?' said Freddie as the taxi drew to a halt near the scene.

'Oh, bugger,' said Noel, his voice full of doom.

'Turn around, Driver!' Marion barked but the driver was already half out of the car.

'Too late,' Marion said, her tone echoing Noel's. A police officer closed the distance between the crowd and the puzzled taxi driver.

Freddie studied the crowd. A grey-haired, red-faced, younger version of Noel pointed at the taxi, his mouth working excitedly. A woman Freddie recognised as one of Marion's daughters marched toward the car, closely followed by...Colleen? And... oh no! Just behind her was Connor!

For a brief moment, Freddie thrilled at the attention. Her family did care! But as the phalanx of angry relatives gathered, she remembered the calls she'd made earlier. The cross messages she'd left.

Many hours earlier.

The sort of attention they would give her was not going to be pleasant. Colleen's face was beet-red. Even Connor looked cross and impatient.

The taxi driver was out of the car and talking to Colleen. Noel, moaning, hid his face in his hands. The keys still dangled in the ignition. The crowd advanced on the taxi, glowering and hectoring. Marion opened her door.

An ember of Freddie's once indomitable spirit sparked. How dare they treat her like an errant child! She straightened her shoulders. They had no right!

'Marion, close the door!' Freddie commanded. 'And hold Monique!' She thrust her shopping tote across the backseat and clambered out of the car with the energy of a woman three-quarters of her age. Then she slid into the driver's seat and shut the door.

She locked eyes with the taxi driver, clicking the seatbelt in place. Then she mouthed 'Sorry' at the nice middle-aged woman, who probably didn't need this in her day.

The taxi driver gaped. Colleen yelled. Freddie glared at her daughter, started the engine and put the car into a fast reverse. Her heart was racing again but this time she knew it wasn't panic. She'd driven all her working life and the taxi felt powerful in her hands.

She turned the wheel hard right and did a U-turn toward the road.

'Freddie! What are you doing?' cried Noel. His face was quite pink, but his eyes were alive with excitement.

'Frederica!' squealed Marion. 'Where are you taking us?' Her voice was more delighted than scared. Freddie glanced in the rear-view mirror. Marion was grinning from ear to ear. Behind her, all their families yelled and waved their arms.

Freddie laughed out loud. She swung the car onto the main road. In truth she had no idea where she was going, or what would happen when they inevitably faced their children. But, all at once, she didn't care what anyone thought.

She met Marion's gaze again and grinned. 'There's life in me yet and I'm going to live it! So I'm doing whatever I bloody-well want!' Her heart sang as she floored the accelerator and drove south under the blazing sun.

#

END

Siren's Fortune

Georgia Willis

'But when does the treasure ship come?' I watched the old fisherman intently as he stitched up the ragged nets.

His long, grey, scraggly beard bounced as he spoke. 'The *Siren's Fortune* comes during the biggest storms, young Leonard. It rides them, ya see, lads.'

'Has it come here before, Joe?' Albert asked, his eyes wide.

'Aye, it has. And it'll come again.' Joe adjusted his seat on the barrel and continued mending his net. 'Long before you whippersnappers were even born was the last time, though.' He squinted up at the sky. 'Looks like it might be soon this year.'

Next to me, Albert clutched at my arm, his skinny fingers scratching at my wrist. I shook him off and looked toward the ocean, frowning. Small, fluffy white clouds drifted on the horizon; crystal-clear water lapped gently at the shore. 'Doesn't look like a storm to me.'

The fisherman grunted and shrugged. 'When it comes, you'd

best hide where no one can find you. The thieving scoundrels on that ship will pillage the town and take whatever they want. Including children.' He chuckled.

Al gasped and looked at me, his eyes shining with excitement. Or more likely fear. I gave him a half-smile. Joe was just trying to scare us; ghost ships weren't real.

'The *Siren's Fortune* sails the ocean in search of treasure.' Joe wagged a gnarled finger at us. 'Takes it back to an island no living man has ever seen.'

Al was lapping up the story, but I didn't believe in treasure islands. If there was a ship, it was run by pirates, and pirates were just people we could rob. Money we could steal to get us out of this hellhole orphanage and crappy fishing village.

'What's it look like?' Al asked as I stood up.

'Where ya going, lad?' Joe asked.

'Leg's cramping. Just going for a bit of a walk.' I placed my hand on Al's shoulder and smiled. 'Be back soon.'

The fisherman snorted and turned his attention solely on Al.

#

I walked around a corner into the heady aroma of fresh bread. Maybe I could nick some before having to head back to the orphanage for dinner-time gruel.

There it was, on a table in front of the baker's shop: a loaf of bread, all cut up, with a jar of bright red jam next to it. I crept forward. No one was around. I could hear a woman scolding a crying child inside the building.

Carefully, I dipped the knife into the jam and smothered a slice of bread. Grinning, I eased the knife down, but it slipped from my fingers and clanged on the table. I gasped and ran around the corner with my prize. When no one came chasing after me, I headed back to the seaside at a leisurely pace, stuffing my face so I wouldn't have to share with Al.

He sat alone on the jetty.

'What ya doing, Al?'

He shrugged. 'Waiting for you.'

'Where's Joe?'

'Said he had to go secure his boat. There's that storm coming, remember? What's on your face?'

I wiped my mouth and saw a smear of jam on my arm.

'Stole a bit of bread. Sorry. Almost got caught, or I would've gotten you some too.'

Al nodded but didn't reply. He got up and dusted off his hands. Odd. Usually he'd get angry at me.

'Come on,' I said. 'Better get back for dinner. You know how the sisters get.' I poked him in the ribs.

'Yeah, we wouldn't want to starve,' he snapped.

'Sorry, Al. It was only a bite, I promise!'

'Yeah, well!' he muttered, then ran.

I swore. Whoever got back to the orphanage last was likely to be on the wrong end of a cane. I chased after him, dodging through the crowd. Al cried out and sprawled on the ground. The butcher, a huge man wielding a large knife, yelled at him. Al scrambled up. But now I was ahead. Al screamed in frustration when I pushed first through the screeching old gate.

'You ALWAYS win!' He ground his teeth.

I shrugged. 'You would've won if you hadn't run into the butcher.' I turned toward the ancient orphanage building. The big steal gate squealed shut behind me.

'I hate you sometimes, Leonard. Why can't you just let me win?' Al growled.

'When you do beat me, do you want it to be because I let you win? Or because you were finally better than me?' I asked without looking at him.

He ran up and shoved me to the ground. 'I am better at some things!'

'Yeah, at eating maybe,' I said, grinning.

He snorted and held out his hand, a small smile playing on his lips. 'Come on, I'll show you how it's done,' he said, the smile breaking free of his bad humour.

When we entered the dining hall, Sister Lea stood at the far end of the long buffet table with two bowls left in front of her, and a cane held firmly in her hands. Our feet echoed on the worn wooden floor. All the other kids watched us hurry toward our meals.

'Where have you been?' she snapped.

'Nowhere, Sister,' Al replied, keeping his head down.

The sister frowned. 'Hands!'

Al and I held out our hands tentatively. The cane came faster than lightning. We flinched with each blow, but to pull away would only result in a worse beating.

'Go. Sit.' She pointed to the bench.

Al reached for his gruel. The cane landed sharply next to the bowl. His shoulders slumped and we trudged to the bench. I learned the lesson and didn't even try. No dinner for us again. Al put his head in his hands, his stomach growling so loud I could hear it.

I stared out the window, bored, but at least not hungry. I felt a twang of guilt about not getting Al any bread, but it passed.

The air grew chilly and I rubbed my hands on my thin, patched shirt. I hated this place and that woman. We went to bed hungry more times than not, and she was never seen without her cane.

I whispered to Al, 'When I grow up, I'm never going to be hungry or get hit ever again.'

Al looked up. 'You'll need to be rich, then.'

I nodded.

Sister Bessy, or the Crone, as Al and I like to call her, waddled to the window near us.

'Storm's coming,' she muttered, shaking her head and closing the shutters.

'The fisherman said the *Siren's Fortune* comes on a storm,' Al said to me quietly, watching the Crone waddle to each of the windows and close the remaining shutters.

I leaned in. 'Well then, tonight we go and find that ship and we steal enough treasure to get us out of this place!'

Al nodded silently, his mouth in a grim line. His stomach rumbled again.

I had my doubts, but anything was worth trying at this point.

#

Our punishment was cleaning up after dinner and practicing our letters. I hated writing so I took my time scraping out the thirty or so bowls into the bin and waited for Al to start washing. Whenever Cook wasn't watching, I'd sneak a mouthful of gruel. When I'd finished scraping the bowls, my stomach was more than full.

Al washed, all under the watchful eye of Cook. I began drying the dishes.

'I'm so hungry,' Al whined.

'Should have scraped the bowls, instead of writing stupid letters,' I said with a giggle.

Al clenched his jaw but didn't reply.

Thunder boomed overhead. The last of the dishes were away and Cook chased us out of the kitchen. We hurried through the empty halls toward our room; we needed to get out through the window before the front gate was bolted shut.

The rain had picked up when we finally snuck into the dorms. The Crone locked the dorm doors behind us. Al and I exchanged a grin and headed for the window. The other boys didn't even blink as we clambered out and into the pouring, freezing rain. We were drenched by the time we snuck around to the front gate and very slowly opened it, avoiding the tell-tale screech.

'You won't leave me behind will you, Leonard?' Al asked, his eyes darting between all the darkened, dripping palm trees.

'You're my best friend, Al. I'll never leave you behind.'

He nodded and flinched as lightning forked through the sky. 'Let's go to the beach!' he shouted over the clap of thunder.

We hurried south with the rain getting heavier and the wind bowing trees to its will. We battled the storm, hiding under what shelter we could. It was late afternoon, but the clouds blotted out the sun, and the town fell into an eerie darkness. No one was around. All the shops were closed and any travellers huddled in the taverns and inns. Not even the fishermen were out; all their boats covered and tied down. The place was like a ghost town.

We ploughed ahead and staggered onto the beach. Sand stuck to our feet. Waves roiled and crashed, leaving white and grey slicks on the soaked beach. The stench of algae and rotting seaweed made me gag.

Albert gasped.

'What?' I yelled.

He pointed through the veil of thick rain. I wiped my eyes and squinted as another flash of lightning thundered through the clouds.

Out in the distance—and getting closer—was a weather-beaten ship.

'My god, it's true!' I gasped. We hid in a bush awaiting its arrival and grinned madly at each other. Shivering, we looked in awe upon the figurehead of a beautiful woman holding a large golden coin.

'It's the *Siren's Fortune*, just as the fisherman said!' Albert yelled, his eyes gleaming. 'We wait till the pirates get off and then sneak aboard?'

I nodded enthusiastically. We would be out of that orphanage and well-fed in no time!

Twenty minutes later, two longboats left the ship and beached themselves right in front of us, smooth as anything. Waves split before them, leaving a neat path through the water.

We fidgeted and waited for the pirates to get off the boats. But nothing happened. The longboats looked empty and the ship sat in the water, a long way from the white sand that looked almost black in the darkness of the storm. The tattered grey sails snapped in the wind but nothing else moved.

I groaned. Maybe the pirates had gotten off in the water and swum in.

I tugged on Al's sleeve. 'Come on, let's go see.'

'N-no!' Albert whipped his arm back.

'Well, I'm going!' I ran out from the bush. This was the first and only time I'd ever seen a pirate ship, I wasn't wasting my chance for freedom. I ran to the water's edge and squinted through the rain at the ship. Its salt-worn timbers creaked under the wind's onslaught. Waves lashed my feet, stinging-cold.

The longboats were too large for me, but a little fishing dinghy was drifting into the beach. That I could manage, even in the storm. I clambered in and loaded the oars onto the rowlocks.

'C'mon, Al!' I yelled, waving at him.

'Leonard!'

I could barely hear him over the rain and the waves crashing on the beach. I turned. He stood on the beach, pale and trembling, gaping at something above my head. I looked up just as a thick strand of fog, like a giant tentacle, slammed into the water next to me. A wave caught my dinghy and flipped me out. I dove to one side, landing deep in the angry surf.

I coughed and spluttered, and glanced back to where Al had been standing. He was gone.

Scrambling up, I searched the beach. Maybe he'd run off. I stumbled for the shore and tripped as a wave pushed me over. I clambered to my feet again.

'LEONARD!'

High above me, Albert was in the clutch of another huge fog tentacle stretching from the ship's deck. He struggled in its grasp but disappeared out of my sight. I clambered into the dinghy and rowed as hard as I could out to the *Siren's Fortune*. Waves and wind battered at me, but I made it to the ship.

The hull was smooth. There was nothing I could use to climb up. I rowed to the other side. There! A rope. Panting, I hauled myself onto the deck.

'Al?'

Thunder boomed above, the sky turning blacker by the minute, and the rain pelted me like hail.

'ALBERT!' No reply. I crept around the deck. Not a person or pirate in sight.

'Al, this isn't funny,' I said quietly. Goosebumps rose on my arms. The storm's noise faded even as winds picked up in intensity. Foreboding rolled through me.

'Leonard…?' A soft voice carried on the wind.

I ran to the gunwale, chasing the voice. Albert stood on the beach, a grim expression on his face. How had he got away from that tentacle? Should I head back to the dinghy and go get him? Where had the two longboats gone? Both had vanished from the beach.

The *Fortune* lurched. I slipped and fell forward, hitting the gunwale. The ship moved, gliding away from the beach. The green-shadowed ocean was already deeper than I was tall.

Albert stood on the beach in the pouring rain, watching silently.

I climbed up on the gunwale and jumped for the dinghy.

A white fog-tentacle shot out and wrapped its slimy self around me, pulling me back. Waves washed over the deck, throwing me from side to side. Whenever I got too close to the edge, the white tentacle grabbed me. I screamed for Albert but he probably couldn't hear me. The rain hid him and he vanished behind a swirl of grey fog.

The storm grew more furious the farther out to sea I got. Lightning lit up the sky; waves and wind pummelled me. I hit every post and barrel on deck. Pain shot through me with every collision. I kept trying to grab something, anything. But every time a wave hit, I lost my grip and was thrown back.

I was going to die.

I crashed into the mast and feebly clung tight. I sobbed between ragged breaths. The ship listed to one side. Lightning tore through the sky again and again. A giant wave twice the size of the ship loomed above me.

I screamed.

Lightning flashed.

A clap of thunder reverberated through my body, rattling my teeth. I squeezed my eyes shut.

The world vanished into blackness.

#

I pried open my eyes. The sea was calm, the sun shone, hot and brilliant, from a clear sky. After a few deep breaths, I released my stubborn grip on the mast, carefully got up and walked to the gunwale. Dried saltwater had stiffened my clothing, leaving me itchy and hot.

Water extended in every direction: bright, clear, blue ocean. I groaned and massaged my shoulder and side. All the bumps and bruises were still there so I hadn't imagined the storm. Where was I? Where was the crew? Where was the treasure?

And how was I going to get home?

I licked my salty lips. Maybe the crew were below deck. I carefully made my way aft. There were two wooden doors: one brown and water-stained, the other of rotting, charred, black wood. The first didn't move, even when I barged it with my shoulder. I rubbed at the new bruise then tried the other. It gave, opening with a loud groan that echoed around me.

Voices whispered from somewhere belowdecks

'Hello?' I managed, though my voice cracked.

I took a step down the stairs and then a second. Gas lamps lit up as I tiptoed further, little flames dancing around me.

'Hello?' I whispered, foreboding rolling through my gut.

Half a dozen steel-barred cages lined the long corridor ahead. Something rattled against the bars on my left; I jumped sideways. A hand shot out of the cage to my right, grasping my arm and yanking me against the corroded steel. I yelped.

'What have we here?' a raspy voice said.

'Let me go!'

Other voices now joined the first. Figures appeared, some with tricorn hats and tattered coats. Some were missing a leg and gnarled pieces of wood stood in their place. Others wore ragged grey breeches and knitted caps. Notched sabres and cutlasses hung at their sides. Their eyes were grey, bleared, or even missing. Teeth broken and blackened. Ghoulish faces and skin dangling.

I clawed at the hand holding me but scraped only my own skin. I screamed and wrenched for freedom. The ghost pirate laughed and released me. I scampered up the stairs and the door slammed behind me.

Once more on the safety of the deck, I sat down. My arm throbbed; a red blistered handprint was left where the ghost had grabbed me. I sobbed and wrapped my shaking arms around myself. How did I get off this nightmare ship?

Night fell and I huddled near the mast, sleep coming in fits and starts. Every creak and noise woke me. The weak silver moon barely lit the rotting timber deck.

Thunder off in the distance made me shiver. Even in the dark, looming storm clouds raged. The ship steered itself toward them. Half-unfurled sails fluttered in the sharpening wind.

I staggered to the wheel and hauled with all my strength, trying to turn it away. It wouldn't budge, instead turning further into the storm. An eerie creaking echoed behind me. I stopped fighting with the wheel and turned toward the sound. Had the ghost gotten out? I crept around and tested the black door.

Still firmly shut.

But the brown door opened so I peeked in. There were no cages, nor any ghosts. Instead, a smoky yellow lamp lit, revealing a cabin with another open timber door.

I stepped inside. A piece of yellowed parchment lay curled on the desk, next to a crusty loaf of bread and a pitcher of water. Beside the desk stood a timber cupboard and a wool-blanketed bed.

I squinted at the parchment but it made no sense. The orphanage sisters had always told me to practise my letters, but orphans were only ever good for thieving or serving rich folk and neither job required reading. Besides, Al was good at letters. If I'd ever needed them, he read for me.

My heart lurched. I'd never see Al again. I'd left him all alone. I'd sworn to him that I'd never do that, and now I had. Why had I been so stupid? The tentacle must have dropped him. If I'd just paid more attention, if I'd never approached the ship, if I hadn't climbed aboard, none of this would have happened.

Tears dripped onto the neatly written note. I studied it carefully, just in case it told me how to get home to Albert.

No luck. Just thick black squiggles of ink. I could make out a few words like 'food' and 'drink', 'rest' and 'ship'. But nothing useful, nothing that could tell me what was going on.

After what felt like hours, I threw the note aside.

With eyes stinging, I sat on the bed, grabbed the bread and gnawed off a chunk. The loaf was filling. So, too, was the cup of water thirst-quenching.

I sighed, laid back and closed my eyes. Sleep would be nice, now. I wriggled under the thick wool blanket, warm and comfortable for the first time.

The ship continued sailing. First toward, then through the storm. This time, neither the thunder nor the bright lightning disturbed me, nor the waves as they lashed the deck. Instead, they lulled me into a deep slumber.

The ship rolled and lurched. Half-asleep, I tumbled to the floor.

'What happened?' I mumbled to the empty room. I yanked the door open. Icy wind cut me to the bone and I slammed the door shut.

Another storm raged outside. Again the air howled and lightning flashed purple and white through deep, thick clouds.

Shivering, I dragged open the closet and donned a thick jacket, pants, and boots.

Braced, I climbed back onto the deck. The wind swept around me but the temperature, although cold, wasn't too biting. The door slammed behind me.

I trotted to the bow. Where was I?

The ship waited close to another beach. Empty again, the two longboats rolled in the surf.

I squinted against the stinging rain. Even though the sunlight was low, the buildings on shore glinted with golden light. So did several fishing boats that lined a dock. I gasped. Were they made of gold? Lightning flashed through sullen clouds and a colourful glistening caught my eye.

The beach wasn't sand. Gems of every colour and shape sparkled in the storm light.

I laughed, ran to the rope and climbed down. The water was shallow and I swam until I was close enough to struggle through the roiling waves. I stood in numbing, thigh-deep water, and staggered onto the gemstone beach.

I whooped with joy and my voice was taken on the wind. I picked up handfuls of the stones and shoved them into my pockets until my pants bulged, then ran to the town. Maybe more treasure lay there.

The buildings *were* made of gold and silver, the walls carved into detailed images. I studied them. Little stick figures on an island, a ship in a storm. Maybe they had something to do with the *Siren's Fortune*.

Lightning flickered and the gold glittered like honey.

The carvings could give me a clue to the ship, but what about the treasure? I couldn't carry a whole building. Maybe I'd just have to take the gems. Or come back another time.

The pocketed gems weighed my pants down. I fished a plum-sized stone out, held it up and giggled. Never mind the carvings, I was never going to be poor or hungry again.

Grinning, I spied a piece of cloth hanging off a golden fishing boat. I tore the cloth free, turning it into a makeshift bag. Any loose metal I could find went into the bag. I didn't dare open any doors since the inhabitants might catch me. When my bag was full, I lugged my bounty toward the ship.

The storm worsened. Rain and ice pelted down as I tied the makeshift bag to my back and climbed back up the rope. It took twice as long as last time. The bag's weight dragged at me. By the time I reached the top, my half-frozen hands were skinned and bleeding.

I hauled my prize into the cabin and chuckled as I tipped the contents of bag and pockets on the bed. This treasure would last me for the rest of my life. I imagined the surprise on Al's face when I showed him.

If I could get back to him, that was.

I grabbed the bread and took another bite. Just as delicious and filling as the night before. I tore the pillowcase into strips and wrapped them around my hands. The bleeding stopped quickly.

Outside, the storm still raged. I hesitated, looking at my warm dry bed. Should I go get more? The treasure won and I hurried out the door, bracing against the cold, my now-empty bag in hand. Holding the rope, I swung off the ship.

A fog tentacle launched out of the deck and pulled me back on board. The boat lurched and left the shore. I swore, watching the glistening beach fade in the distance.

My teeth chattered and my feet slipped from side to side. I stumbled back to the cabin and changed out of the wet clothes into a too-big shirt and pants from the closet.

When feeling returned to my hands, I packed my treasure into a stronger bag.

Then I waited. And slept.

#

Blinding lights and booming thunder woke me again. Was it all storms these days? How did I steer the ship back home to Albert and our bright freedom? Or maybe I just needed to find any town where I could start again. I could always find Albert later.

I clambered onto deck and smelled the fresh air, but something wasn't right. Something in my stomach gnawed at me. Trying to shake the feeling off, I walked around the deck, but by the time I got to the bow, I was exhausted. I slouched against the gunwale. Weakness sapped my bones and I could barely raise my arm to wipe the sea spray from my face.

'What's happening?' I croaked.

A piece of paper flew into my face. I pulled it away. The note from the cabin. Still indecipherable. I growled and threw it aside.

Someone walked past me. I shot to my feet, gaping, wide-eyed.

People strolled around the deck, swabbing timbers, stitching canvas sails. One man stood in the crowsnest high above. Another, in a large tricorn hat, stood at the helm and directed the ship toward the next storm.

Another man in sailors' rags walked past.

'Hello?' I said.

He ignored me. I grabbed at another man but my hand passed straight through him. I gasped. The barrel showed through his misty body. Every man on deck was nothing but rags and mist, just like those in the steel cages I'd first seen belowdecks.

Where they ghosts? I fumbled for the gunwale. My hand slipped and I fell.

I stared at my hand. Through my palm, the deck gleamed in the stormy light. I shook my hand and it grew solid for a few seconds.

Thin, white tendrils of fog drifted from my hands into the old wooden boards.

The ship was drawing my energy into itself.

Was I going to turn into one of the ghost sailors, too? I should have listened more closely to the fisherman and his story. A tear ran down my cheek. Would I ever see home again?

I mustered my strength and crawled back to the cabin. My loot was still sitting in my bag on the bed. I pulled myself into a seated position against the bed—it was too much effort to crawl up there— and drifted off to sleep as the ship sailed on.

\#

Something jabbed me in the side. Blinking, I frowned at the tall figure standing above me. The pock-cheeked, thin features of a man in his twenties, grinned at me. He seemed familiar.

'Well, well.' The figure knelt. 'So, the stories were true.' He laughed.

'Do I know you?' I croaked.

'Of course!' The man stood, picked up the bag of treasure and peered inside. 'Is this all you got? Where's the rest? You were supposed to visit three islands!'

I frowned. Why was this man so familiar?

'Gah! You ate the food, didn't you?' He glanced at the half-eaten loaf. 'Idiot! You still couldn't help yourself. Greedy little thief!'

A page of parchment floated to the floor next to me and the man looked down at it. I reached for the letter, but he snatched it up first.

'Do you know what this says, Leonard?'

I shook my head.

He snickered. 'I guess not. You were never very good at letters, were you?'

'Al?' I struggled to get up but groaned and slumped onto the bed. How had he found me? Why was he so much older?

The man sneered. 'Yeah, it's me.'

'How?' I pointed at him; his face, his broad shoulders, his rough shirt and grey pants.

'Time moves differently here.' He gestured around the ship. 'I had plenty of time to read the letter and get off the ship before the *Siren* left that day.' He shrugged. 'And, with what the Joe, the fisherman, told me while you went and stuffed your face at the bakery, I knew how to get around the curse. The ship needs a soul for every journey. But you can give it any old soul. So, it was me or you. And I chose you. You climbed aboard all so willingly.' He chuckled.

'I came to save you.' I whimpered.

Al tilted his head, a smirk on his face. 'A good thing you did, or it would have been my arse on the line with Joe. He needed someone to provide the *Siren* a soul so it wouldn't raid the town. I needed a job. I've been working for him on the fishing boats for fifteen bloody years. Waiting for you to get back.'

He hefted my treasure. 'I expected more. If you hadn't eaten the food you would have been able to get three times as much. Suppose this will do.'

'Wait, Al!' I stretched a hand toward him. 'I'm coming with you.'

'Not in this lifetime, Leonard. You're stuck, kid.' He walked to the door and spoke without turning around. 'But you got your wish. You'll never be hungry again.'

'Al?' I called, the wind catching my voice.

A single tear trickled down and fell through my face. I watched through cabin door as Al grabbed the hull's rope. The same rope I'd scaled to save him.

He paused and looked at me. 'You were right, you know. It is much more satisfying waiting till I'm better than you to finally beat you.' Then he disappeared over the side of the ship.

The *Siren's Fortune* lurched again.

I took one last shaky breath, ready to yell for Al, to beg him to come back.

Instead, the tricorne-wearing captain appeared before me, cat-o-ninetails in hand.

'Get to work, boy, or join the others down below.' He leered. 'Time to go find another soul.'

#

END

Marvin and the Twist of Fate

Mandy Chandler

Madame Fontaine, the Great Oracle of all unicorns, peered into the deep, black scrying pool, shadowed by thick forest, and decreed Marvin's fortune in a dispassionate monotone:

I see a maiden fair with auburn hair.
She will groom and bind your hair.
Then take you home and keep you there.

'Wait! Whaat?' cried Marvin. 'That can't be it!' The poetry was bad enough, but the fate it predicted was nothing short of insulting. 'I'm the son of Ruth and Edgar Goldhorn—your clan leaders! My brother Edward rides with the great knight Sir Windermere, and my sister Eugenie married noble Ragnar of Ruevenden. Surely, I'm not destined to be some girl's pet?'

'*Adopted* son.' Madame corrected. 'You're not fit to polish the hooves of a *true* Goldhorn. They were the last of the *real* kings.' She narrowed her amber eyes at him. 'Before the sacred golden Pentatheron was stolen and we noble unicorns were reduce to living in shitty little villages like Orp.' She glared at the scattered collection of thatch huts as though they were a personal affront.

'Well that was 400 years ago,' Marvin muttered. 'You can't blame me for someone stealing our 500 gold pieces.'

Madame swished her elegant silver mane and matching tail. 'No, but you're definitely not a Goldhorn. To start with, you're totally the *wrong* colour. That garish rust coat and blue mane and tail! Ugh!'

'Anything else you'd care to point out?' he said sarcastically.

'Yes.' She sniffed. 'Your legs are too short. You'd never win a race. I warned them when they adopted you. He's nothing but trouble, I said.' She turned so a beam of sunlight fell on her pure white body and impossibly long legs.

'Many times, …' growled Marvin. She was such a show-off.

'*And* I was right! You've been thin-skinned and thick-headed all your life. No good at magic either, except when it results in ruination for others—'

'Now hang on a minute. I didn't mean to make your house *permanently* disappear! Digby dared me to do it. Who knew I'd be so good at vanishing spells? As you're so fond of saying, I'm usually shithouse at spells.'

'My house *and* my prize-winning rose garden.' She sniffed. 'All gone. Do you *know* how disgusting it is living with my slovenly sister, Lavinia, and her 13 cats? No, as far as I'm concerned, my prediction is a better fate than you deserve. I'd have banished you to the coal pits of Azania. Then we'd all be safe from your disastrous spells and stupidity. Instead, you'll be languishing in the arms of some maiden. Be thankful.'

'Oh, pshaw,' hissed Marvin. He wasn't going to settle for this rubbish. He'd create his own destiny. He'd follow his secret dream to find that most desired and elusive of all things—gold.

He hid a grin.

Legend had it that the one who restored the Pentatheron to its rightful place in the Goldhorn's palace would be the next king of the unicorns.

Forget being a pet, he'd be king and then they'd all be sorry for the way they treated him. Yes. That would show Madame—and everyone.

'Now go away,' Madame said, sticking her horn in the air. 'I have important things to do.'

Marvin kicked defiantly at a rock lying close to the scrying pool's edge, hoping to send it whizzing into the sacred pool, just to annoy her.

He missed, lost his footing on the slippery bank and tumbled into the water.

'Ha-help!' he spluttered, gasping for breath as water sloshed up his nose. 'I can't swim!'

Madame only gave a gleeful cackle and transformed into the shape of her familiar—a large, leathery phoenix. She flapped off, still screeching with laughter.

Marvin thrashed and fought helplessly against the whirling current. No good. He gulped one last breath as the icy water closed over his head. Exhausted, he let it drag him down into unfathomable depths.

#

When the spinning stopped, Marvin opened dry, gritty eyes. Flies jostled against his eyelids and stung his flanks. He lashed at them with his tail. His mouth was parched and his head ached. The smell of dust and sweat filled his nostrils.

'Ho—ly shit!' He squinted into the glare of a white-hot sun and took in his surroundings. 'Where the hell am I?' The pool and the lush forest of Orp were gone, replaced by a great expanse of red desert that shimmered in the heat.

I can't be dead, can I?

A worse fate dawned on him. *That old nag better not have sent me to the coal pits. Nope, Azania has black earth and purple sky—not red dirt and azure sky like this place. Hmmm, blue sky...* He tried to recall his geography lessons. The only one place he'd ever heard of that had blue sky was the human world, 'Urth' or something like that. But he'd never heard of anyone going to Urth.

Wait a minute, maybe this is all just a dream? That's more likely. Better get out of the heat, though. Dreaming or no, he was dying of heat, hunger and thirst.

On unsteady legs he ambled toward a nearby village where a faded sign read: 'Welcome to Bungaloori.'

The place appeared deserted—must be sheltering from the heat. Marvin took advantage; he helped himself to a long drink from a nearby trough, then followed the most heavenly scent of ripe apples to a wooden storage shed. Now he *knew* it was a dream—red apples were by far his favourite food, and damn hard to find back in Orp. But, in this cool shed, several barrels brimmed with the beauties. Marvin gorged on them then decided he'd better try to get back to reality. *A decent sleep should do the trick.* He lay down on a comfy pile of sacks. *Next stop Orp.*

#

Bang! Bang-bang! Bang!

Marvin jerked awake. *What's that racket? Where am I?* He

remembered falling into the scrying pool and finding himself in a strange land. *I'm in some sort of shed.* The smell of apples filled his nostrils.

No, no, no! I can't be here! Am I still dreaming? He smacked himself upside the head with a silver hoof. *Ouch! Nope, definitely awake. Damn.*

He peered round the door. More loud bangs and shouts—and were those human voices? Yep. Squinting into the brightness of the setting sun, he saw four men sweeping through the town on horseback. The riders had masks over their faces and held guns aloft, firing wildly into the air. Terrified men and women scurried into the relative safety of the public house as the horsemen pounded down the dusty main road. The bandits dismounted and barred the pub door, locking the townsfolk inside. They then headed into the local bank and emerged shortly after with several bags of loot, which they slung over their saddles.

Two lawmen approached, guns drawn, and attempted to trade fire with the robbers. But being outnumbered and outgunned, the lawmen were quickly overpowered and frogmarched back to the lock-up. The robbers mounted their horses and, with great whoops of victory, rode off into the desert.

When they were gone, Marvin crept past the pub, where the townspeople appeared to be making the most of their time—glasses clinked and ale flowed. He reached the place where the bandit's horses had been hitched and spotted a small pile of coins glinting in the light of a full moon. They emitted a rich yellow glow that whispered of their immense magical power.

GOLD! Right there on the ground. It wasn't much, maybe twenty pieces, but it was a start.

Helloooo destiny! Marvin gave a mental whoop. He scooped up the coins, relishing their rich metallic flavour, and deposited them in his whatchamacallit—a secret pouch every unicorn had in the pit of their right foreleg.

Now for a transformation spell to blend in with the locals. Transformations were tricky and only lasted if he stayed awake. But humans were notoriously skittish around unicorns, so he'd have to try. He hesitated, recalling the time he'd transformed Digby into a toadstool. Poor Digby still had a distinctly mushroomy odour.

Marvin shrugged off his fear and found a likely candidate on a nearby poster of a strikingly handsome, lantern-jawed man named 'Jack Ryder'. With such a good-looking character, what could possibly go wrong? He screwed his eyes tight and spoke the magic words:

'Soli transformata adonis!'

He felt a tingling sensation all over and a tightness across his rump. He looked down to see his chubby behind crammed into Jack Ryder's black leather chaps. But two shiny silver hooves protruded from the ends and a bright blue tail stuck out the back.

He tried again.

'Soli transformata adonis!'

This time, his front half transfigured, but his shadow still showed two large ears and a horn sprouting from beneath a cowboy hat.

Okay, third time's the charm. He took a deep breath and with great gusto spoke the magic words once more.

'Soli transformaaaata aaadooonis!'

There was a crack like a gunshot, and he successfully transformed into the dashing fellow. His magical horn was now a magical black riding crop held tightly in one meaty fist. He grinned a wicked grin at his handsome self, reflected in the window.

He was about to swagger to the pub, when an advert for the Bungaloori Horse Race, caught his eye.

They may not have gold in Orp, but they certainly had races. And races meant gambling. And if there was one way to turn 20 gold coins into 500 coins with very little effort, that would be it. This was almost too easy.

'You there!' hissed a voice.

In his excitement, he had wandered up to the open door of the lock-up. Marvin peered into the gloom and saw the two lawmen trussed up in the middle of an empty jail cell.

'Release us this instant!' the voice demanded.

Marvin stepped into the cell. The lawmen gasped.

'A-aren't you *him*?' one asked shakily.

'Him who?' asked Marvin.

Y'know, Ja-Jack Ra-Ryder?'

'Crickey, Bert! What would the greatest bushranger of all time be doing here in Bungaloori?' asked the other.

'Actually, I'm here about the horserace,' said Marvin.

'He's here about the race, Dave.'

'Shut up, Bert,' said Dave, turning to Marvin. 'Now, look here, um, Jack, if you want to ride in the race, that's fine, but I can't see why you'd risk it. It's only a little exhibition race, no prize money.'

'I don't want to ride in it,' said Marvin. 'I need someone to help me fix it. Then I can bet on it and win money that way.' He narrowed his eyes. 'You two will do.'

'But we can't fix races—' protested Dave.

Whoops, yells, breaking glass, and several very loud crashes drifted in as drunken townsfolk broke out of the pub. The lawmen exchanged anxious glances.

'Okay, okay! Just set us free, so we can get the town back under control.'

'Right,' said Marvin. He touched his riding crop to their bonds, hoping like hell that this time his spellcasting would work. The last time he used this spell, he had blown a watermelon-sized hole in the barn door. Probably best not to mention that.

'Chooonnnngaaaiii!'

There was a small red flash and the two men jumped up, yelling. The smouldering rope fell limply around their feet.

'Shit! What was that?' cried Bert.

'You *could* have just *untied* the ropes!' said Dave, rubbing his wrists.

'Ingrates,' Marvin grumbled.

The officers grabbed their truncheons.

'Wait here,' Dave ordered, and the pair headed off into the chaos.

Figuring they might change their minds and arrest him if he stayed, Marvin headed back to his shed where he stayed up all night practicing transformation spells on a variety of fruit and vegetables, and one unfortunate rat.

#

The next morning found him, still as Jack Ryder, lounging on the front porch of the lock-up—his chair casually tilted back against the wall, his boots on the rail. The two cops arrived, luckily just before Marvin dozed off. That could have been disastrous.

'Fancy Jack Ryder showing up like that last night?' Dave said, heading for the steps.

'Yeah,' agreed Bert.

'We probably should've arrested him. What with the price on his head an all.'

'We still could—' Bert murmured pointing to the porch. 'He's still *here.*'

'Crickey, what'd we do now?' Dave gaped. 'Thought it was a bad dream.'

'You were about to arrest me,' said Marvin, 'but *we've* got a deal, remember?' He wagged his riding crop at them. The two men took a step back. 'I helped you last night, now you two have to help me fix tomorrow's race, right?'

'Okay, okay! Just be careful where you point that thing!' said Bert, eyeing the riding crop.

#

'What you need,' mused Dave, perching on the corner of his desk, 'is Thunderbox to win.'

'What's a Thunderbox?' asked Marvin and the two men burst into fits of laughter.

'Not what, *who*!' cried Dave. 'Thunderbox is a horse, of course.'

'He's a bit of a local legend. A real beauty. Thoroughbred. Pure black, with a white splash. He's got promise, but he's inexperienced. Odds on him to win are around 12:1.'

'Those odds will do nicely.' Marvin did a quick mental calculation. All he had to do was ensure Thunderbox won the race and he'd turn 20 gold coins into 240 gold coins. He'd be almost halfway to his goal. He pictured himself back in Orp and the fools who ridiculed him chanting: *'All hail, King Marvin the Magnificent!''*

'Okay, who is the favourite?' he asked.

'Oooh, *My Fair Lady*!' said Bert. 'What a gal. A chestnut mare who can run like the wind.'

'Any others we need to eliminate?' Seeing their faces, he hastily added, '*Temporarily*, of course.'

Bert consulted the race sheet, 'Gelding called *I'll Have Another* has been doing well. You'd need to slow him down. *Kevin Almighty* is good. But he's overdue for a spell.'

Marvin was surprised that horses also did spells, but there was no time to dwell on that.

'Okay, we'll need a laxative and a sleeping draught,' he said.

'Never take those together!' said Bert, wide-eyed.

'I can get them.' Dave threw Bert a concerned glance.

'Right,' Marvin said. 'Get enough laxative to give the mare the trots and just enough sleeping potion to slow down the gelding. We won't worry about *Kevin*. Bert, I'll need you to distract the jockeys.'

Both men nodded.

'And d'ya have any rum?' asked Marvin.

'I have a bottle at home,' offered Dave reluctantly. 'Why?'

Marvin grinned. 'I just like it.'

Dave sighed. Marvin outlined the rest of his plan then headed back to his shed for some sleep. He locked the door and feasted on the delicious red apples until his belly ached.

#

The following day, after several attempts and a great deal of swearing, Marvin transformed into the swagman from a 'Billy Tea' poster. Not nearly as dashing as Jack Ryder, but the swaggy blended in better at the track.

There, he bet all his gold on Thunderbox for the win. Forget butterflies, an entire school of slippery eels churned in his stomach as he handed the coins over.

He carefully stowed the betting slip in his whatchamacallit. *This is it, no turning back now. Kingship or bust. This plan had better work. I'm so not going to spend my life as someone's pet.*

In search of some peace, he snuck away from the bustle of the track into the quiet coolness of the stables. He breathed in the dank aroma of horse and hay, which both comforted him and added to his misery by bringing on a sharp pang of homesickness. He slumped down in the fresh straw of a stall.

'Just 'til I feel better,' he murmured as he drifted off.

#

A commotion on the far side of the stables roused him and he got groggily to his feet.

Marvin peered over the side of his stall. A couple of jockeys were settling a chestnut mare and a grey gelding into their stalls. *Must be the competition.*

The men began to walk down the row toward his stall.

Shit! His nap would have reversed the transformation spell.

Glancing around he saw a race program on the stable wall. He focussed on a picture of Thunderbox and hissed the magic words.

'Soli transformata equisteris!'

There was a soft poof and his rump transformed into the rear-end of a black stallion. A second poof and it reverted to his familiar plump brown rump with the blue tail.

Shit! Shit!

The men were nearly upon him. He tried again.

'Soli transform-a-a-ta equestris!' he intoned with greater emphasis. This time there was a loud pop and the faint smell of coal

dust. The men turned toward the sound, but before they could investigate, a familiar voice piped up.

'Oi! G'day Victor, Terry!' Dave lumbered over and whisked them away to the clubhouse.

Marvin let out a sigh. *Phew, that was a close one. Never thought I'd ever be so happy to see Dave's ugly mug.*

He was just about to transform back into himself when a shrill voice cried out.

'Crickey! What a beauty!'

A young lady with unruly auburn curls came charging toward his stall. A wide grin covered her freckled face. Her blue eyes gleamed.

Marvin's own eyes almost burst from their sockets.

Shit, shit, shit, shit, shit! The bloody auburn-haired maiden had caught up with him, and just when things were going so well. There was no time to bolt. He just stood there gaping as she clambered up the gate.

'I can't believe I'm going to ride him in the race today, Dad!'

Wait, what? Ride me in the race? But there was nowhere to run.

The strapping shape of the real Jack Ryder sauntered over.

Oh, great. This just gets better. She's the daughter of a violent bushranger? Marvin stomped a hoof and glared at the girl, hoping she'd run away. No luck.

'Take it easy, Georgie,' Jack growled, but his eyes smiled fondly at the girl. 'If you're to pass for his jockey, you'd better pipe down and get dressed in these silks.'

'Where's his real jockey?' she asked.

'It's all taken care of, no worries.'

I guess it's sleeping drafts all round today.

'Stick to the plan and be ready at 2pm,' Jack instructed. 'Soon you'll be an initiated gang member *and* you'll have this beauty for your own.' He pointed at Marvin then kissed her on the forehead.

While they were talking, Marvin noticed the large black head of the real Thunderbox showing above a stall at the far end of the stables. Had he been there all along? Marvin took a deep breath.

Play it cool. Focus on the gold, and get rid of Thunderbox!

Luckily, he was *very* good at disappearing spells.

While Georgie's dad continued his pre-race briefing, Marvin focussed on Thunderbox.

'Disintegratum transperatum!' he hissed through clenched teeth.

'Bless you!' said the girl.

The real Thunderbox disappeared in a puff of black dust.

Marvin's stomach roiled and he shivered. How quickly things were spinning out of control. Now he was going to be *in* the race, not just betting on it. *And* he would be ridden by *the auburn-bloody-haired girl!* He had no choice but to go with it.

Jack Ryder's parting remark added insult to injury: 'Oh, and tidy him up a bit, will ya? The brushes and ribbons are in the pack.'

Brushes! And ribbons? Really? Ugh! Fate was a bitch. Marvin silently shouted all the swear words he knew.

He stopped abruptly as the enticing aroma of ripe red apple wafted across. Powerless to resist, he grudgingly ambled over and took the fruit from her. As he devoured it, she vaulted the gate.

She moved slowly, talking in soothing tones about his fine coat, his sturdy body and his graceful head. Marvin lifted his head and tossed his sleek black mane, preening. Yes, she was idolising the mask and not the real Marvin, but he couldn't help wallowing in her adoration.

She expertly slid the cold steel of the bit between his teeth and the harness over his head. He whinnied loudly, shook his head and chomped at the bit; snorted, but it did him no good. He couldn't even do a vanishing spell on the harness because the bit made it hard to speak the words.

'Easy!' She crooned in a tone that reminded Marvin of his mother—the proverbial titanium hoof wrapped in rabbit fur.

He didn't want to hurt the girl. *Focus on the gold, the win, the prestige of being crowned King.* He pictured Madame's cat's-bottom face when he returned home triumphant. The image calmed him.

Then out came the damn brushes and ribbons. He wriggled and writhed beneath Georgie's skilful ministrations. No good. The girl got his mane and tail braided with emerald satin ribbon. His coat shone and she worked a checkerboard pattern onto his rump.

'There!' she exclaimed. 'Aren't you a beauty?'

Ribbons or not, Marvin had to agree. Pity it wasn't his real body. She'd probably hate that, like everyone else did.

She quickly changed into matching green racing silks and cap, then saddled and mounted him with the ease of a seasoned horseman. Despite his humiliation, Marvin thrummed with anticipation as they headed out toward the main arena.

#

At 2 pm sharp, the starter gun cracked. They were off. With the favourite scratched at the last minute due to an upset stomach, and *I'll Have Another* stumbling out of the gates as though he'd had one too many, Marvin got off to a good start. Georgie was light as a feather. She moved with grace and ease.

Marvin forgot the ribbons and the girl. Exhilarated, nostrils flaring, he charged. With 400m to go he was neck-and-neck with the leader. They tore down the final straight. Hooves thundering.

Georgie's crop tapped his rump. He surged on. Divots flew. His heart pounded. He crossed the finish line at top speed and won by a short half-head.

The crowd roared. Georgie spurred Marvin to a victory lap. On the far side of the track, she urged him to jump the fence. Still buzzing with adrenalin, he did as he was told. The crowd let out a collective gasp.

Marvin sailed over the fence and raced on, into the desert. There'd be more than enough time to go back and collect his winnings later. He wanted this feeling of freedom and unspeakable joy to last forever.

He'd won a race *and* earned half what he needed to become king!

#

Just on sunset, finally spent, he slowed to a walk near a stand of boulders. Georgie dismounted and made a campfire. She took off the bridle and pulled a huge leather satchel from a cleft in the rocks. From the bag she produced a drink of fresh cool water and a bag of oats.

They planned this well. Shrugging, Marvin slurped and munched.

After he'd had a good feed and long drink, she tied a leather lead around his neck and looped it round the trunk of a nearby gum tree. Then she was back at him with the brushes, grooming away the sweat and dust, humming as she worked. Marvin was too spent to protest and he had to admit, it felt good to have the grit of the day wiped away. As soon as she was done, he sank down gratefully onto the soft red earth. Keen as he was to get back to town to claim his winnings it was late, and he needed sleep. He'd rest for a while, wake up before dawn, and be off on his way to gold and greatness!

#

'Crrrriiickey!'

The shout jarred Marvin awake. He squinted up at the silhouette of Georgie, standing over him, arms akimbo. The sun was already well up and a blush of hot sunlight swept pinks and oranges across the desert.

Damn. The transformation spell was broken and he was no longer a svelte black thoroughbred, but a chunky, rust and blue unicorn. Marvin lifted his chin and tried to ignore the sinking sensation in his belly.

Georgie poked him with her riding crop.

'What the hell happened to my thoroughbred?' she demanded. Then, turning to the desert, she hollered: 'Ha, ha. Very funny switching him for this weird-ass nag! The hideous dye-job and fake horn are a bit much though!' She reached out and tried to wrench Marvin's horn away.

'Don't!' bellowed Marvin. 'It's not fake. I really *am* a unicorn. Name's Marv—'

'Oooo—kaaaay!' she cried, still addressing the hills. 'That's just freaky. The joke's over now, ya hear me. Show yourselves, shitheads—' No reply came.

She balled her fists and stomped her feet and swore impressively.

Marvin's patience had worn thin. He had no time to knock about here listening to the girl whine. He had to head back to town to claim his gold.

'Listen,' he said, trying a firm, but reasonable tone, 'I'm sorry I'm not the horse you wanted, but I really must be off now.' He touched his horn to the lead, vanished it, then turned to go. But she blocked his path.

'Wait a goddamn minute. Just *where* do you think *you're* going?'

'Back to Bungaloori.'

'Forget it,' she said. 'I'm not going back to that shithole. Besides, do you know what they *do* to horse thieves?'

'Nobody asked *you* to come,' said Marvin. 'I'm going alone.'

'You're not going anywhere, Marv. As long as *I'm* without my thoroughbred, you're the only ride I have, and I'll be damned if I'm covering five miles of desert on foot. Here.' She shoved a bag of oats and a pan of water in his direction. 'Eat up, and have a drink, then we're heading off to camp.'

'Thanks,' Marvin tucked right in, continuing his protest between mouthfuls. 'But I'm...' *smack, smack* '...still not...' *slurp, smack* '...going...' *slurp, slurp* '...with you...' *smack, slurp* '...though.'

'Yes, you, are,' She scrunched up her eyes and pinched the bridge of her nose with two long thin fingers. 'Can't believe I'm *arguing* with a bloody horse!'

'Unicorn.'

'Huh?'

'You're arguing with a bloody unicorn. You know, horns, magic, silver hooves...' He waggled a hoof at her. '*And* this unicorn is heading back to Bungaloori. Now get out of my way.'

'Oh, really?' She snorted. 'Well, *Mr Unicorn*, good luck getting back there. You won't last a day alone in the outback!'

'Just watch me.' He pushed past her and headed into the desert.

'Other way.'

He reluctantly turned and stomped off the way she pointed.

#

After a day's hard walking, he had become quite lost. In the fading light of dusk, a tree root sprung to life beneath his hoof and sank two gleaming white fangs into his shin. Pain shot through his leg. He whinnied shrilly and stomped on the evil stick. The world started spinning and he slumped down in agony.

#

He woke to a squawk and the sound of large leathery wings flapping nearby. He warily opened one eye.

'Oh, piss off, Madame Phatty!' he moaned.

Phatty belched a short burst of fire that singed Marvin's forelock.

'Hey!' Marvin shook his throbbing head. He tried to stand up, but a thick grey mist clouded his vision and he slumped back down.

The phoenix squawked and snapped her powerful jaws.

'What do you want from me?' he shouted. 'Aren't I suffering enough? I've got no gold, no glory, and hardly a hope of surviving the night, all because of that *stupid* girl.'

Phatty cocked her head, merely eyeing him with glittering amusement.

He groaned. 'I can't believe you expect me to stay with *her*. She's exasperating, overbearing, and bossy. Now go away. I'm tired and I'd like to be left alone to die in peace.'

With a squawk the phoenix belched another burst of flame. Marvin winced, but the flame caught a nearby pile of twigs. Phatty flew off, leaving a bewildered Marvin with a comforting campfire.

The warmth and light of the fire, soothed Marvin's aches as well as his temper. Had Madame Fontaine just *helped* him? Could he have been wrong about her?

What if he'd been wrong about Georgie too? He remembered the way she had treated him: the apple she'd given him, her soft voice, her gentle touch, how good she'd made him feel, the exhilaration of the ride, and what an exceptional rider she was. She'd known how to read the course, when to hold back, and when to spur him on.

Bitter tears rolled down his cheeks. Damn it, they'd won that race together. They'd made a great team, but he'd been so focussed on getting his winnings that he'd left her alone in the desert.

She was right, she *had* been tricked out of her thoroughbred. *He*'d tricked her by pretending to be something he wasn't. And vanished poor Thunderbox.

Obviously, she'd been disappointed to discover her svelte black thoroughbred, was only a frumpy, overweight unicorn with an uncanny ability to suck at magic spells. But hadn't she asked him to stay anyway? And she'd given him food and water and pointed him in the right direction—even *after* she'd seen him as an ugly unicorn. Would it have been so terrible just to see her safely to her campsite? At least he wouldn't be here, dying, alone in the middle of nowhere. And nor would she.

He cried himself to sleep.

#

He woke to the intoxicating smell of apples. He opened one crusty eye. An auburn-haired girl was kneeling over him, tying a bright red ribbon around his leg. *Argh. What is it with girls and ribbons?* He struggled to get up, but she pushed him gently back down.

'Ea-sy, mate.'

'Nuh-no, ra-ribbons.'

'Nah, mate, no ribbons. Just my old red scarf to check the venom.'

'How'd you find me?' asked Marvin weakly.

'Dad's gang tracked you, of course,' said Georgie. 'Your campfire helped. I told you, you wouldn't last a day alone in the outback.'

'I'm sorry I left you out there.'

'S'all right, Mate.'

'Sorry about your horse,' he said.

'I'm buggered if I know what happened to that damn horse,' she said. 'But they accepted me into the gang, anyway. And, hey, I guess a unicorn might be useful.'

'Oh, I could be. I am particularly good at making things disappear.'

'Hmmm… funny that.'

'No, I didn't make Thunderbox …' He cleared his throat. 'Well, it's complicated.'

'Look,' said Georgie. 'We've both been through a lot. Let's get you fixed up first, then we'll figure things out.'

'Why are you being so nice to me?' he asked.

'It's what mates do!'

'We're mates?'

She patted his flank. 'Of course, we are.'

'Not a pet?'

'No, Marv. You're too big and ugly to be a pet.'

An arrogant retort sprang to Marvin's lips, but he suppressed it.

She had saved his life and she wanted to be mates. That meant she liked *him*—not the fake hero he'd tried to be, but the lumpy, bumpy, oddly-coloured unicorn that he really was. He supposed, at least for now, he could look past the ribbons and brushes. Besides, she was right: he needed her to survive this place.

He rested contentedly beside her and peered up at the stars.

'Hey, Georgie,' he said after a while.

'Hmmm?'

'You wouldn't happen to know where I could find 500 gold coins, would you?'

High above, he could just make out the fiery tail of the phoenix flying up and away into the night sky and shaking its leathery head.

#

END

How to Catch a Scoundrel

Caroline Molachino

'I hear Tom's not working as a labourer for the landscaping company anymore.' Beryl pats at her iron-grey ponytail and slides me a glance over her graduated lenses.

I swivel around to face her. 'But I did weeks of baby-sitting to call in the favour to get him that position.'

'Apparently he started up a new business?' Beryl does a bad job of pretending disinterest by focussing on the Discreet Investigations website she's updating.

I blink. 'What sort of business?'

Beryl sighs. 'Tiffany.' She rolls her chair across the concrete floor of her converted garage until she's only centimetres away from me.

'You were young when your parents died,' she says. 'Too young to be your brother's full-time guardian. He was only fourteen, but now he's an adult. You have to stop being so overprotective. You have to stop rescuing him. Let him learn from his own mistakes.'

'It's all very well for you.' People with big families just don't get it. 'I only have Tom. I have to protect him.'

Her eyes narrow. 'Your constant mothering is undermining his confidence.'

'Feel free to tell me how you really feel.' I smooth my blue shirt and grit my teeth.

'I'm sorry, love. But I'm always going to be honest with you.' Her gaze softens. 'Your mother was one of my dearest friends. I love you like family. I can't watch you drive Tom away like this. He's such a gorgeous boy, inside and out. But you know he's too kind-hearted for his own good. Always believing people's sob stories and getting caught up their dramas. He needs you more than he realises. But if you're not careful, you'll lose him.'

I spin back to my laptop then snap it shut. 'I'm heading off to my compensation case.' Better being stuck in my car for the next eight hours spying on some malingerer, than staying here to be lectured.

Beryl exhales loudly and rolls back to her desk.

I gather my things and head for the door.

But it's difficult to ignore Beryl's rigid posture and clenched jaw. And I'm struck by how appallingly I've just treated the kindest, most supportive person in my life. She gave me a job. Taught me detective work. Even lent me the money for bond on the crappy unit I'd shared with Tom. It wasn't her fault he'd moved out and didn't want to talk to me.

I pause in the doorway.

'Sorry for snapping,' I mumble. 'And thank you. For everything. I do appreciate it.'

'I know, I know.' She waves me out. 'I've got a meeting in five minutes. I'll switch the phone through to you, if that's ok?'

'Sure.' I don't tell her I'm going to call Tom. He probably won't answer, anyway, and she'd only roll her eyes at me.

Outside, the sun beats on my head as I dash for the tree shading my rust-bucket car. I dial Tom's number and the ringtone buzzes five times in my ear, then stops.

'Yo,' he says.

I nearly drop the phone. 'Ah...hi. Beryl told me you quit your job.'

He sighs. 'Not that it's any of your business, but yes, I did. I was sick of living on the poverty line.'

I click my tongue as I unlock my car. 'I gave you free board. You shouldn't have moved out.'

'And I was sick of your nagging, too.'

I rub my forehead. 'So what's this about a new business?' I pull open the creaking door and climb in.

'I'm making better money now,' he says. 'Paying off my debt.'

'What debt?'

He pauses. 'Nothing for you to worry about.'

'What debt?' Why is this the first I'm hearing about this? I fidget in the seat, the torn vinyl burning me through my skirt.

'It's not a big deal.'

'Tell me!'

'Urggh. Why do you always have to know everything about me?'

I wait, pulling at a loose thread on the steering wheel.

A puff of frustration echoes through the phone. 'I invested in a cryptocurrency scheme and it turned out to be a scam. I owe someone a bit of money.'

My hand stills. 'How much?'

He says something indecipherable.

'I didn't hear that. How much?'

'Twenty thousand.'

My hand slips off the wheel and hits the dash. I cover my mouth to stifle a swear word. 'When do you have to pay it back?'

'Yesterday.'

'You're not serious.' He's always playing tricks on me. This is a joke.

'Just forget about it. I shouldn't have told you. I've gotta go.'

'Wait, I—' But there's only silence on the other end of the line. I phone him back but he doesn't answer.

How could he be so stupid? And who has he got himself caught up with? Criminals? The Mafia? I know nothing about these things. Beryl and I only deal with spouse-busting and insurance fraud. What if he's in danger? Thoughts crowd my mind as I sweat in the car.

I need to get hold of twenty thousand dollars. Fast. I've already saved about fifteen for my law studies. I straighten, staring down the tree-lined suburban street. If I could somehow get another five...

My phone rings and I answer it without checking the number. 'Tom?'

'What's that dear?' The voice is high-pitched and breathy. 'I'm looking for Discreet Investigations. Do I have the correct number?'

Oh, of course. Beryl diverted calls to me.

'Sorry.' I switch to professional mode. 'Yes. You've got the right number.'

'Wonderful. My name is Mabel Winterbottom,' she warbles. 'And I would like to hire a private detective.'

'Certainly. What services do you require?' I picture a frail old woman, possibly in her eighties.

Mabel sighs into the phone. 'I believe my boyfriend is being unfaithful to me. I need to know one way or the other. I don't have much time left in this world.'

The poor thing! I chew on my thumb nail, a guilty idea forming. I'll work freelance, take some cases on the side. Beryl needn't know. This might be the perfect case. I could squeeze her in between jobs and Beryl will be none the wiser.

I nod, and shift in my seat. Then I inject a confident tone in my reply. 'You've come to the right place Ms Winterbottom.'

'What a relief to hear you say that, my dear. When can you start?'

'Tomorrow.'

No need to feel guilty. I'm doing this for Tom. I have to protect him.

#

The next day, I arrive at the address given to me by Mabel Winterbottom. After staring through an iron gate at a palatial mansion, I double-check the address in my notebook. When I press the intercom button, a man's voice barks back at me.

'Yes?'

'It's Tiffany Goode, from...' But I'm not working for Discreet Investigations: this is freelance. 'Tiffany Goode the Private Investigator.'

'Identification.'

I flash my ID at the security camera. The gate slides across, and I roll up the driveway toward the gothic-style mansion. I cut the engine near a lion statue the size of my car, and climb out.

At the front door I press another buzzer. The door creaks open and I hesitate at the sight of a giant in a business suit. He has one glass eye, and the black circle in his earlobe frames a view to a bifurcating staircase behind him.

A prickle of apprehension runs down my spine, but I force out a smile. 'Hello.'

He says nothing. Instead, he leads me across marble floors into a room adorned with multi-tiered chandeliers. Classical music drifts out of concealed speakers, and a grand piano sits in one corner. The coffee table looks like it's made out of solid gold.

Eventually my eyes settle upon Mabel Winterbottom, and I only just manage to contain a gasp of surprise. She sits primly in a high-backed, red-velvet chair. Her white hair is so round and bouffant that it's almost double the size of her head. Dressed entirely in black, she looks like someone who never quite let go of her youthful goth stage. Even her make-up is severe and theatrical. Plastered into the crevices of her wrinkled skin.

From the phone call I'd imagined a sweet little old lady wearing spectacles and a floral dress.

'Thank you, Gerard. That will be all,' she says delicately. He leaves on silent feet.

'It's lovely to meet you Ms Winterbottom,' I say.

'Please, call me Mabel. Thank you for coming, dear.' She gestures for me to sit in the chair opposite her, as a puff of her expensive perfume engulfs me. *Poison* if I'm not mistaken.

I do as I'm told, retrieving my notepad and pen from my bag. 'We should get straight to business. Could you tell me about your...uh, boyfriend.'

'You probably think I'm a silly old woman.' She clutches a veiny hand to her chest. 'He is a lot younger than me.'

'How old is he?'

'Mid-twenties?'

I retain a neutral expression. 'What's his name?'

'Devon D'Amore.'

Probably an alias. 'Have you been together long?'

'A few months.'

I tap my pen on my notebook. 'What makes you think he's cheating? Has his behaviour changed somehow?'

Mabel's lips press together, accentuating the wrinkles beneath her nose. 'Gerard saw him with another woman at the coffee shop near the local art gallery we frequent.'

'Did you ask him about it? Sometimes there's a logical explanation.'

'Yes dear. He denied it point-blank. He said Gerard must have been mixed up.'

'I'm sorry if this question is upsetting, but is it possible he sees this relationship as more of a friendship?'

'Good Lord no, dear. We're engaged to be married.'

I almost lose my poker face.

Mabel leans forward. 'You see, this is why I need to know if he's being unfaithful to me.' She pulls a tissue from a box and dabs at an eye, where her lashes are crusted with black mascara.

'I'm so sorry to have to ask you this...but...' I chew my thumb nail.

'What dear?'

I almost lose my nerve, but why else would a twenty-year-old man date a wealthy old woman? 'Have you ever, um given him, gifts or...money?'

'Oh, a little bit here and there.' She waves a bony hand dismissively. 'I can hardly take my money with me when I die now can I?'

What a scumbag, taking advantage of an old lady! 'Do you have a photo of him?'

'I'm not really one to go around taking photographs.' She wrinkles her nose. 'What are they called? Selfies? No, our relationship transcends physical appearance. We like to discuss philosophy, and the arts. That's what I love about Devon. He's an old soul in a young body.'

Or so he pretends to be. 'Could you describe his physical

appearance?'

'Oh!' She claps her hands. 'He is so delightfully arty and disorganised.' Her face glows. 'But you would be needing specifics. He has the most mesmerizingly green eyes and glorious, sand-coloured hair. In need of a haircut I'm afraid. He's about average height? And terribly handsome.'

'Can you give me his home address?'

Mabel shakes her head. 'Unfortunately, I've never been to his abode.'

I try a different tack. 'What does he do for a living?'

'He's an entrepreneur, my dear. Nothing specific.'

I pencil the detail into my book. 'Would it be possible to organise to meet him here and I'll follow him afterwards?'

'No, my dear. You see, we had an argument when I accused him of cheating. We're not speaking at the moment.' She swipes at an invisible mark on her leather pants.

'Could I have his phone number?'

'Of course, but there's no point in ringing. It's disconnected.' Her sculpted eyebrows pop up. 'Oh! You could try the opening of the Altro Mondo exhibition at the Stephanie Sartoni Art Gallery. He's bound to be there. I'm too distraught to go out.' She dabs at her eyes again. 'But please, don't let anyone know you're a private investigator. This is highly embarrassing for me, as you can imagine.'

'Of course. This is all strictly confidential.'

Mabel confirms the details of the opening and I jot them into my notepad, hiding a sigh. This is the least amount of information I've ever had to go on for a case.

Then I think of Tom—the only family I have left in the world. Tom, who owes someone twenty thousand dollars and might be in danger.

Somehow, I'll make it work.

But the matter of money for this case is still to be discussed. I clear my throat. 'Given the complex nature of this case and the importance of discretion...I'll need to charge more than the standard amount.'

Mabel nods. 'Of course. Name your price, dear.'

She can always say no. I swallow. 'Five thousand for proof either way.'

Her eyes narrow and she stiffens. But then she holds out a bony hand. 'It's a deal.'

After wiping my sweaty hand on my skirt, I shake on it.

#

Two nights later, I'm reversing into a carpark across the road from the Stephanie Sartoni Art Gallery. I cut the engine, straighten my scratchy blonde wig and reapply my red lipstick. After doing an internet search for Devon D'Amore and coming up with nothing, I've been left with no choice but to go under-cover to catch him.

I take a deep breath. It's been a long two days, keeping secrets from Beryl while getting nowhere on my cases with her. Five thousand would mean a lot to her business.

But I'm doing this for Tom.

I climb out of my car and cross the road. Hiding behind a small group as they enter, I avoid the beak-nosed woman checking invitations, and make it through the door. I swipe a pamphlet from a stand and start mingling. With bare floorboards and zero furniture, the gallery is a hollow space and conversations echo around the room.

It's more crowded than I expected. I search for a handsome,

twenty-something man with sandy hair but see no one of that description. I approach two white-haired women who are holding pamphlets and discussing the artwork like regulars.

'Have either of you seen my ex-boyfriend Devon?' I fake a whiny, rich-kid accent. 'I need to get my apartment key off him. I've tried to phone him but he won't answer.' I pout. 'I don't know how else to get my key back.' My bottom lip wobbles. I could have been an actress.

'You poor thing. I saw him about ten minutes ago near the Bella Canaglia.'

The other woman nods.

I pretend to know what they're talking about. 'Thank you.' I wipe my dry eyes and move in the direction they've pointed. What if they tell Devon an ex-girlfriend is looking for him? My heart thumps but I keep searching.

Finally, I spot the back of a floppy-haired man in dark trousers and a lilac shirt. Is it him? The woman he's with looks about sixty, with dyed brown hair and wearing a cream suit with pearls. Her arm is hooked around his elbow.

What's with this guy? Has he got a fetish for older women?

I meander closer, pretending to photograph a sculpture but actually snapping the couple. Someone steps into my line of vision. I turn a page of my pamphlet and make a show of studying it. I'm close enough to eavesdrop now.

'Oh, Devon, you do make me laugh,' says the pearl-wearing woman.

Confirmation! Now, if I can just position myself a little closer; get a look at the guy's face...take a better shot of him somehow.

But no luck. Devon and the woman move on and start chatting with the white-haired women I spoke to earlier. They glance at me suspiciously.

Damn. It's time to go.

I squeeze through the crowd and race out the door, barely checking the road before hurrying to my car. Back in the driver's seat, I open the image and zoom in. I've only got the back of the guy's head, but it's a clear shot of the pearl-wearing girlfriend. I groan.

It's not enough.

I rip off the wig and clean my face with some wipes. Then I throw an old jumper over my dress, and lace on some sneakers. Dragging one of Beryl's cameras out of a bag, I slouch back in the seat and wait.

#

An hour later, people start spilling out of the gallery. I bolt upright in my seat, and shoot a few useless pics in the semi-dark, before spotting the lady in the cream suit. D'Amore is obscured by other people. Then the two of them stroll off in the opposite direction to the rest of the crowd. Away from me.

I throw the camera onto the passenger seat—it's too obvious to carry—and jump out of my car. Then I follow at a safe distance, but pause when the couple reach a taxi rank. I snap a blurry photo on my phone, just as the subject kisses the woman on the mouth.

Bingo.

The jerk! He must be a third of her age! Is he conning these women out of their money?

What a douchebag.

He leans in for another kiss. I press the camera button on my phone. This is surely all the evidence I need. The five thousand dollars is mine!

I zoom the image in closer to make sure it's clear. Then I reel backwards with a gasp.

It's Tom.

My brother is Devon D'Amore.

Devon D'Amore is Tom.

My stomach clenches and I swallow the urge to scream at him, to tell him what an idiot he is. It won't help. Not right now. I need to think...need to work out what to do next.

I make it to my car and clamber in. As I flop back into the seat, I stare into space, my thoughts swirling.

My brother is a scoundrel and a con artist.

My brother owes someone twenty thousand dollars.

I squeeze my eyes shut and rub my face, straining my brain. For five minutes I sit. How did I fail so badly in raising him that he thought defrauding old ladies was a smart thing to do? How can I fix this? Then slowly I open my eyes.

I'll pay off his debt, then convince him to change his ways. Start afresh. Get him back into the landscaping job. He can move back home.

I take a deep breath and send him a text.

We need to talk.

Hours later—when I'm tossing and turning in bed—he replies, agreeing to meet me the following day.

#

After a sleepless night, I sit opposite Mabel, my hands planted on my lap as I try to control my jiggling legs.

Stick with the plan.

Get the cash and get out.

She'll never know my brother is Devon. She'll forget about him and move on with what little life she has left. Hopefully.

The old lady adjusts the ruby choker at her neck, her scarlet dress the same colour as the chair she sits in. 'I'm surprised to see you so soon, dear.'

'I took a couple of risks. They paid off.' I slide my ridiculous report across the table, full of blurry, sub-standard photos of Tom— or Devon D'Amore, the two-timing scoundrel and con-artist.

Mabel's eyes narrow, and she studies me like I'm a cockroach she's about to squash under her shoe. 'It's him.'

'I'm sorry about this.' I gulp. 'But at least you're able to protect yourself from this...man.'

The corners of Mabel's mouth twist into an unconvincing smile. 'There will be the matter of payment, then. Gerard will fetch the cash.'

'Oh, a bank transfer would be—'

'*Gerard! Cash! Now!*'

A piece of spittle hits me in the cheek and I recoil, clutching the chair's armrests.

'*I said now!*' Mabel's face is the same colour as her dress, and a vein pulses at her neck.

Gerard walks in with a yellow envelope, his glass eye fixed on me. He hands me the package and, for the first time I notice the gun holster bulging under his jacket.

With trembling hands, I take the envelope and stuff it into my bag without counting the notes. 'Right.' I smile weakly. 'Thank you.' I stand up. 'It was a pleasure...'

The old woman stares into the distance, her eyes bloodshot and lips a thin, blood-coloured line.

'Good-bye, Mabel.'

She doesn't respond.

I follow the gun-wielding giant out. 'Good-bye, Gerard.'

He says nothing.

Outside, I jump in my car and accelerate down the driveway, gulping as I glance in the rear view mirror.

Have I just made a deal with the devil?

#

Arriving back home, I race up the stairs, not bothering to close the door behind me. Inside, I pace. A train screeches into the station across the road and I throw my hands over my ears: the noise is like fingernails down a blackboard. I continue to pace in the stuffy apartment, wringing my hands and muttering like a crazy woman.

An agonising thirty minutes later, Tom walks through the door.

'I saw you last night,' I spit out. 'With that old woman.'

He frowns. 'So, you're stalking me now?'

'I can't believe you'd do this. After all the sacrifices I made to raise you properly.'

He throws his arms wide. 'I knew you'd react like this. That's why I didn't tell you!'

I grind my teeth. 'You're scamming women out of their money. How do you expect me to react?'

'What are you talking about?' He squints at me.

'You're tricking rich women into dating you. Pretending to care about them. Conning them out of their cash.'

He starts, eyes wide. 'I'm not conning anyone!'

'Then what are you doing, hanging out with older women?'

He swallows. Then straightens, and takes a deep breath. 'I'm a paid companion.'

My jaw drops. 'You're...an escort?'

'You don't need to make it sound seedy. It's purely platonic. I like these women, and they like me. They're lonely, and spending time with me makes them happy.'

I digest this information as I stand there, slack-jawed.

Tom is an escort, not a con artist.

And somehow, it makes sense.

He always had such a kind heart, always wanted to cheer me up when I was down. Has the rare knack of being able to make people laugh when they're feeling sad.

'I make good money,' he says. 'And it's only temporary. I was saving for a house deposit. I wanted you to be proud of me.'

'But...' Mabel said she and Devon were engaged. I shake my head, my brain still foggy.

'Anyway, why were you following me?'

'I was working freelance, earning money to pay off your debt. I wanted to help. I was on a job for Mabel Winterbottom.'

'Why would you work for her? She's a sociopath!'

I glare. 'You're the one dating her!'

He groans and rubs his face. 'She seemed normal at first. But then she got delusional, acting like we were a couple, forgetting she'd hired me. One night she spiked my drink and tricked me into signing the cryptocurrency documents. When I told her it was over, she tried to blackmail me. Said she'd drop the debt if I stayed with her...that she'd kill me if I cheated on her.' He swallows. 'She's the one scamming me, Tiff.'

The blood drains from my head.

'Tell me you didn't do anything stupid,' he says. 'Tell me you didn't give her any evidence of me with other women.'

'I might have...'

'You might have what?'

'I negotiated a contract of five thousand dollars,' I croak. 'For proof you were cheating. Only I didn't know it was you at the time.' My voice is barely a whisper.

'But you didn't give it to her. The evidence. When you saw it was me...you didn't give it to her.'

I gulp in some air and rub my burning chest.

Tom's eyes widen. 'You did! Why would you do such a stupid thing? I'd already earned half the money. I was going to pay her back. She's probably going to put a hit on me!'

'She wouldn't!'

'She's a retired criminal. Didn't you check her background? I can't believe Beryl would put you in this situation!'

'She didn't. This was all me.' I take a half-step toward him. 'But don't worry. I can fix this.'

'You can't fix this. You'll just make things worse. He scrubs a hand through his hair, his eyes glassy. 'How many times have I told you not to interfere in my life?' His face crumples. 'I've gotta get out of here.'

'No! Don't go.'

He stares at the floor, shoulders slumped. 'I can't do this anymore.'

I almost stop breathing, as a cold shiver runs through me. 'What do you mean?'

'This.' He points to me. 'Us.'

'No!' Panic coils through me. 'I can't lose you. You're my only family. Please. I'm sorry.'

He turns toward the door.

I hurry after him, tears streaming down my face. 'Wait!'

But he's half-way out the door.

'I was wrong!' I say.

He slows.

'I know that now.' I stare at the back of his head. 'You might not need me but the truth is, I need you.' The full realisation dawns upon me. Beryl was right. About everything. 'I've made so many mistakes. But I can change. No more interfering. No more rescuing. Please stay.'

He turns around, still looking at the floor.

The silence drags on while I wait.

'On one condition.' He finally meets my eyes. 'Together, we bring Mabel Winterbottom down. I give her the 20K, get the cryptocurrency docs back. But I'll be hooked up to Beryl's spy equipment, and get the old lady on tape confessing to drugging and blackmailing me. Then, we take the evidence to the cops.'

I nod slowly. It's a good plan. Suddenly, I can breathe again. This time it's my brother and me—together—against the world. I smile. 'Condition accepted. And I'll find a way to pay the 5K to Beryl.'

He nods and steps back through the door.

Back home.

'As long as I'm in charge,' he adds quickly.

'Of course!' But I cross my fingers behind my back.

Just in case.

#

END

To Ashes

Monica Schultz

I always pick my next victim before Saifi dances, but today I'm running late. Papa will be livid—again.

It's not my fault. The crowds of Milan have not been the same since last summer. The men are stiff and restless, keeping their distance from our musicians, even if their hands are busy drumming; and the shadows are always watching.

I pause at the edge of the crowd, checking for Duke Gian's guards and their trained dragons. We can't afford to have them show up again this week. One more ruined performance and the people of Milan will write off the Romani as too dangerous to watch.

I shiver and drag my eyes from the hidden spaces under dark archways. No time to worry about that. Papa is here, drumming for Saifi, and he always notices when my head is in the clouds. I weave my way through the growing throng, searching for the perfect mark.

There. A large man. Focussed on Saifi. He pushes off the pillar of the cathedral and inches closer to Saifi's dance space. I follow. He's dressed in a bright blue doublet, pockets bulging, silken undergarments burst at the seams. His two chins sink into the fat of his neck; a sure sign that his purse can afford enough meat for a week. My stomach rumbles at the thought, empty even after eating Mama's leftover breakfast scraps.

The man hugs the outskirts of the crowd, his broad shoulders tense and gaze wary as he peers at the musicians. I become his shadow, mimicking his confident stride just as Papa taught me to do years ago. Buried within the crowd, my familia do the same, each waiting for the perfect moment to strike.

The moment Saifi captures their victim's heart.

With nothing better to do but wait, I watch her. Mid-morning sunshine glints off Saifi's golden bangles with every flick of her wrists, mesmerising even the most cautious men. Unlike my plain patchwork skirt, Saifi wears red silk. The fabric hugs her curves, revealing a body none would suspect of birthing a child only six months prior. The perfect daughter-in-law.

As the tempo swells, I copy her movements, practising. The tips of my braids brush my waist as I tilt my head back. Our hips copy every drum-beat. The panpipe sends me twirling, feet light on the cobblestone street. Saifi's angelic voice sings a simple folk tune over the hoots and hollers of the crowd. My lips silently echo her words, but I am painfully aware I was not born to sing.

The song rises to a crescendo. Each musician lends their voice to a chorusing cry of *oprey* that calls the children to join the dance. I stumble to a halt. The simple word snatches me from my daydream. My eyes flicker to Papa. His brows draw together, dangerous as thunderclouds, casting his face in stormy shadow. Through the tangle of his coarse, black beard, his lips mouth four dreaded words.

Get to work, Charani.

With a heavy heart, I lift my skirt, dancing once more, acting the part of an innocent child. I slip through the crowd, focused on a single point.

A blue doublet.

I pitch forwards and stagger into his arms. Fingers faster than light, I pluck his leather purse, tucking it into the fold of my waistband. The man shoves me away, spewing a string of curses. I stand still, blinking my long lashes in my best impression of a clumsy girl.

'Coglione!'

Moron is better than being called a thief. Dusting his clothes free of me, the man spits at my feet. His eyes dart back to Saifi.

I jump back, a smile plastered onto my face for Papa's sake. Papa's fingers fly across the drum skin, urging Saifi to dance wilder than a burning flame. Slowly I work my way back through the crowd, fighting to keep a frown hidden.

Noblemen do not spit.

Before I reach Papa, a new cry stirs the crowd.

'Gavver!'

I freeze, searching the shadows for soldiers. The music falters. Saifi collects coins from the cobbles, ending the performance. Romani jump to their feet in panic. Tales of the Duke's rising power are enough to send us scrambling without a fight, regardless of the lost coin. Onlookers hurl insults at our departing backs.

But we are not quick enough.

The Duke's new favourite pets are upon us. Three black dragons, the size of bullocks, barrel through the crowd, steel clad soldiers close at their heels. The dragons' handlers follow and shout instructions to their animals. The dragons hunt with their noses to the ground. Have they caught my scent?

'Heavens bless me...' I whisper.

My feet grow roots, legs useless trunks. A lone dragon turns toward me. Smoke pours from between its snapping teeth. Empty black eyes lock onto mine. Transfixed, I watch as the nightmarish creature rears onto its hind legs, standing taller than two men. Inky black wings obscure the sky and the dragon's maw cracks open.

Hot air envelops me, laced with the stench of rotting meat. Blood pounds in my ears. Bursts of orange flame leap to life in the pit of the dragon's throat.

'Papa!' I scream, stumbling backwards.

Papa's large fingers clamp around my wrist and wrench my arm almost out of its socket. The flames miss me by inches. He yells in my ear, spit flying. But I need no further encouragement.

We run.

#

The canal is quiet when we finally arrive home. I trudge a few steps behind Papa and Saifi. Reflected on the water's shimmering surface, our little corner of Milan is usually a kingdom grand enough to house hundreds of Romani. Today they are just tents of every shape and size crammed together in the back of an alley. Empty fire-pits line the street, smouldering in the midday heat, abandoned under the threat of dragons.

Before our tent flap can fall shut, Papa turns on me.

'What were you thinking?' He throws his hands up as he stomps across the rugs.

Saifi and I stop, eyes wide. Papa plants himself at the squat table beside Mama.

'I've never seen a clumsier pickpocket!' he says, causing Mama to wince. Her arms tighten around Babik, shielding my infant nephew from Papa's rage. Saifi's shoulders loosen. She is not the target of Papa's anger. With a sympathetic glance at me, Saifi hurries to the back of the tent to change, leaving me with only Mama for protection.

Papa glowers at me. 'You're lucky it was Saifi dancing today, or else that man would have caught you quicker than a wounded dog.'

I lower my eyes and stay silent.

'And are you trying to get yourself killed? Standing there waiting for a dragon to use you as a toothpick.'

'Sorry, Papa,' I murmur, barely audible over Babik's gurgling. He tugs at Mama's clay necklace, shoving fistfuls into his little mouth.

'Sorry doesn't put food on the table.'

'Vano.' Mama's voice is both gentle and stern at the same time. Her grey eyes hold Papa's even as she pulls the beads from Babik's mouth. 'Charani is just a child.'

'Pfft. She is more of a woman every day. The noblemen see it. They do not trust her anymore.'

I baulk, shaking my head. 'I still have time.' But his words hold an undeniable truth. High cheekbones now define my once-round face and it won't be long before my skirt no longer fits the shape of my hips.

'Tell her,' Mama whispers.

'Tell me what?'

Papa shifts wearily on his stool. 'I've made a deal, Charani. We couldn't offer much of a dowry, but Šaban has agreed to take you as his bride.'

'Šaban? But he is so old. Surely, Mama, no!'

'It is a good match.' Mama's reply is steady though she will not meet my glare. 'He has a plan to travel north. Join his vitsa as a farm-hand. You'll never hunger again.'

'I'll never see Milan again, either.'

'But you'll be safe,' Mama says, with a sad smile, 'The dukes of the north do not use dragons.'

I turn to Papa. Eager to prove my worth, I slide the leather pouch from my waistband and drop it into Papa's expert palm. He grunts, brow furrowing.

'I can still make us money here, in Milan,' I insist.

Papa opens the pouch and spills its contents across the tabletop. Dull bronze lira.

'Is this all? What about the debt collectors? Milk for Babik? New clothes for Saifi and your Mama?'

I gulp against the lump in my throat, blinking back tears. 'But he wore silk!'

'Doesn't matter what he wore if I still have an empty stomach does it?'

I kneel before him and rest my head in his lap. 'Maybe I am too old to steal at the dances, but I can find other work.' My words are smothered in his faded cotton pants. Daring to lift my gaze to his stony face, I say, 'I could even dance like Saifi.'

'Saifi is one of a kind. Besides, you do not have the face to win the hearts of Milanese men.'

I flinch but remain at his feet. 'Please,' I whisper, 'Just give me a chance.'

Papa jerks away and turns his face from me. 'No.'

I rock back onto my heels, the word a fist in my stomach. My throat constricts.

'I won't do it.' I rise, hands clenched. 'I won't marry him.'

'You will marry Šaban or you are no daughter of mine.'

I suck in a lungful of air and hold my breath, blinking rapidly to keep my eyes dry. Mama rests a hand on Papa's shoulder, though I don't know who she is trying to steady.

'You would never do this to Saifi,' I say, choking on my tears.

'Saifi needs no help to earn coin for this family. Some are born with talent.'

With each word from Papa, I take a wobbly step backwards.

'We just want what is best for you,' Mama says, but the frown between her threaded brows reveals her lie. She knows Papa thinks with his stomach first.

Behind me, wind through the tent flap curls around my ankles, inviting me to flee into the open arms of Milan.

For the second time today, I run.

#

The cobblestones are rough and uneven beneath my tired feet, yet they don't trip me. Still, I keep my eyes down as I brush past shop boys and merchants, hunching my shoulders against their curious stares. I have already broken Papa's golden rule once today; a thief must always remain invisible. Usually it's easy as a girl, but everyone notices one that's alone and crying.

Ducking inside an alleyway between shops, I finally straighten. Now that my breathing has steadied to the occasional hiccup, the aches of my body present themselves. I lean back against the stone wall and press the heels of my hands into my eyes until all I see is black. Papa's cruel words replay in my mind.

I'm not good enough. My heart falters. I'll never be good enough.

But I must be. Somehow. I don't want to marry and leave Milan. I bite my lip until the sharp pain chases away tears.

'But the Duke... he'll kill us,' says a nearby voice.

My ears prick at the name of a familiar enemy. With a deep, trembling breath, I wipe my eyes dry. Now that I am listening, the tradesmen's bickering is easy to hear over my own pitiful sniffles. Their voices echo against the alley's close walls though there is no-one in sight.

'Gian will never know the difference,' a second voice replies. 'All it would take is one dragon egg and we'll be living like kings!'

A smile creeps across my face at the voice's promise. Visions of mountains of decadent food swim before my eyes, causing my mouth to swim with spit. Curiosity takes control.

I inch forwards, following the hushed argument. Poking my head around the corner, I see them. Two men, dressed in the Duke's dark uniform, perch on the edge of a wooden cart and pass a hunk of bread between them. Their backs are to me and to their load of straw.

'He'll notice,' the older man says. 'He's paying for them.'

'A single egg means nothing to a man like him,' his companion whines, his voice like a child's. 'He spends twice as much on breakfast alone. But to us? It's enough to set us both up for life. No more pulling carts.'

My breath hitches. Papa could have anything his heart desired; even Saifi could not offer such a gift. I stare at the straw, each strand fresh and golden. My gaze locked onto the straw; I carefully step between piles of rubbish to silence my approach.

'Who'd be crazy enough to buy a stolen dragon egg?'

'Black market. Look, I know a guy. It's a done deal. I just need to know you're in.'

When I am less than a breath away from the cart, glints of onyx wink at me from beneath the straw. Just one egg could easily fill my skirt. How many are there?

'Too risky,' the older man says. 'You're a dead man if you're caught with a dragon egg.'

My fingers twitch. Do I dare snatch one? I glance around. There are no soldiers. The Duke will never know, and Papa will see I am not a worthless daughter.

I reach into the straw, silent as a mouse. I seize the closest egg and finch at its unexpected warmth despite its smooth, stone-like appearance. It slips neatly into the fold of my skirt. A thrill dances down my spine and I stroll away from the cart, my skirt bulging.

With each step toward home I can feel the egg's fluttering pulse against my stomach, reminding me I am more than enough.

#

Romani crowd the canal once more by the time I arrive home. They sit in clusters before their family fires, cooking supper. The scent of roast meats wafts toward me and my stomach growls. I have not eaten since this morning.

With each step closer to home, my giddy smile fades. Doubts press in. What if this is another mistake? I suppress the voice. Placing my hand on the egg, I draw comfort from its warmth before pulling back the tent flap.

A gust of fresh air follows me inside the tent, stirring loose tendrils of Mama's hair. She and Papa speak with their heads bent together. Papa glances up. His expression melts from surprise to anger in seconds, his lips pressed into a line so thin they disappear inside his beard.

'Where have you been?' Papa's gaze flicks to the bulge in my skirt.

I hesitate. Now that my eyes have adjusted to the dim interior of the tent, I spy the coins spread between Papa and Mama, counted into neat piles.

'We don't have to worry about money anymore.' I withdraw the egg from my skirt, cradling it against my chest.

I explain all that I heard this afternoon. Papa's mouth drops open and Mama's eyes bulge.

'The men were clueless, Papa.' I try to reassure them. 'They never heard me coming, and they were certain Gian wouldn't know the difference.'

Papa curses, slamming his fist into the table, 'He always knows, damn it! How can you be so daft?'

'Papa, it's ok.' I hold the egg out so he can see the hope hidden in its dark sheen. 'All we have to do is sell it and everything will be fine.'

'It is NOT ok!' Papa smacks the egg out of my hands.

I yelp and fall to my knees to bundle the egg back up. Trailing my fingers along the shell, I stare daggers at Papa. Who knows what a damaged egg is worth?

Papa curses softly, pinching the bridge of his nose. 'As sure as day, they'll be here soon. Hide anything stolen,' he orders Mama. 'Charani stay put, you've done enough.'

I do as I'm told, and inspect the egg. A hairline crack becomes visible in the light. A bubble of anger forms in my stomach. If only he'd trust my judgement just this once. Yet still Papa paces before the tent flap, glowering at me and my egg.

Silence stretches between Papa and I, becoming a chain that binds us. Outside, screams pierce our tent's thin walls and the chain snaps. Papa curses again. I clutch the egg close. My heart echoes its fluttering pulse.

Soldiers burst through the tent flap, their armour clanking. Instinctively, I tuck my egg back into my skirt where it is safe.

'What business do you have here?' Papa demands, despite the slight tremble of his hands.

The lead soldier rakes Papa with a sneering gaze. 'One of Duke Gian Galeazzo Sfroza's dragon eggs has gone missing during transport. Our dragons smelled something on the straw that lead us here.' Behind the soldier, adult dragons loom, slobbering as they sniff the air. 'What business did you have with our carters?'

The dragons pull at their chains, eager to devour us should the soldiers prove us guilty. I glance at Papa, but I can't catch his eye. He is already sweating, beads pooling on his brow. He swallows.

'Forgive us, sir. Twas our daughter,' Mama stammers, squeezing Papa's hand.

'She thought to sell it,' Papa says. 'We beg your pardon, my lord.'

'Mama? No!' I cry. 'That's not true. Say it's not true.'

'We had no part in it,' Papa continues.

'Your dragons frighten my parents, good sir,' I say, but the damage is done.

The soldier inclines his head toward Papa and strides across the room to me. I stumble backwards, out of his reach. Heart thundering, I dart for the back entrance. Straight into Papa's waiting arms.

'Let me go! Mama, please?' I squirm but Papa remains firm.

'You went too far this time, Charani,' Mama says, tears welling in her eyes, 'Our family is not safe with you in it.'

She reaches into my skirt and rips out my egg, handing it to the soldier.

'Thank you for your honesty, gypsy.' The soldier deposits the egg into a pouch secured to his belt. 'We'll take care of the little thief, now.'

Papa transfers me to the soldier's gloved hands as easily as he would trade stolen coin for a fresh cut of meat. My stomach sinks and I search Papa's face for any sign of remorse. He turns away, comforting Mama.

The soldier drags me from the tent.

Outside, Romani men gather, makeshift weapons in hand. They form a last line of defence against the dragons should they attack the tents. As we pass, they shuffle back, knuckles white around torches and hunting knives. My heart bursts in two at the sight of their defiance; a stark difference to my own parents. I look at my home, waiting for Papa to emerge; to realise his mistake. My legs buckle and I stall to give Papa more time.

Yet he never comes.

Limp in the soldiers' arms, I let them drag me. The skin on my knees scrapes against the cobblestones and tears blind my vision.

#

By the time we reach the piazza, the sight of dragons has drawn a crowd. Sobs wrack through my chest, but my wails are not enough to drown out the delight of curious citizens.

'Vermin!'

'Thief!'

'Cut off her hands and she'll never steal again!'

'Cut of her head and she'll never breathe again!'

Their laughter cuts through my sorrow, forcing me to take in my surroundings. Duke Gian's castle looms in the distance, lending an ominous air to the simple chopping block erected in the piazza's centre. On either side of me, soldiers march, weapons sheathed at their hips.

'Filthy gypsy!' a new voice shouts. A rotten tomato splatters against my cheek.

I flinch, jerking in the soldiers' grip. Blinking the tomato juice from my eyes, I catch sight of my assailant. A peasant, like most of the crowd.

Except one. The corner of a familiar blue doublet catches my eye.

Another man pegs a chicken egg. The egg shatters against my chest, knocking any lingering misery free. The stench of sulphur leaves me gagging. Without my blanket of heartache, the bubble of anger transforms into a cloud of rage.

I remember every time I sacrificed my own needs for my family. Every time I accepted less food. Every time I worked longer hours. Repaid with barely a grunt of acknowledgement from Papa, and empty promises from Mama.

No more. From now on, I'll steal for me.

But first, to get free of these soldiers.

The dragons take their place on either side of the chopping block. My mind churns. There are dozens of escape routes, but only one if I take the dragon egg.

And I want that egg.

I jam my feet into the cobblestone street and wrench my arms free. I yank at the egg pouch. The leather straps break. The soldier grabs for me but I dart out of reach. Before he can bark any orders, I slip into the crowd.

People jump out of my way, but it's not me they retreat from. The dragons chase, flames scorching the cobbles in my wake. Fear fuels my aching limbs. The scrape of dragon claws on stone erases thought. Smoke billows around me until I falter, coughing.

Desperate to shake them, I leap over fruit carts, sending their contents flying. Yet the dragons charge through. Ahead, the street draws to a dead end. The canal forms a barrier between the heart of Milan and the outer slums. Squeezing my egg tight, I jump in to the murky water feet first.

I surface, spluttering. My long skirt drags me down. I fling my arms through the water to stay afloat, but it is of little use. I never learnt to swim. The dragons pace at the water's edge. Teeth snap and they stretch their necks out over the water. Claws rake across the water's surface. Their stubby wings flap uselessly.

I glance behind them. It won't be long before the soldiers reach us, and they can swim. Holding my breath, I succumb to the current.

The waters force me under. I flail, kicking furiously. My lungs burn. Murky water stings my eyes as I search for the surface. Darkness creeps into the edges of my vision. I must breathe.

There. A pinprick of light flickers at the end of a tunnel that pierces the canal wall. I squeeze through a narrow opening.

Surfacing, I spit and suck in a lungful of air. Blazing torches light the cramped space. I hunt for anything to grab hold of. The chattering of rats draws me to a ledge. I splash through the water. My limbs quiver with each clumsy stroke. Hauling myself out of the water, I flop onto my stomach. I lie there, panting. Water drips from the ceiling onto my cheek. I flinch away and slump against the wall.

I gingerly extract my egg from its pouch. Its smooth surface has splintered into hundreds of jagged cracks. I blow hot air onto my egg, praying no water has seeped past its shell. My egg. The first stolen treasure that is entirely my own.

Squawk.

I jump, fling the egg away and scramble back. The egg smashes against the cobblestone, releasing more unpleasant chirps and squawks. I crawl over cursing under my breath. The egg is broken. Worthless.

All my plans are wasted.

Shards of shell fall to the ground, revealing a moving black lump. My breath stills. Fear locks my joints.

The perfect first meal for this fearsome monster, small though it is.

Yet, instead of chasing me down, the little creature rolls over, licking slime from his scales with a long, forked tongue. Once clean, he burps a spark of flame, charring the surrounding shell. A giggle bursts from my lips. The dragon cocks his head and fixes a golden eye on me.

I break into a grin. Perhaps there's space for a new plan. Trained by the Duke's men, these dragons are the Romani's worst nightmare. Yet, what if a Romani trained the dragon? Could he protect me?

'Glad I found you.' A gruff voice echoes through the tunnel.

I turn, fanning out my soaked skirt to block any view of the dragon. 'Who goes there?' I call into the dark, my heart racing.

'A man no one steals from,' the voice replies. A familiar face appears in the flickering light.

I gasp.

'Please, sir,' I beg the man in the blue doublet, 'I will repay any debt.'

'After your performance in the piazza, I'm sure you will.' He inclines his head and inspects me, his eyes narrowed. 'With the correct training, you could be an asset to the Court of Miracles. But first, we must keep moving. Come.' He turns and waves me toward a half-open door. Fresh air trickles through the gap. Tempting.

'Wait.' I hesitate. It's dark beyond the door, not the sort of place guards lie in ambush, but I won't be someone's asset again. I eye him suspiciously. 'What sort of asset? What's a Court of Miracles? Who do you work for? What do they want from me?'

The man holds out his hand. I catch my breath at the sight of a golden coin. With a flick of his wrist, the coin disappears. I step away, ending his performance before he can pluck the coin from my ear. I've seen this trick. There's no miracle in it.

'You're a thief?' I ask.

'A court magician,' he says.

He offers no further explanation. I cross my arms, waiting.

Finally, he grimaces. 'I was ordered to collect the dragon before he hatched...but now...now I need you too. The hatchling will perish without his bonded master. That's you.'

A small smile tugs at my lips. I raise my brows. 'Then you'll feed me? Keep a roof over my head? I'll have silk to wear, like you?'

The man massages his temples and studies the dragon as it peers around my skirt.

'Yes,' he says with a sigh, 'but, you'll work for the Court.'

I scoop up the dragon. The little beast croons and nestles into my chest.

'I'll work for the Court,' I say. I'm no stranger to hard work. 'But on my own terms. I won't be anyone's servant or slave. Ever.'

'Fine, fine.' The man holds up a hand in a gesture of surrender. 'We must go. It'll be harder to leave Milan unnoticed after curfew.'

I lift my chin. 'I won't leave Milan.'

'You'll come back. It's just for the training.'

I nod, my chest tight.

'You must name the dragon if he's to survive the night,' he says.

The hums and dragon leans into my touch. Warmth shoots up my arm, chasing away any doubts.

'His name is Liberto.'

A sly smile curls the man's lips and he nods, leading me to my future.

#

END

Two Truths

Jem McCusker

**There are two types of truth in this life. Hers and mine.
It's up to you to work out which one's the lie.**

My mumma was two things in this life. Well, three if you count being my mumma.

She was also a bitch and a gardener.

Not the water and fertiliser type, although she did plenty of both. She was the type that liked to plant the seeds of doubt and then watch them grow.

Her lies went down as smooth as a glass of sweet iced tea on a summer's day.

Her voice sounded down the hall. I tied back my flyaway brown hair and hastily flipped over a biology textbook. Open textbooks, notebooks and sticky-note reminders, their contents highlighted for reference, littered the desk's surface.

I stroked a college pamphlet then opened it.

I was meant to be studying for my senior year exams. Human anatomy. What it took to keep the frail human body living. The liver. The lungs. The heart.

Did she even have one?

A footstep fell outside my room. Mumma spoke in low tones. I hastily returned the pamphlet to its home under my mattress.

I pushed away from my desk. The wheels of my chair caught on the blue, shag pile rug. Its shade was not dissimilar to the veins in my bone thin hands.

My stomach grumbled and the pounding in my temples increased. I peeked out my bedroom door and saw her, leaning across the kitchen counter, phone to her ear.

Her hair sported no greys thanks to regular top-ups from her friend Medium Brown L'Oréal. She was unnaturally thin, with shoulder bones jutting out beneath her tank. Her arms bordered on skeletal. She insisted on wearing pyjama shorts so short you could practically see her butt cheeks. At a size eight, I was obese compared to her.

She spoke again. Some poor bastard was caught in her sights and she was running him down to anyone that would listen. I heard the sharp changes in her tone as she manipulated her audience.

First sadness.

'I just don't know what to do, Sherry.' She sighed heavily.

Then fear.

'He followed me into the staff kitchen. Honest to god, my heart was in my throat.' She hiccupped on the last two words. Paused. Waited.

Next, resignation.

'I can't say anything. You know how these things go. I'd be the one sacked. I can't afford that. As it is, Lilly-Mae's grades are falling even with me paying for tutors. I need to suck it up until she gets a job.' A long silence ensued as she listened.

Then, finally, aggression broke through.

'I'll document everything that happens. Once Lilly-Mae has finished high school I'll be in a better position to take the bastard on. I'll record him and send it to his wife. Let them battle it out.' Her lips curved into a satisfied smile.

Aggression was always favoured; savoured after a slow build. The victim status needed to be solidified first for aggression to pack its true punch.

She wasn't done yet. I'd have to wait. I closed the door carefully and flopped onto my bed, the old mattress springs squeaking despite my lack of weight.

Too hungry to study, I gazed blankly around my small room. Dream catchers hung from the bed posts and an assortment of crystals filled the shelves, a measly scattering of approved novels in between. The scent of sage lingered in the air, tickling my nostrils while cleansing my tainted spirit.

Finally, the back door opened with a bang. She saved her biggest lies for blue skies, the backyard, and the absence of my hearing.

I slid off the bed, hoping to find some real food. The brain shakes I'd been living off for the last two weeks were revolting. Mumma said they helped focus the mind and were filled with omegas and proteins. I'd never felt less focused. Even now, my body trembled; my fingers ghosted over acne on my chin. The only benefit I'd seen was a shrinking of my already narrow waist.

I tiptoed to the kitchen. Mumma was good with tricks. Sometimes she'd slam the door and wait, just to catch me.

The lime green paint on the kitchen walls assaulted the eyes and the combination of yellow and brown curtains hanging over the windows made it worse. Mumma was always promising we'd sell up and move somewhere better when I finally started contributing to the household income.

On the fridge, today's alphabet letters read, *love and light.* I rolled my eyes and made quick work rearranging them. Then I tugged on the door; it gave slightly but went no further. Frowning, I tried again, but no luck. I looked up the side of the door. A padlock had been installed.

Clenching my fists, I kicked the fridge and cursed, beating it with my hands until my flesh swelled, red and angry.

I looked over to the cupboards. They now held the same locks.

I closed my eyes and sucked a slow, shuddering breath. This had to stop. Three weeks ago, I had never considered a different life. With another Sunday looming—a Sunday alone with James—I couldn't continue living this way. A life of silence, without voice. Without choice.

I opened the cutlery drawer, took out the small paring knife, and went back to my room.

#

Peace could be found if you knew where to look for it. For me, it was the sound of rain on our old tin roof during a blackout. Shadows moved about my bedroom, dancing to flickering candlelight.

'Lilly-Mae, come here.'

I should have known better. The woman had a sixth sense for peace. Not the nurturing kind. Rather the rip it from you bodily until you bled kind.

I straightened and hurried down the narrow hall to her room. Wind battered the house, the windows groaning, as if the very elements were railing against Mumma's meanness.

Mumma sat staring at her reflection in her vanity mirror. She turned her head, stroking the line of her cheekbone. Her face was etched in shadows. In that moment, I imagined they revealed the monster she truly was.

Then the fierce winds dropped away and with them the darkness. She was a woman once more. She glanced toward me.

'Look at that, the power's back on. I thought we'd have to wait until morning.'

I shrugged. The less I said, the less she could critique.

'I'm volunteering at the nursing home tonight.' Her shrewd eyes narrowed. 'I've left some brain shakes on the kitchen counter for you.'

'Okay,' I mumbled, scuffing my foot against the carpet.

She stood and placed her hands on my shoulders, holding me back. Her eyes searched mine. For what, I couldn't say. My gaze fell to the chain around her neck. The key to the kitchen cupboards and fridge hung from it.

'I had a call from the school earlier. They want to see me on Monday to discuss you.'

My stomach flipped. I fought my body's urge to tremble. 'Probably all those brain shakes. My homework has improved.'

Her nails dug into my skin. The sickly odour of stale wine wafted across my face.

'Never lie to me, Lilly-Mae. The truth always comes out, eventually.' She let go and I stepped away the minute her nails released their pressure.

'Of course not, Mumma.'

'Celia and Albert across the road will be keeping an eye on the house for me.' She checked her reflection and adjusted her hair.

'Make sure you get to bed early. Big day with James tomorrow.'

'How's Albert's blood pressure?' I asked. I didn't want to get her started on James.

'Oh, you know, he's doing little to manage it. Relying only on his blood pressure tablets. Celia worries for him.' She dismissed the couple with an airy wave of her manicured nails.

'Poor Celia,' I said, unenthusiastically. 'Well, enjoy your night at the home. I'll be studying and then heading to bed early.' I hurried from the room.

Her volunteer work at the nursing home was a second skin. She wore it to project the image of a kindly woman that cared about others. She never wore that skin in our house.

My pulse beat rapid-fire and warmth pooled in my belly.

The school had acted quickly and now I must as well.

#

I waited in my room for a good forty minutes after her headlights vanished down the narrow street. Just in case. Then I snuck out the back door, blending into the shadows of the neighbouring hedge. I scanned the street. No-one about. Good. I dashed across the road.

Celia and Albert were both hard of hearing and considered our neighbourhood safe. The back door was rarely locked.

I crept through their house while they watched television, the news blaring. I peeked into the dining room. They were both laid up on recliner chairs, fresh cups of tea beside them. Everything about the house screamed 'old people live here'. The shelving was crowded with family photos, doilies under ornaments, and a statue of Jesus. A large confederate flag was framed on the wall.

I took my backpack off. Carefully opening the cupboards, I took a little of everything. A half packet of biscuits, some two-minute noodles. An apple, a banana, a hot chocolate sachet. A small long-life milk. From their medicine cabinet, I grabbed some paracetamol and other supplies.

I was nearly home free.

Then I heard the groan of the recliner chair.

'I need to take my pills,' Albert said.

Thank God the old man was slow. I had just enough time to open the laundry door and cram myself into the broom closet with the Hoover and mop. A few minutes passed. I heard a faint crash and hoped it was an opportune distraction.

'Al, you're a fool. It's all over the tiles,' Celia exclaimed.

Shit. In a second they'd come looking for something to clean whatever he'd spilled. I cracked open the closet door, pushing the mop and bucket into the middle of the laundry floor.

Moments later, I heard the bucket roll away. I peeked; coast was clear.

I slipped out and sprinted across the street, moments before headlights turned into our driveway. I fumbled with the back-door lock. It finally gave. I rushed to my room and pulled out an old shoe box from the back of my closet. My hoard went under the craft materials inside and I shoved the box back in its place.

A car door slammed. I jumped into the bed, pulling the blankets up to my chin, and closed my eyes. My heart pounded and the hint of a smile tugged at the corners of my mouth.

But my angst was for nothing. The clink of a wine glass being set on the counter and the sound of wine pouring told me I had got away with it—for now.

#

Mumma wasn't one for mornings. In that respect we were alike. For her, it was the hangover. For me, it was the smell of booze seeping from her pores.

Her lipstick was smudged around the corners of her mouth. Her disposition was no different to most mornings: bitchy with a touch of self-loathing.

She stood in front of the fridge and removed the key-necklace. Her fingers brushed the newly organised fridge magnets. *Go in Peace.* She frowned and yanked the door open.

I eyed the contents inside before trudging over to the blender, scooping out the brain shake powder and adding water. I thought back on the evening, careful to school my features lest she sense my happiness. I was exhausted and my body hurt, but it had been worth it

'Lilly-Mae are you listening to me?'

My mother's voice sent chills racing up my spine, ripping me out of my daydream. 'Uh, sorry. Trying to remember my poem for English Lit on Monday. Got caught in the zone.'

'Oh, I didn't realise you were doing poetry this semester.' Mumma poured a coffee, propping herself on the stool beside me.

'Yeah, we have to write our own poem and recite it next week. I just need to get my note cards ready.'

'Don't leave it to the last minute like everything else you do. You've never been the brightest so don't lower yourself further with poor organisation. At least you have your looks.' She swept a hand over my hair.

I'd had the same hair cut my entire life. I'd never coloured it. I longed to get caramel highlights, maybe even a fringe.

'I won't, Mumma. Do we still have the prom dress fitting

tomorrow?' Nothing cheered Mumma up more than the idea of dolling me up. I hadn't chosen the dress or the colour. Choices were something other people had.

'You've got a little more weight to lose. I'll push it back another week,' she said.

That was what I heard every week. Nothing was more important to Mumma than public image. Didn't matter if I failed my final exams, as long as I looked good doing it.

'Make me one of your shakes. I swear my pants are tighter this morning.' Mumma smiled at me. The smile she saved for taunting. The one that said, question me, I dare you?

That was a battle I'd never win. Whatever answer I gave would be wrong. I had one week of exams left, my prom and then graduation. When I graduated, I planned to be at the top of the food chain.

'Vanilla or chocolate?' I asked, unable to meet her gaze.

'So, you're saying I am fat? That I've put on weight and need shakes to lose it?' She pushed back from the counter, storming around the small kitchen.

I was on dangerous ground. She didn't like it when her taunts went unanswered. She considered it a sin.

'No, no. I just…I thought you know, that—

'Oh, save it, you little bitch.' She spat the words.

I didn't resist when she grabbed my ear and hauled me to my room. She pulled the lighter from her pocket and took down a sprig of dried sage from my shelf.

'I can't have you inserting all of this negative energy into my life.' She roamed around my room, waving the smouldering sage to smudge out my energy.

To erase me.

One more week and I'd be erased completely.

#

An hour later she returned and rummaged through my closet. I sat on the bench seat, looking out the window. The morning sky held a strange glow today. A glow it had no business keeping. The colour of burnt orange; reserved for days when the sun had reappeared after a storm.

'James'll be here soon. Wear the white tank. You're coming along up top. Don't let it go to waste.' Mumma tossed the top onto my bed.

I looked between it and the door.

'Don't be silly,' she said. 'Get changed. It's nothing I haven't seen before.'

I picked up the tank and turned my back to her, trying to hold onto a shred of modesty.

'If you're lucky he'll kiss you today.' Her eyes lit up, not from joy but the scent of money.

'He's twenty-seven. He's old.' I said.

'A rich twenty-seven-year-old. You'd be lucky to catch him. Don't waste an opportunity.' She raked me up and down before fluffing my hair. Then she picked up the eye shadow and started prodding at my eyelids. 'This will make your brown eyes pop.'

I didn't want my eyes to 'pop' or to kiss the old dude. But today wasn't about what I wanted. It never was.

This was the third week in a row she'd sent me out with James. I vowed it would be the last. I wanted to date boys my own age. He'd made it clear that he was more than interested and assumed I was interested too, because I kept going out with him.

'You make me sick.' She tilted my chin, her eyes narrowing. 'I bend over backwards to give you a better life. To give you the opportunities I never had. And all I get from you is attitude. Don't screw this up for us.'

'Us?'

'Yes, us.' She wrapped her hand tightly around my arm. 'Family is forever. I've lost prime years of my youth raising you. I intend to have a more comfortable retirement; he comes from old money. Old enough for me to see out my days in luxury.'

'Of course, Mumma.' I tried to twist free, only for her to squeeze tighter.

James pulled into the driveway in his midnight black Jeep with tinted windows. I feigned enthusiasm and rushed for the door.

'Life's not a fairy-tale.' She yanked me back and whispered. 'There's no Prince Charming. No fairy godmother. Just me. Best remember that.'

She pushed me out the front door.

#

'Hi Lilly-Mae,' James said. 'I'll have her home by three, Anna.

Mumma tossed her head and smiled in a forced way. 'Don't be silly, James. You two enjoy yourselves, now.'

We took the highway. Nothing but grey road and cars ahead. I'd never been one for small talk and didn't intend to start now. He had the radio on low and tapped his fingers on the steering wheel.

I didn't know why James wanted to spend time with me. He was good looking. Tanned skin, neat blonde hair. He worked out. His eyes were a touch too close together and his nose sat a little crooked, but he should be able to find someone his own age.

'How's school going?' he asked. 'You must be looking forward to graduation.'

'Ah, it's fine. Stressful trying to cram it all in.'

'Your mumma said you don't have a date to your prom.'

'I'm going with a group of girlfriends. None of us have dates.'

He signalled, taking the exit toward the coast. Obviously Mumma knew we were going to the beach, having selected me the tank and skirt when I much preferred shorts and t-shirts.

Eager to change the subject, I asked about him. 'So, how's work going?

'Good. Busy. I won't bore you with the details.' He stole a glance at me.

I'd seen this look on our previous two Sunday outings. The look that said, *I'd like to see what's under those clothes.*

I had to think of something. The silence was too loud and the stare too long.

'I'm thinking of enrolling in a Bachelor of Engineering program next year, so I'd like to know.'

'Really? I didn't think your grades were good enough.' He focussed on the road, fingers still thrumming on the steering wheel.

'I have excellent grades,' I replied sharply, straightening and facing him.

'Oh…It's just your mum said you'd never really excelled at school.' He cleared his throat.

'You caught me. I'm a complete dim wit. I'm only dating you for your family money and the hopes of a comfortable life.' My tone was dry, eyebrow raised.

He pulled the car over on a side street, not far from the beach. 'So, we're dating then.' He unclipped his seatbelt and leaned toward me.

Fuck.

'No, we're not dating.' I folded my arms.

He shifted back in his seat, and clenched the steering wheel until his knuckles turned white.

'You're a tease. You know that.' The words came out short and choppy.

'No, I'm a seventeen-year-old girl that does not want to date you. My mumma wants me to date you.'

His hands dropped, along with them, the anger. 'You mean that? Your mum? Not you?' A

'Look.' I sighed and relaxed my arms. 'I'm sorry. It's just when she gets her mind caught on something she pushes and pushes.'

'Fuck. I'm sorry. I wouldn't have kept asking you out if I'd known.' He slumped. .'Want me to take you home?'

I'd expected him to be an asshole about it. I really shouldn't have said anything so soon. Now I'd missed out on a real lunch.

'Say something. What are you thinking?' he asked.

I answered honestly, with a half-grin. 'That I'm really hungry and now I've missed lunch.'

'Well, I could eat. Friends eat lunch, yeah?' A wry grin tugged the corners of his mouth. He started the engine and drove cautiously into traffic.

We pulled up at a nearby diner. I inhaled the scent of greasy fries and burgers, salivating. James steered us to the coffee house next door. We waited by the *Please wait to be seated sign*. The café was practically empty.

'Table for two?' The waiter asked.

'Yes. We'll take your least romantic table setting, please,' James replied, a surprisingly disarming grin on his face.

The waiter smiled. 'Try table number four in the friend zone.'

I laughed. Lighthearted, honest laughter without a trace of fear. It felt good. I even managed to order my coffee with a smile.

'So, tell me.' James looked over the rim of his coffee cup. 'Why is your mum so keen on playing matchmaker?'

The brief spark of happiness blew out. Tears pooled and I blinked them away. She hated me crying. Said it made me look ugly.

'She's just…' I managed, 'very attached. She's not dealing well with the idea of me going to college. She told me outright I couldn't go. She thinks if I meet a nice boy, I'll stay.' I hurriedly wiped a stray tear.

James took my hand in his. Nothing untoward. A symbol of friendship. Support. 'Is there anything I can do?'

'Not really. I have to find a way to reassure her. She's been spiralling lately. The only time I'm allowed out is with you or to go to school. I think she's scared of being on her own.'

'Look if you need any help, let me know. It's the least I can do. My intentions haven't been entirely pure,' he said. 'When your mumma approached me, I was visiting my grandfather at the nursing home. Grandpa was dozing when your mumma started telling me about you.'

I cringed, trying desperately not to imagine how that conversation went.

James grimaced. 'I saw it as an opportunity. I've spent my entire life in the south. Country Clubs. Garden parties.'

'How awful for you,' I drawled.

'Point taken. But I've been trying to transfer to the New York office to get out. My parents won't hear of it. Want me settle here. Keep the family business going.'

'Why don't you just leave?'

'Money. Until I take my place on the board, they have a tight leash on it. However, nothing gets you sent away quicker than a good ol' fashion scandal.'

'Enter me. Seventeen. Poor, single parent family.' Just another pawn to be moved across the board in someone else's game.

'I never intended; you know...anything, untoward. I knew it wouldn't take long for word to get back,' he said. 'It was Grandpa's idea. He understood me.' James shrugged. 'Once he heard about you, he encouraged me to date you then get out of town.'

I looked down at our joined hands. Somehow, I'd linked mine with his. I felt him staring, looked up and saw nothing but kindness with a dash of shame.

'I can't think straight.' I said, pulling my hand free. 'This is all just a bit much for me right now. Mind if we order? I'm starving.'

'Sure. Hope you don't mind me saying but I swear every time I see you, you're thinner.' He blushed. 'I don't mean that you needed to lose weight. You were already thin. Have you been sick?'

'No, it's okay. She's got me on these shakes. Brain shakes she calls them. Says they're filled with omegas and proteins. They're not. They're diet shakes. She's obsessed with the prom.'

His jaw went slack, his hand squeezing mine again. 'That's not normal, Lilly-Mae. It's your senior year. You can't study if you're hungry.'

Sympathy was not something I was familiar with. A strange sensation settled over me. I'd heard the word comfort and suspected I was feeling it for the first time.

'Don't get me started.' I gave a wan smile. 'My teacher asked me why I hadn't applied to any colleges. I tried to brush her off. She kept pushing and I ended up telling her there was no way Mumma would let me leave. She gets so worked up about it, it scares me.'

I crossed my arms. The bruises on my right arm from when

she'd grabbed me earlier were beginning to turn purple and nasty.

The lump in my throat built and tears flowed. I buried my face in a napkin as sobs racked my body. 'The school…c-called her. Want her to c-come in Monday to talk about it. I told Mumma about my teacher and now she's furious. Said she won't allow anyone to question her choices for me.' The crying took over, my nose streaming. No doubt the mascara had smudged beneath my eyes. She'd be so mad I'd messed up my makeup.

But the floodgates had opened.

#

Not much was guaranteed in this life. Two things I did know. Life was about choices and sacrifices. I was about to make mine.

Monday morning I wandered into the kitchen, blinking in the sharp light. The shake ingredients waited for me on the counter.

'Well, tell me how it went yesterday with James? I noticed he kissed your cheek when he dropped you off,' Mumma said, pausing to look at me while she poured milk into her coffee.

'It was good. He might come by this evening. If that's okay with you, of course?' I didn't allow my excitement to show. My shoulders slumped. She preferred it when she thought she held all the cards.

Truth was, by the time James and I had finished lunch I'd decided I was a willing accomplice in his mission to bring shame upon his family name. He wanted away from his family. I understood the feeling.

'He absolutely can,' she said. 'I was worried you didn't have enough to lure and keep a man. I'll chaperone tonight. Keep you on track.' She sipped her coffee, malicious delight in her eyes.

'Thanks, Mumma. You always know just what to do.' I turned

on the blender. She wandered out of the kitchen, smiling.

I couldn't stomach another shake and set it on the counter. Then I went quietly to my room and took an apple from my bag and the paring knife from its hiding place in one of my textbooks.

The door burst open. Mumma stalked in. A hound, sniffing its prey. She focused on the apple; the knife in my hand.

'Where did you get that?' she all but yelled, ripping them from my hands. She opened the window and threw the apple as far as she could.

'Yesterday.' I cringed away. 'When I was out with James. I'm just so hungry. I can't focus on my exams and I shake all the time.' A lone tear escaped.

'I'm doing what's best for you.' She brandished the knife at me. 'Your prom dress is a size six and by God you *will* squeeze that butt of yours into it.' She grabbed my ear, pulling me out to the kitchen.

'Drink it.' She handed me the shake I'd left untouched.

'No.' I tried to sound firm but my voice shook.

'I said drink it. We can't afford waste in this house.' She pushed the cup at me, the knife still in her other hand. Its sharp blade tipped, just inches from my chest.

I stepped toward her. Toward the knife. Meeting her forceful gaze with one of my own. I set the shake on the counter. 'It's disgusting. Why don't you drink it? See what you've had me living off these past few weeks.'

'Fine.' She drank it in one go.

I took satisfaction in watching as she tried to mask her facial expressions to hide the distaste.

'There.' She slammed the empty cup onto the bench and wiped her lips, smearing scarlet lipstick onto her cheek. 'Nothing wrong with it.' She stood nose to nose with me. The tip of the knife now pressed against my belly. I didn't dare breathe.

'You'll get nothing to eat today. You had a choice and you've chosen to go hungry.' She stormed from the room, slamming her bedroom door.

The silent treatment wasn't unusual. I'd always pretended it unsettled me. It didn't. It allowed me some peace. I bided my time and went to my bedroom, flicking open my textbooks.

She'd taken the bait upon first offering. I'd played out all the scenarios; had back up plans in place. But now, they were unnecessary. Relief coursed through me.

Hours passed before I finally heard groaning from her bedroom. I rushed in.

She lay on her elegant bed, deathly pale, her body wracked with shivers, perspiring profusely.

'Are you unwell, Mumma?' I asked from the door.

'Call...call an ambulance. Something...something's wrong.' Her fingers twisted the sheets.

'No, Mumma,' I said.

Her eyes grew wide. She tried to sit up but her arms collapsed beneath her weight.

'Why not?' Her voice quavered.

'I'm taking my life back. I learned how from the best.' I sat on the edge of the king size bed, just out of her reach.

She shook her head, trying and failing again to sit up.

'That's right, Mumma.' I smiled sweetly. 'I'm making my own choices now. You were getting in the way.'

'What did you do? You can't do this to me. They'll investigate, find out.' She heaved out the last words along with her stomach contents. Vomit oozed at the side of her mouth; dribbled down her cheek and neck to pool in her hair.

She coughed, the bile gurgling in her mouth.

'No, they won't. I already told you, I learned from the best. I've established myself as the victim both with James and my teacher, Mrs Brown. You know, the one that wanted to see you tomorrow?'

She nodded shakily.

'But oh, I played it up.' I shook my head, sighing. 'Made sure they saw I was resigned to my life. Said I understood your worries and how you needed me. How the idea of me leaving you left you so distressed. So unhinged that you couldn't take it anymore. And they bought it.' I patted her leg. 'And you helped. Thanks.'

She gaped. 'What?'

'Remember the sexual misconduct story you've been telling about a colleague at work.'

Her eyes widened but no sounds came from her open mouth.

'Altogether it paints the picture of a disturbed woman that took her own life.' I rose and brushed at my shirt, wiping her away. 'But here's the final punch. My true assertion of aggression was in that fucking diet shake. Albert across the road is missing a few blood pressure tablets.'

I smirked. 'Old people can be so absent-minded. No one will know except you and I. Maybe I'll tell them you made two shakes. That when you went to the fridge, I switched the glasses because yours had less and you never noticed. They'll say you plotted to kill me. Yes, I think I much prefer that. I've been a victim my entire life. I can play the part a little longer.'

Stripped bare at last, I looked down at her, knowing her unblemished skin wouldn't reflect her sins, it would hide them. A shiny wrapper over damaged goods.

Her eyes rolled back; her body twisted and pulsed. Just for a moment, her eyes rested on mine. Then she sighed one last, rattling breath. A death film coated her eyes.

She died knowing I had stolen back all she'd taken away and that was enough for me.

She would keep a while yet. I could call the ambulance later. Play the distraught daughter when James arrived this evening.

For now, I had a new life to prepare for. I returned to my room and flipped open my biology textbook.

The human heart.

Was it necessary to know what kept a human heart beating when you had already learned how to stop it?

#

END

Vagabond

Cassandra Kelly

Feronia stood with mouth agape and eyes wide at the sight of the billowing sails, and smoke, and the noise of chugging engines. As each airship came to rest on Hampstead Heath the crowd around her cheered and clapped. What might it be like to fly so high and look down on the world, soaring above all the misery?

So lost in the spectacle was she that she forgot the emptiness in her belly and the crowd of rich pickings around her—the wealthy and great had turned out in droves for the 1860 aeronautical exhibition.

'Are you enjoying the show?'

Feronia turned and glared. 'No.'

'Really? You seem focused on the event.' The woman, not much older than Feronia, spoke in a manner as refined as her appearance. Fair hair and pale skin contrasted with her blue dress, matching hat and parasol. No doubt the woman had a pedigree as long as her arm.

Feronia screwed up her nose, aware of her own tattered attire.

The dun-coloured dress she wore didn't disguise the dirt from the streets. Patches of material, some of it stolen, covered the holes. Why did she feel ashamed? It wasn't her fault that she came from a father unknown, a seaman whose only legacy to Feronia was her olive skin. A strand of her dark wavy hair blew across her face. She brushed it, and her shame, aside.

'Well you're bloody wrong.' Feronia avoided the woman's gaze, instead noting the position of her purse.

The woman recoiled. 'My, my. Unpleasant little thing, aren't you?'

'I ain't little, I'm seventeen.' Feronia drew herself up to her full height of five feet five and added, 'And I'm not a thing, I'm a person.'

'You're certainly amusing. Do you do tricks?'

Feronia clenched her fists. 'Amusing? I ain't here for your amusement, lady.'

'No. You're here for the airships. Are you with anyone?'

'Does it bloody well look like I'm with anyone?'

The woman kept staring, her gaze dropping to Feronia's bare and dirty feet.

Feronia moved her hands to her hips, fists still clenched. 'I ain't got shoes. So what? I like being barefoot.'

In a soft tone the woman said, 'You must also love airships. How long did it take you to walk from London? Two hours?'

Feronia crossed her arms. 'I live near here.'

The woman raised an eyebrow. 'Your accent places you close to the East End.'

'What's it to you?' Feronia paused. 'Matter of fact I came up yesterday and took my time about it.'

'My husband owns an airship.' The woman no longer looked at

Feronia, instead staring at a vessel flying overhead.

Feronia tried to sound uninterested. 'I suppose it's only a small, old one.'

The woman turned back to her. 'It's a large new one. My husband is Lord D'Vanth.'

'Supposed to be impressed, am I?'

'He's a philanthropist.'

'I ain't into that sort of stuff.'

The woman stifled a laugh. 'He uses his wealth to help the less fortunate—people like you. Can you read?'

'Yes,' Feronia lied. 'I could read since I was two.'

'Clever girl.' The woman stared at her until Feronia grew uncomfortable.

'What?' she snarled.

'You've had a hard life, I see that. Would you like an opportunity?'

Feronia let her hands drop to her sides and changed her tone to one she used when she wanted to be agreeable. 'What sort of opportunity?'

'To fly. To learn how an airship works—to see new lands.'

Feronia tilted her head to the side. 'What's the price?'

'Nothing wanted in return at all. We—Lord D'Vanth and I—use our wealth to perform charitable acts. We consider it our Christian duty.'

Feronia had heard of the benevolent rich but wasn't sure they existed. 'I ain't gotta go to church or nothing?'

'No church.'

'Where's this airship?'

'Are you interested?'

'Course I bloody well am.'

'What's your name?'

'Feronia.'

The woman took a card from her purse and handed it to her. 'Feronia, be at this inn at 6am tomorrow.

#

Feronia found someone to read the address on the card and set off to find it. She traipsed along the narrow cobblestone street, past rows of shops and houses. The inn occupied a corner and an archway beside it gave access to a courtyard beyond. She slipped a hand through a slit in her dress and felt the dagger strapped to her thigh. Her lock picks, in a pocket on the sheath, were in place. Satisfied she had the means to escape if she needed to, she entered the courtyard.

Two pipe-smoking drivers waited by wagons which were hitched and ready to go. Beyond them stood a stable, and the smell of hay, horse dung and pipe smoke lingered in the air.

A gaggle of girls in various states of vagabondage stood or sat on the grey stone paving, with Lady D'Vanth in attendance. She appeared plainer than previously, now dressed in brown with a simple corset and hat. Glasses perched on her nose and she held a ledger and pencil. Reassured by the presence of so many other girls Feronia walked to Lady D'Vanth.

'Good morning, Feronia.'

'Where's the airship?'

'We'll get to it. We're waiting on one more.' Lady D'Vanth marked something in her book and looked at her pocket watch. 'Never mind, it's time to leave. Everyone on the wagons.'

Feronia climbed onto the second wagon. As it departed the archway and rattled onto the street, a freckle-faced girl came running, her skirts gathered and clutched in one hand as she reached out with the other.

'Wait!'

Feronia ignored the girl's outstretched hand. Another girl grabbed the latecomer's wrist and hauled her aboard.

'Ta. Had trouble finding the place.' She sat on the floor and nestled in amongst the girls, her questioning gaze fixed on Feronia.

#

The airship, moored in the expansive grounds of a Georgian manor house, came into view before the house itself. The ship's twin keels rested on the grass and two pairs of bat-like wings were folded back against the hull. Three short masts supported a yellow balloon secured with netting.

Lady D'Vanth hadn't lied; the ship showed no signs of age, and Feronia had to shift her gaze from bow to stern to take it all in.

To her dismay, the wagons took them past the airship, behind the house, finally stopping by a low building of red brick—a wash house. Inside, new clothes awaited; clothes more suitable for clambering around an airship.

Under Lady D'Vanth's watchful eye, the girls washed. Soap and half barrels of cold water had been set up for the purpose. Feronia shivered as she immersed herself. She sniffed the soap, screwing up her face at the sickly scent.

She had secreted her dagger under the bench as she undressed and, once clean, she tucked it into the waist band of the baggy pants she'd been given. A short, plain brown dress and lighter brown pinafore went over the pants. The clothes were new but the fabric cheap, and it scratched her skin.

Lady D'Vanth led her herd of freshly-washed girls around the manor to the airship, where a man with a handsome beard and engaging smile stood waiting. Feronia noted his tailored clothes, his expensive, shiny shoes and the gold chain of his fob watch.

He lifted his hat. 'Good morning, girls. I'm Lord D'Vanth. On board you'll address me as 'captain'. The airship is the *Ortus*. After boarding you'll be assigned to one of the crew who'll be your instructor for the voyage. Now, I don't want to come across as a tyrant but you'll do exactly as you're told; there's no place for disobedience when you're a thousand feet up. Obedience is safety. Your crew will answer any questions you have.'

A door opened into the side of the vessel. The girls followed Lord D'Vanth inside and up onto the deck, where they gazed about at the ropes and pulleys and polished brass fittings.

Lord D'Vanth called for their attention. 'Who can read?' Several of the girls put their hands up, including Feronia. 'You look capable,' he said to her. 'You're assigned to the navigator. And you...' He looked at the young woman who'd been the late arrival. She hadn't put her hand up. 'What's your name?'

'Alice.'

'You'll be the cabin girl for myself and Lady D'Vanth.' He looked at the other girls, assigning them to the helm, boilers, and as deck and kitchen hands.

'There's a lot to learn, but don't be concerned. You're in safe hands. We're flying first to Egypt to take on coal from a depot there, and then on to India before reaching our destination in Singapore. On the way you'll be trained as aeronauts to assist in flying the vessel.' He tugged on a rope as he talked. 'You'll also be schooled in the good graces. There are many English men in the colonies and outposts of the empire, but few English women. If you make yourself pleasing you may find a presentable and wealthy husband. If you excel as crew we may keep you on as a paid aeronaut. We're going up now, you can look over the rail as we ascend, but when we're underway you'll join your instructors.' He moved to another rope and gave it a tug. 'Any questions?'

'Do we get fed?' asked one of the younger girls.

Lord D'Vanth tousled her hair. 'Three times a day.' The girl grinned.

Another girl asked, 'I've heard of air ship pirates. Will we get attacked?'

'A vessel this size is safe enough, and we do have weapons stored below if we need them.'

There were no more questions and, as the *Ortus* increased altitude, every girl looked out over the railing. Squeals of delight and fear carried across the deck. A smoke haze hung over London and the girls became quiet, awed by the altitude and the view. Feronia searched for landmarks, found the Tower of London and located the area where she'd lived. She spat. With any luck she'd never have to go back.

The air grew colder and the girls drifted away to assume their new duties. Feronia was the last to leave the railing and she heard Lord D'Vanth berating an aeronaut for having a lantern three inches from its correct position. Everywhere she looked spoke of tight discipline and exacting standards. She'd have to watch her step with that one.

She asked Lady D'Vanth where she could find the navigator and was directed to the chart room below deck. Light entered the room from a single window above a narrow bed which doubled as a bench seat. A cabinet of map drawers took up one wall and a table occupied the centre of the room. A lantern on the far wall provided extra light and pipe smoke filled the confined space.

Feronia squeezed herself into the room and introduced herself to the navigator, who lay on the bed reading and smoking. A long scar, from brow to chin, marred the woman's otherwise attractive features. Her fair hair, cropped short, did nothing to enhance her appearance.

'Call me Abby. Done any navigation?' Abby put down her book and stood.

'No.'

Abby laid out a chart and set brass weights on the corners. 'This is a small scale map of the Mediterranean. We're following this line here to Egypt and once there we use another map. There are larger scale maps of the areas along this route. You should look at them in your free time. If I call for a map, you'll fetch it and place it here.'

'The blue stuff is water?'

'You've never seen a map before?'

'No, but I know about them and all about different places and stuff. Spend a lot of time talking to the soldiers at the barracks, I do. They even show me their weapons.'

Abby rolled her eyes. 'I bet they do. Fetch some tea and I'll explain the maps.'

#

Feronia had better things to do with her free time than shuffle through a pile of musty charts. The passageways and rooms on the airship invited exploration and she took every opportunity to do so.

The other girls spent their spare time on deck, peering over the railing at the view. At night they shared a single cabin; hammocks strung along its length, paired one above the other like double bunks.

Feronia took a top one, swinging it into motion to drift off to sleep.

Many areas were off limits to the girls and Feronia found those even more fascinating. Locked doors were no obstacle to her curiosity; she used her lock picks to gain access.

One room proved harder to enter than the others, the lock being complicated. The room reeked of gunpowder and gun oil. In the light from the lamp in the passageway she saw it was filled with weapons, ammunition and firkins of powder. She stroked the handle of a pistol. Nice size. It would do if she needed one.

Muffled voices from a room next door interrupted her thoughts and she pressed her ear to the wall. She could hear Lord D'Vanth.

'I don't care. Treat them well. If they're happy they'll fetch–'

'But we're getting rid of them. It's a waste of time training them.' She didn't recognise the crewman's voice.

'The one I've got is stupid, I'm sure.' Abby's voice. 'We'd be better stuffing them in a cabin until we can offload them.'

Feronia clenched a fist.

'You know only too well why we don't do that. I want them happy and compliant. Now, go and don't question me again.'

Feronia relaxed on hearing Lord D'Vanth's support of the girls' training, but Abby? Calling her stupid? And wanting her and the other girls confined to the cabin? Bitch. The conversation disturbed her.

She slipped away and hurried back to the chart room where she pulled out a pile of charts and placed them on the table. She leaned over them as the door opened.

'Good to see you doing what I suggested.'

'Yeah. A bloody good girl, I am.' Feronia pointed at the red circles around some of the locations. 'What are these?'

Abby peered over. 'Lord D'Vanth's business. Nothing for you to be concerned about. Come. I'll teach you how to use a compass and show you the helm. The helmsman only needs a compass heading, and it's our job to provide it. We don't take the charts up on deck as they'll blow about. The helm is that round thing on the deck with spokes that looks like a cart wheel. It has a compass by it.'

#

The pyramids captured Feronia's attention as the *Ortus* flew over them. They were more magnificent than Buckingham Palace—still, a lot of work for a rich cove's grave. Warm air whipped up from the desert and fine grains of sand pattered against her face.

'Bloody good view isn't it?' Alice stood by her elbow, looking up at her.

'What do you want?'

'Nothing. I'm just saying.'

'Why say it to me?'

Alice didn't answer at first. When she did, Feronia could barely hear her. 'I like you.'

'Why? I never helped you when you ran after the wagon.'

Alice shrugged. 'I've been watching you. You're strong, and you're wary of them and don't care much for their authority.'

'Whose?'

Alice nodded in the direction of the captain's cabin.

Feronia frowned. 'What are you getting at?'

'I need help.'

'With what?'

'Them.'

'What the bloody hell are you talking about?'

'The captain—and her. I think they suspect.'

'You're as clear as muck. Get to the cut of it.'

'They think I can read.'

'Can you?'

Alice glanced over her shoulder and whispered. 'Yes, but don't tell anyone.'

'Why would they care if you can read?'

'Because I read something. I read—' A voice called out to her. Lady D'Vanth. 'I got to go.'

Alice ran off and a few minutes later Lady D'Vanth joined Feronia at the railing. 'Lovely girl, Alice, isn't she?'

'I suppose.'

'Do you find her chatter bothersome?'

'No more than most.' Feronia kept her focus on the sphinx.

'What was she chatting about?'

'The view.'

'Hmm. It's a good view. I sometimes take it for granted. Are you enjoying flying?'

'Yeah. I love it up here.'

'Good. We like our girls to be happy.' Lady D'Vanth walked away.

#

'We're going to Bombay. Plot the course for me,' Abby instructed.

'Where's the map?'

'Find it and do the route. I'll watch.'

Feronia sorted through the maps, pulled one out and laid it on the table. 'This one?'

'Good guess. Where's Bombay?'

Feronia scrutinised the map. She knew they were heading east and east was the right hand side of the map. She pointed. 'Here.'

'Kabul? Kabul is in Afghanistan. You can't bloody read, can you?'

'What of it?'

'You've been wasting my time. I don't know how you managed to bluff your way this far.'

'Because I'm clever. Anyway, I can read the 'N' and 'E' and 'S' and 'W' and know what they mean, and I know numbers.'

'I should report you to the captain but I don't suppose it matters.'

'Why? Because you're chucking us all off the ship anyway?'

Abby looked away. 'Yes. You'll all find husbands.'

'We were told we could become aeronauts if we wanted.'

'Not many get to do that.'

'How did you do it?'

Abby, who'd bent over the map, stood straight. 'I learned to navigate—except I could read when I came onboard.'

'I want to stay.'

'You can't.' She pointed at the map. 'This is Bombay. Plot the course and estimate the flying time.' Feronia set to work as Abby slumped on her bed, stroking her scar.

'How'd you get that?'

'Accident.'

'What sort of accident?'

'You ask too many questions. Don't go getting yourself killed.'

'Killed for asking questions?'

'Do your job.' Abby picked up her book and ignored Feronia.

#

Abby remained quiet about Feronia's illiteracy and Feronia did her best to learn the place names. After a couple of days she could recognise Bombay and Singapore on the maps, as well as many other names.

At Bombay, cargo had to be despatched and received. Two adjoining cargo holds, fore and aft underneath the *Ortus*, allowed goods to be lowered by means of winches. The girls were barred from the cargo area, due to coal and gunpowder being stored there, so they watched from the deck as the exchange took place.

Feronia, fascinated by the bustle of activity, the strange language and clothing, leaned wide-eyed over the railing. Some workers wore cloth wrapped around their loins, and turbans on their heads. Most went barefoot. An old woman begged by a stack of crates while a group of men, dressed in silks of every colour and sparkling with gold jewellery, stood with their backs to her, watching the transfer of cargo. Feronia frowned. The gap between rich and poor wasn't confined to England.

#

A week later the *Ortus* approached the Nicobar Islands—green gems on a clear blue sea—far removed from the grey smoggy slums of London. Feronia could see natives paddling canoes near a sandy shore.

Intrigued by the possibility of a better view through the cargo hatch, she snuck into the forward hold. She was about to lift the hatch when she heard someone entering, and crouched behind a crate.

'Feronia?' Alice's voice.

'What are you doing here?' Feronia rose.

'I followed you. I need to talk to you.' Alice clutched a book.

'About?'

'That woman who's training you. The cut on her face—she did it herself.'

'Why would she?'

'I'll tell you why. It's got to do with what's in this book. This ship ain't right.'

'Yeah. Something's off. So what's in—'

Footsteps sounded in the corridor outside.

'Hide!' Feronia ducked through the door, into the adjoining the hold and crouched behind another barrel. A single ray of light from a ventilation hole gave scant illumination. She heard the sound of a scuffle and a short sharp scream from Alice.

'I've got her.' The voice of a crewman.

'What are you doing, snooping in here?' Lord D'Vanth.

'I wasn't snooping. I wanted to be alone.'

'Who's here with you?'

'No one.'

'I heard you talking.'

'I was singing.'

'It didn't sound like singing.'

'I know. It's why I like to sing alone.'

Feronia smiled at Alice's quick thinking.

'I found this book.' The crewman again.

Silence, and the sound of a hard slap and Alice gasping. One of the men murmured something. Feronia crept to the door, held her breath and pressed an ear to the timber.

'Why have you got this?' Lord D'Vanth asked.

'I never seen it before.'

Another slap, and the sound of something hitting the floor.

'Who have you told about it?'

'No one. I swear.'

'Open the hatch.'

Feronia assumed Lord D'Vanth spoke to his crewman.

'We'll throw you out if you don't tell the truth. I'm sure the natives are friendly, especially to a young woman.'

Feronia cringed. What a bastard.

'I'm telling the truth.' Alice's voice, desperate.

'Last chance.'

'It's the truth.' The sounds of a struggle. Alice's scream, cut off, muffled. Were they really going to throw her out? For a moment Feronia froze with fear and indecision. She snuck to the hatch in her hold and lifted it a fraction.

The *Ortus* flew low over the main island, barely above tree top height. Waves lapped a golden beach. Something dropped from the *Ortus*.

A girl. Alice.

Feronia saw her splash into the ocean. Alice surfaced, struggled against the waves, but reached the shore. Feronia let out a shaky sigh.

The sight of Alice lying curled up on the sand receded into the distance. Trembling, Feronia lowered the hatch and remained quiet until she could steal away safely.

#

She stalked back to the chart room, her fear receding and anger rising. 'Tell me about the scar.'

Abby didn't look up from the book in her hands. 'It's none of your business.'

'Tell me or I'll give you a matching one.' Feronia held her dagger inches from Abby's face.

'You'll be hanged for this.'

'Tell me.'

Abby put down the book, staring at the knife tip. 'You're a fool.'

'Tell me.' Feronia placed the dagger tip below Abby's eye, resting it against her skin.

'I did the scar myself.'

'Why?'

'So I could stay onboard.'

'What do you mean?'

Abby took a deep breath. 'I didn't want to get sold. No one would buy me with a scar like this.'

'Sold? This is a slave ship?'

'Yes. You'll all be sold when we arrive at Singapore.'

'I should bloody well kill you.'

'It's not my fault. I was like you when I came onboard. I wanted to stay free.'

'By helping slavers?'

Abby spat her reply out. 'I had to. If I didn't, I'd be killed.'

'What happened to their old navigator?'

'He died in a fight.'

'Fight?'

'The voyage before my first one, some of the girls broke free and attacked the crew. Now the D'Vanth's have the charade of training you and finding you husbands. Keeps you all compliant. They still didn't have a navigator on my first voyage—the captain did it. He trained me.' Abby breathed heavily, her eyes on the dagger tip. 'Then I learned this is a slave ship, so I cut my face open. Have you noticed all the girls are pretty? I ain't so pretty now.' Abby's eyes were red with tears and one rolled down her cheek. 'I got whipped for this. If I hadn't been so good at the maps I would've been tossed over the side.

Feronia looked down at Abby. 'I don't want to be a slave.'

'What choice do you have?'

Feronia lowered her dagger and leaned back against the map table. 'I have an idea. Will you help?'

Abby stared at her hands, clenching and unclenching her fists. 'If it's a good plan. I've been wanting a chance to get back at the bastards.'

Feronia outlined her idea.

Abby agreed. 'Needs some tweaking but we can do it.'

'I'll talk with the girls. We'll need their help.'

#

Late at night, as most of the aeronauts slept, Feronia crept out of the bunkroom, followed by a line of girls. She led them down to the cargo hold and had them take the metal coal buckets. Each bucket she half-filled with coal. The girls also carried away bolts of linen, sugar and saltpetre. As each girl exited the cabin Feronia ensured they knew where they were to be and what they were to do.

After the last girl left, Feronia made her way to the room where the weapons were kept and picked the lock. She armed herself with colt revolvers and a Sam Browne belt sporting a naval cutlass. She took a third colt for Abby.

No sound could be heard in the corridor apart from the creaking of the ship and the muffled chugging of its engine.

Abby reported to her at the map room. 'The girls have begun setting fire to their coal. With the saltpetre, sugar and cloth it's really doing the trick. I've got most of the interior doors and hatches open and the smoke is going everywhere.'

'Good. If this doesn't work we'll have to try shooting.' Feronia handed over the colt. 'Give me a few minutes to get in place.'

Outside the captain's door, Feronia waited. Somewhere on deck a crewman shouted and the ship's bell sounded. D'Vanth's door swung open. Lord D'Vanth, in his dressing gown, leaned out, mouth open. He saw Feronia standing with two pistols levelled at his chest and froze.

'Inside.' Feronia waved the pistols at him. He stepped back, colliding with Lady D'Vanth who'd appeared behind him.

'You, m'lady, take his belt and tie him tight. If I think you're slacking I'll blow his brains out.'

Lord D'Vanth snarled. 'You ungrateful bitch! This is piracy.'

'Better a pirate than a slave.'

Abby joined her in the cabin and they secured Lady D'Vanth.

The commotion on the deck grew louder.

Shouts of 'Fire! Fire!' echoed through the ship. Smoke curled around the door frame into the cabin.

Feronia gave Abby a nod.

Abby ran onto the deck yelling, 'Ship's about to blow! Captain says abandon ship! Take her down. Lower the boats.'

The helmsman pushed a lever and the airship's nose dropped sharply. The *Ortus* descended to the ocean. Lifeboats dropped. Men, roused from their slumber, jumped over the side. Flames billowed from open hatches and smoke filled every part of the ship.

A small explosion sounded from below deck. Screaming, the helmsman and remaining crew deserted their posts and launched themselves into the ocean.

Feronia left Lord and Lady D'Vanth bound and gagged in the

cabin and joined Abby, who now gripped the helm.

'Are all the crew gone?'

'I think so. The girls are searching the ship.'

'Turn us about,' Feronia said.

#

Flying back over the Nicobars, Feronia had Abby circle the island where she'd seen Alice drop. The *Ortus* flew low over the sand so the women who had no crew duties could watch from the railing.

'There she is!' A woman pointed.

Feronia spotted Alice running along the beach, waving with both hands at the airship, screaming for help. A band of natives, armed with bows, pursued her.

'Get the *Ortus* over her and hold course.' Feronia left Abby at the wheel and dashed to the aft cargo hold. She lowered the winch rope.

Alice sprinted for it, but the ship flew too high. The rope fell short. Feronia looked forward and swore. The ship was nearing the rocks at the end of the beach.

No time to run back to Abby to give instructions. Feronia wrapped her legs around the rope and hung upside down. She slid down to the hook. Alice, her face red, and covered with sweat and sand, leapt, her hand reaching out.

Missed. She fell flat.

'Again!' Feronia screamed.

Alice picked herself up and ran. Arrows thumped into the sand around her.

Feronia slipped a few more inches down the rope. Her heart pounded. Her hand clawed at the air.

Alice jumped. Feronia grabbed her wrist. Held tight. Hauled her upwards. Alice climbed over Feronia's body. Arrows thudded into the hull.

Sweat ran into Feronia's eyes and she hung, still dangling. The rope jerked. Feronia clung to it. Alice had the winch, pulling her to safety. Feronia collapsed on a coal sack, shaking and panting.

Alice released the winch handle and threw herself into Feronia's arms. 'You came back for me.'

'Wasn't going to leave you behind.'

'What's happened?'

'We took the ship. They were going to sell us as slaves. We made a lot of fire and smoke and set off an explosion to make the crew think the ship was burning and about to blow.'

'Where are they?'

'They took to the lifeboats. We have Lord and Lady D'Vanth prisoner.

Alice grinned. 'I know what to do with them.'

#

Feronia assembled the new crew on deck to witness the proceedings.

'Stop complaining,' she said when Lady D'Vanth protested. 'It's traditional.'

Lord D'Vanth snarled. 'You rogues. You'll all hang.'

'Save your breath for swimming, cap'n.'

The *Ortus* flew alongside a beach, low over the water.

'I can see sharks down there,' said Lady D'Vanth.

'I think they're dolphins,' said Abby. 'Anyway, you'll be close to the beach and in water you can stand in.'

Alice smirked at the pair. 'I'm sure the natives will be friendly.'

Lord D'Vanth inched along the plank.

'Too slow.' Feronia prodded him with the cutlass. He tried to dodge it, and fell, screaming.

'You next, m'lady.' Feronia gave a theatrical bow.

Lady D'Vanth glared at her, saying nothing as she stepped onto the plank. Down below, her husband had reached the sand. She jumped and the women cheered as she splashed into the waves. Feronia, Alice, and Abby grinned at each other.

As the sight of the marooned couple receded into the distance, the women returned to their duties.

Abby turned to Feronia. 'Where now?'

'Alice found this book.' She showed it to Abby. 'Belonged to Lord D'Vanth. She says it lists the sale of every girl for every voyage—where they were sold and who to.'

'The chart in the map room, the one with the red circles you asked about a while back—it shows the buyers' locations.'

'He's a tidy bloke, that Lord D'Vanth. We'll be paying these places a visit. You navigate. Alice and I have another task to attend to, first.'

A short while later, Alice and Feronia dangled over the stern on a swing seat, with brushes and paint pots in hand. They turned to each other, grinning. In place of *Ortus*, big black letters now proclaimed the vessel as the '*Vagabond*.'

#

END

The Thirteenth House

Caitlyn McPherson

'*Begin anew. Never again,*' I murmur.

The scrawled crimson words dribble down a pale marble wall in sluggish lines. Down to the broken, bloodless body strewn across the dais steps. Between his torn flesh and exposed bone there's not much left of the victim to recognize. His face is still masked—as the Twelve always are—but his white robes are sprayed in gore and muck.

Still, there's no mistaking the gold-dusted skin or the signet ring of Aquarius.

It's almost laughable. That death has finally come for one of the Twelve who've ruled over the planets, stars, and all the dark-space between since first light was birthed. They're supposed to be infinite and untouchable. Yet here lies Aquarius, little more than a bloody footnote on the floor.

Stars, what a mess….and that smell! Putrefying guts, and blood.

Reaching for the silver chain wrapped around my neck, I follow the links down to the timepiece hanging at its end. A reminder of a promise made. It's a habit really, running my thumb over the engraved cover. So much that I've nearly worn the carvings smooth.

Popping open the worn silver casing, I consult the dial, then address my assistant, who stands nearby.

'Time of death must've been around…' I tap as I do the calculations '…around 0120 ante meridiem. Yes?'

Tanith briefly glances up from her datapad, her tawny eyes calm as always, her ebony-skinned face expressionless. She nods in affirmation and returns to reviewing the case files without adding any further input. She's never been much of a talker but, after years of working together, we're so attuned to each other that words are hardly necessary.

Pocketing the timepiece, I squat before the body and inspect it more closely. Apart from the sliced abdominal cavity there are two large, chest entry-wounds that could have been the cause of death. I lean closer, tucking my long mousey hair behind an ear. The wounds are neat, sharp holes. Precisely located over heart and liver. The skin is already blackening, the body swelling. I snap a few quick photos to refer back to later.

Click, click, click.

Stars, the stench of rot is too much to bear. Reeling away, I put some distance between me and the body before taking another breath.

'You look pale, Detective Ophidia.'

The dark voice triggers something almost instinctive and my spine snaps straight in response. Capricorn, the current Ascendant House sovereign, assesses me from the council chamber's archway. I'd been so engrossed in my examination I'd almost forgotten he watched us. Though his expression is hidden behind one of those featureless masks that all the House rulers wear, the arms crossed over his broad chest tell me he's not impressed.

'I was told you two are the best, yet you're pale as the corpse before you. I want this whole affair sorted out immediately. If you can't stomach the task, I'll summon another who can.' His dismissive tone echoes across the marbled chamber, betraying no emotion, no empathy. Stone cold as the rest of this place.

It's not the first time someone has remarked on my complexion but it's the first time it's been thrown at me as an insult. I bristle, my fingers digging into my datapad to keep myself from flipping him a rude gesture. Tanith must sense my internal struggle because the corner of her thin mouth quirks upwards in amusement.

'Your Grace,' I say as calmly as I can, 'I assure you my pallor has nothing to do with the case. And there is none better for *this* job, than us. Now...' The screen of my datapad lights up as my fingers hunt for the records I need.

Thousands of years worth of information should be available. This could take awhile.

There are some things everyone knows about the Twelve. Like, they're immortal, powerful and each rules over one of the Zodiac Houses. They align their court with the movements of the planets and stars, taking turns to rule as Ascendant over both humans and the other Houses with every rotation around the sun.

So, considering it has taken this murder investigation for me to gain access to the court records on the Twelve, I'm appalled by how grossly incomplete they are. The files barely extend past all that commonplace information. They don't even broach the humans' Millenium rebellion, or the slaughter that followed when the Twelve regained control of the planet. Someone has wiped the archives— and the Twelves' hands—clean of that bloodshed.

This is exactly the kind of corruption I swore to end when I began my career as a crime scene detective for the United Earth Authorities. But how do you bring the most powerful beings in existence to justice for a list of crimes spanning centuries? If I'm honest, most of humanity will probably consider Aquarius's death a step in the right direction. Not that I'd admit that out loud.

Tanith clears her throat, reminding me we have a task to complete. I focus on the datapad. It takes a few more moments of digging through the documents before I find something useful: a detailed layout of the Court of Stars. Although maybe it would be more accurate to call it a fortress. A maze of corridors, halls and chambers. All under tight security.

'Well?' Capricorn presses, his fingers drumming a steady beat over his bicep. Clearly I've maxed out his patience quota for this sol. That makes two of us.

Pushing back the opening of my overcoat, I prop a hand on my hip. 'Who else has access to these chambers?'

It's a stupid question. One I already know the answer to before he gives it.

'The Twelve.'

'And security detail?'

'There are no guards if that's what you're asking. Humans are flawed creatures of wavering loyalty. We learned that a thousand years ago.' His hand flicks dismissively. 'Biosecurity, however, is unfailing. The entire palace is fitted with DNA-scanners. Only Celestials can pass through these halls without triggering the security systems.'

I manage to refrain from remarking that Aquarius's cadaver is evidence to the contrary. Clearly the Celestials, and their systems, are not nearly as perfect as they've deluded themselves to believe. But I'm not fool enough to provoke Capricorn by pointing this out. The Twelve aren't exactly known for their ability to be humble or understanding. Or compassionate, for that matter.

But the biosecurity does leave a very narrow list of suspects. Surely even Capricorn can see that? I'll need to send Tanith ahead to locate the remaining rulers if we're to speed up the process of elimination. My gaze flickers to her and she gives a small nod. She knows what she needs to do without me saying so.

Turning to Capricorn, I widen my stance in preparation for the resistance I'm no doubt about to face.

'And where are the other Houses now? We need to start conducting interviews and confirming alibis immediately.'

Capricorn's head tilts ever so slightly and it's not hard to imagine his eyes narrowing at me.

'You dare question us, *mortal*?' He hisses the word out as though it's sour on his tongue.

Stars...If only I had a mask like his to hide behind. I'm not entirely sure I can keep my expression neutral. This asshole takes *ant under boot* to a whole new level. I pinch the bridge of my nose and take a steadying breath. Focus. Just get the damn job done. I won't have to deal with this walking, talking piece of shit much longer.

'Your Grace.' I raise my chin and stare directly at the blank mask. 'The murder of one of the Twelve is something that should be impossible. At least, for a human. But perhaps not for one of you. Can you honestly account for the whereabouts of each House at the time of the death?'

He falls unnaturally still and I can practically hear the cogs grinding as he mulls over my question. If he wants this messy situation resolved, he'll have to swallow his pride and allow us to work.

It's a whole tense minute of him clenching and unclenching his fists before he concedes with a curt nod. 'You better be right Detective Ophidia. If you're wrong...'

He leaves the threat unspoken and begins tapping away at a device on his wrist.

Asshole.

Tanith takes this as permission to leave and begin conducting her search of the Court. She slips out through the main entrance and a door closes behind her with a soft click. My fingers instinctively seek my timepiece necklace to draw comfort. She'll be back. I trust her to take care of things on her end. I just have to concentrate on doing the same. This is the murder case to end all others and our names will go down in history if we get it right.

Capricorn finishes typing and addresses me. 'Don't make me regret this decision.'

He's marching toward a set of doors at the chamber's far end before I can respond. I run a hand through my hair and grimace before chasing after him. The datapad I drop into my coat pocket.

The entrance he approaches is not the one we came through on arrival, but another, leading deeper into the Court. One of many we now have his authorization to pass and investigate beyond.

The red-oak doorway is imposing with its floor to ceiling height. It's made more impressive by the House sigils—twelve exquisite carvings—that cover every inch. The level of craftmanship is unrivalled. From the soft woollen curls of the Aries ram, to the gleaming silver scales on Pisces's fish, no detail has been spared. The Twelve might believe themselves superior to humans in every way, but only a human has the capacity to create such masterpieces.

Capricorn presses a golden hand to the door handle and my attention snags on the carving below. A woman, her arms and legs flung wide, holding an ebony snake that circles around her. Not the first time I've seen this symbol. It's not uncommon on Earth and it stirs up an old, painful memory. My fingers itch to touch the image, trace along each dip and groove in the woodwork for a moment.

Then Capricorn shoves the door open with a groan of timber.

The carving swings out of sight. Only once the doors clunk to a stop does Capricorn stride into the sanctum beyond.

I'm not really sure what I expected to feel in this moment, but awe and reverence wouldn't have been my pick. I thought I'd fortified my heart against anything regarding the Twelve but there's something unmistakably sacred and otherworldly about the space that I can't deny.

Stepping over the threshold is like waking up from a coma and experiencing the world anew. Every sense is amplified and I not only smell the sweet, spicy fragrance of starlight, but feel and taste it. Warm and honeyed. Like my first ever bite of warm apple cinnamon pie. Like coming home.

I hardly know where to look first, but I drink it all in greedily. The sanctum is a large tridecagon—thirteen walls forming a near circle. The floors are silver-lit up from beneath, giving the appearance of moonlight shining through frosted glass. Enough light to see by, yet it keeps the room shrouded in shadows.

Each of the thirteen, white-marbled walls bleeds up into the darkness of a very real star-flecked sky where Capricorn's constellation currently shines. In the room's centre lies a mahogany table encircled by thirteen chairs—well, thrones. Hanging above, like a chandelier, is a gold orrery clock. Moving slowly; planets and moons rotating and spinning in a timeless dance around the sun.

But as eternal and enchanting as it all is, there's something odd that's captured my attention.

Thirteen. Not twelve.

Thirteen seats and thirteen walls.

And let's not forget the thirteenth symbol carved on the entry door: the familiar serpentine image. Anyone with half a brain can see it doesn't add up.

'Who is this?' A woman's sultry voice cuts through my assessment.

I should've noticed them milling about in the shadows and plucking at a table overloaded with ambrosia. There are four of them—Pisces, Libra, Virgo, and Scorpio—all dressed in the regalia of the Houses. Resplendent, immaculate, untouchable white.

It's a joke, really. If corruption has a colour, it's definitely white. No other colour stains as easily.

Capricorn stalks past everyone and takes his place at the table, folding his arms and legs in the same manner that a toddler stomps its foot. He makes no comment on the absent other Houses. Interesting.

'This is Detective Ophidia. She's here to investigate Aquarius's murder.'

All their eerie, faceless masks round on me with unnerving focus. My chin inches a little higher. I refuse to cower before them.

'You allowed a mortal here? Have you taken leave of your senses?' Scorpio demands, his silver goblet dimpling under the pressure of his thick fingers.

Capricorn's hands curl into fists. 'Watch your tongue, brother. I have no more love for this situation then you but this mess won't solve itself. The detective thinks that one of us is the culprit.'

Virgo laughs, a sound that is more caustic than melodic. 'And you believe her? You are many things Capricorn, but a fool is not one of them. Now be done with this nonsense and send her away. She smells too much of mortal filth.' They fall to arguing amongst themselves.

I'm not at all surprised that they're not taking this seriously. They're more concerned with me intruding in their space and interrupting their shallow lives than with the death of one of their own.

My pocket buzzes so I draw out my datapad and open the message from Tanith.

Tanith: Aries asphyxiated in bedchamber. Message left at scene suggests Taurus, Gemini, and Cancer are deceased as well.

A second message comes immediately after.

Tanith: Also, I thought you might want to see this... Open attachment

The attached image fills the screen. Another message, scrawled in blood, upon a wall. Only, instead of words, it's a symbol. Similar to the one I spied on the door: a circling serpent, mouth on tail. A crude image of a woman in the centre.

Shit. There's no more time to waste.

'Your Graces,' I say, raising my voice to cut through theirs. 'I'm afraid things have escalated. The sooner this interview begins, the sooner it ends.' I gesture to the seats around the table and hope they'll cooperate.

I don't mention the most recent list of victims, though I'm interested in gauging their reactions to the news. I have some more pressing questions that need answering before I deal with that.

Their heated arguing simmers down with the reminder of my presence. They clearly have no love for each other, but they're all unified in their distaste for me. They're eager to have me gone, so they take seats. Five out of thirteen.

Thirteen...

Chasing my prior observation, I circle around the table following the order of the Houses, mentally tallying as I go. Aquarius (dead), Pisces, Aries (dead), Taurus (dead), Gemini (dead), Cancer (dead), Leo (dead), Virgo, Libra, Scorpio, Sagittarius (dead), Capricorn and...

I stop before the thirteenth throne, leaning past it to better examine the constellation—gold, obsidian, and diamonds—inlayed into the wood. The shape of a woman inside a circling snake. It's beautiful but so ridiculously over-polished that my reflection glowers back at me from the shiny surface. There's a rich earthen scent to the timber. One that might be alluring to someone with expensive tastes. I find it to be rather musty and outdated.

'Who sits here?' I ask.

Virgo spies where my attention has fallen and her clear-water voice fills the sanctum.

'That's the seat of Ophiuchus—the Serpent Bearer—the Thirteenth House.'

My gaze snaps to her. She's apparently more invested in scrutinizing the polish of her nails than in this investigation, but her information is a step in the right direction.

'But there's no record of a Thirteenth House,' I argue.

'Of course not. Ophiuchus was denounced long ago. Her power was stripped away and the name erased from all records.' She explains with an air of boredom.

'Why?'

'I fail to see how this information correlates to your investigation,' Scorpio cuts in.

He fails to see a great many things. All of the remaining Twelve do. Their heads are so far up their own arses they don't understand the shit they're in.

Stars! I'm going to need my teeth checked out after this is over. It can't be good how much I'm grinding them. My fingers find purchase on the cool metal timepiece hanging around my neck, helping to centre me and clear my focus. I need a level head right now.

'Because, your Grace, of the messages left behind at the crime scenes. The one above Aquarius: *Begin anew, never again.* That refers to the Ouroboros.' My gaze narrows on the constellation before the thirteenth seat. Ophiuchus. The Serpent Bearer.

I frown. But, throughout history, Ouroboros has always been set apart from the Court; with no separate symbol or sigil. The Serpent, itself. Devouring its own tail in an eternal cycle of beginnings and endings, death and rebirth. Almost-forgotten guardian of time.

'Now,' I say, 'you tell me there's a Thirteenth House known as the Serpent Bearer and I'm not supposed to question a possible connection? If the Serpent Bearer partnered with the Serpent Ouroborus, not only would they have the ability to bypass your bio-security to commit the murder but they have a motive too.' I smile thinly. 'You did throw the Thirteenth House out, after all.'

There's a subtle shift in the room's atmosphere and, for the first time, they appear uneasy. I watch each of them closely, assessing their reactions with interest.

Pisces is the first to speak. 'Don't be ridiculous. They've both been gone a millennia or more.' But he exchanges a swift look with Capricorn.

Capricorn's blank face turns to me. 'Wait. You said crime *scenes…*'

Guess the cat's out of the bag. I pull up the last message on my datapad and project it for everyone to see.

Libra gasps. 'That's not possible…'

'What about Sagittarius and Leo? Everyone was called to the sanctum, but they haven't shown,' Virgo points out, her voice a tad higher than before.

'I've sent Tanith to go track them down. Now…' My thumb grazes the bezel of my timepiece. 'Tell me why the Bearer was banished?'

The five share a collective glance, clearly deciding how much information to reveal in light of the growing list of deceased. It must be grating every nerve that they have to tell me even the smallest secrets, but they have little choice if they wish to save their own skins.

'Ophiuchus was…not like us,' Pisces begins. 'One of the Houses in the Court of Stars, yes. But Ophiuchus preferred to spend time amongst the mortals, rather than here at court with us.'

The corner of my lip twitches. 'Oh, yes, strange indeed. But hardly a crime.'

'Ophiuchus's crime was sedition and heresy!' Capricorn snaps. 'She disagreed with our governance of the mortals. Called us tyrants and oppressors. Said we'd lost our way. That ruling meant we were supposed to take care of the people!' Capricorn sneers. 'As if giving order to your chaotic lives wasn't enough!'

'We let the insults slide for a time,' Libra adds as though she genuinely believes it was gracious of them to do so.

Scorpio says, 'But then Ophiuchus began rallying the humans together to form the Millennium rebellion. Even tried to get Ouroboros involved—the one Celestial supposed to be outside of everything. Ophiuchus wanted to tear down what we'd established.' He smacks his goblet down, spilling gold wine over the table. 'Ungrateful wretches.'

'So that was that,' Pisces finishes. 'We stripped Ophiuchus of her power and banished her to the Abyss.'

I narrow my eyes. There is *so* much more to the story. They're either knowingly omitting details or they never cared enough to remember and I don't know which option infuriates me more.

'And the humans who rebelled?' I'm impressed my voice

doesn't crack given how hard my shoulders are shaking, 'What you did to them after…' My fingers clamp on my timepiece. 'The word slaughter hardly seems to suffice. It was the near-extinction of humankind!'

'How do you know that?' Capricorn demands. 'That was a millennia ago and the records—'

'Were wiped?' I interject with a hiss. 'Yes, I know…It's kind of in my job description to find things others try to hide. But that's inconsequential. What I really want to know is—'

A knock on the door cuts me off. The heavy panels split and golden light from the hall beyond filters in for a brief second. Tanith steps into the room. It's hard to make out in chamber's starry gloom but her usually-flawless sable suit appears darker in patches, like she's been splattered in something.

It's a relief to see her and I feel it from shoulders to toes as the tension leaves my muscles.

'Ah, you made it. Did you find Leo and Sagittarius?' I ask.

With raised eyebrows, she surveys the room: wall to wall, floor to ceiling. She appears to be as curious and bewildered with it all as I was.

'Well?' Scorpio barks, tapping his index finger against his chair arm.

Tanith's tawny-eyed attention slides to him, her expression turning cold. But it's her voice—soft and wispy from disuse, with the hint of bite—that seems to freeze him.

'Oh, I found them, alright.' She flicks her onyx curls over one shoulder.

'Where are they?' Pisces asks, sounding understandably confused.

But Tanith ignores the question. She shifts her weight from side to side in an almost hypnotic manner, her attention rivetted on me as she waits for my instructions.

I guess the game is up.

No more pretending.

My heart flutters. I'm trembling as I lightly stroke the top of Ophiuchus's throne. Like everything else that's beautiful in the world, the throne was crafted by humans. With sweaty, calloused, perfectly imperfect hands. My heart warms with fondness and my fingers tighten with purpose.

The snake-head feet scrape loudly as I pull the chair back. It's so satisfying watching the remaining Twelve cringe.

But not nearly as satisfying as finally taking my seat.

'How dare you, *mortal*!' Scorpio splutters.

I roll my eyes. 'You don't even know who I am.' I lay my feet on the tabletop and cross them there, just to piss him off.

Tanith takes this as her signal and moves toward the table.

One.

Slow.

Step.

After.

Another.

A funeral march.

Each click of her heels counts down to the moment of revelation. None of the others mark her movements, their attention is locked on me: The one who has rattled their perfect little web. Except I'm not the worthless insect they were expecting.

I let out an exaggerated sigh for dramatic effect. 'Honestly, I'm disappointed you didn't work it out. Though I suppose it has been a long time since we saw each other last. And I guess you thought I was dead. You tried hard enough, after all.'

One by one, understanding dawns on them.

Capricorn exhales through clenched teeth. 'Ophiuchus.'

'It's Ophidia now, if you don't mind.' I retort, crossing my arms.

'You!' Scorpio slams his palm against the table then stabs an accusing finger at me. 'You killed Aquarius and the others! How could you do that to your own?'

'I think that should be obvious by now.' I flick a dust smote from my coat sleeve.

'Murderous human-lover!' Virgo screams, her voice echoing loudly across the marble walls. Libra anxiously digs her long fingers into her chair, her masked gaze alternating between each speaker.

Pisces's calm façade cracks, much like his voice as he asks, 'H-how did you escape the Abyss?'

'A great question.' I applaud mockingly. 'Well, I had some help.'

I raise my timepiece for them to see. The metal casing pirouettes slowly on its silver chain, revealing the well-worn engraving on its cover. An image of the Ouroboros, the Serpent; gold eyes and jet body barely visible.

'Striped of power and separated from my friends. Banished to a place no mortal could reach.' I shrugged. You thought I had no hope of escape. So did I.' Bitter mirth curls my lips. 'I spent a long, *long* time just staring into the depths of the universe. But the thing about the Abyss is, when you stare into it long enough, eventually something looks back. That's when Tanith here found me.' I pointed at my assistant. My friend. My co-conspirator.

Tanith glides over and takes up vigil at my right. No one speaks but I can tell they're finally taking note of her. Uneasy awareness creeps into every one of them. They're afraid.

Good.

They should be.

Even without the blood splattered all over her, the inhuman and unnaturally graceful movements should trigger anyone's warning bells.

I shift in my seat and turn to share a wicked grin with Tanith. 'Or maybe I should call you, Ouroboros?'

Capricorn jumps to his feet, his head shaking frantically. 'N-no!''

Libra hugs herself and begins weeping. Pisces makes an awkward choking sound and the other two are frozen still.

Without further preamble Tanith sheds her human guise like an old skin. It splits and peels away, giving birth to a large obsidian serpent with slitted gold eyes. Her head rises high above, her forked tongue darting out to taste the fear tainting the air.

I lean back in my seat, taking it all in. It's been a long time coming but we finally did it. Made it back to where it all began; to where it will all end. There will be no more Court of Stars, no more Ascendant Houses and their ruthless domination of those who live Below. It's time for a new beginning.

'Begin anew, never again,' I whisper.

And the Ouroboros uncoils and strikes.

#

END

The Fastest Bum in the West

Jan-Andrew Henderson

Once upon a time, there were three brothers who ran a building yard in Ipswich. Their names were Wiggly, Bob, and Fugly Mutterfunk, and they had a young stepbrother called Boring Norman, because his job was drilling holes in planks. At least, that's what they told him.

Everyone complained they were cowboys, so the brothers decided they'd better act the part, not wanting to disappoint their customers.

Business was brisk for, whenever the trio ran out of work, they'd drive around in a pickup truck, breaking windows and knocking down lampposts.

Then, one day, the annual Line Dance and Rodeo came to town. Wiggly read about it in the local paper, which he had borrowed from his next door neighbour's letter box. He also borrowed the letter box, so he could go over and fix it when his neighbour grumbled about the draught.

'Says here there's prize of a wooden koala for the person who can stay on a mechanical bull longest!' he roared. 'Bet I can win that!'

'And just how do you figure to beat me?' Bob retorted. 'I'll be entering too.'

'I'm gonna superglue my bum to the saddle.' Wiggly pulled an economy sized tube of adhesive from inside his trousers, where he kept it to impress the checkout girls at the Coles supermarket.

'Darn! That's pretty clever.' Bob scanned the shelves of their office and grabbed a jar of nails. 'I'll just have to use these.'

'You can't hammer them into your butt!' his brothers gasped.

'I know. I was gonna nail you two in the coal cellar.'

The door opened and Boring Norman entered. He wore an apron that said *Kiss Me Quick, 'Cause I Smell*, and chicken slippers—which had been birthday presents from his brothers. Norman would have liked the slippers better if they hadn't been made from his pet chooks.

'Hi guys,' he said. 'I've ironed your Stetsons and polished your air guns. Remember that they're not toys, so use them in a responsible and safety conscious manner. I've only got two birds left.'

'Ehmmm. One actually,' Fugly replied. 'I sold the other to our neighbour. He's using it to block a hole in his door, where his letterbox was, till I get round to sorting it.'

'I rescued those chooks from a bag floating in the river.' Norman pouted. 'Someone saw three reprobates in weird hats throw it off a bridge.'

'There you go using big words again,' Bob scowled. 'Anyone would think we let you go to school.'

'Right, stepbrother.' Wiggly ran a comb through his moustache, then fastened the hairy strip to his face using the superglue. 'We're off to the Line Dance. When we come back, we want the longhorns dry-cleaned.'

'And all the grazing land mowed,' Bob added.

'Don't you think you're taking this cowboy thing a bit far?' Norman glanced out of the window where his last chicken was hopping around miserably with a pair of plastic horns attached to its head. 'We don't actually have cows or a ranch. We've only got a back yard and it's concrete.'

'Yeah…well…Just have a snack ready when we get back! Nothing fancy.' Wiggly turned to his brothers. 'Gophers?'

They nodded vigorously

'Yup. Gophers. Gophers on toast.'

'Ehm...This is Queensland, remember?' Norman reminded them. 'There aren't any gophers in—'

'Or we could always have chicken soup.'

'You want your gophers grilled or deep fried?' Norman sighed. 'I'll check at Aldi.'

'Sautéed.' Bob patted his cheeks. 'You know I have sensitive gums.'

'Can't I come to the Line Dance with you?' Norman pleaded. 'I've done all the housework, hosed down the beds and even cleaned your toilet.' He thought for a moment. 'I'll need to get more industrial solvent from the supermarket too.'

'Of course not,' Fugly scoffed. 'Line Dancin' is for proper men.'

'Seriously?'

'Of course,' Bob bristled. 'Men with leather chaps, tight jeans and big droopy moustaches, like the ones we just stuck on.'

'You fastened it to your knee.'

'I got sensitive lips too.'

'Anyway, you ain't a proper man.' Fugly laughed. 'You can't

burp like us.'

'You can't shoot like us,' Wiggly added. 'And you can't ride like us.'

'That's because you ride in taxis and I don't get paid.' Norman wouldn't give up. 'I want a shot at the real thing. To win first prize on the mechanical bull!'

'Yeah?' Wiggly slapped his stepbrother on the forehead. 'If you're such a great rider, how come we never see you on a horse?'

'Cause we live in the middle of a city.'

'What about Potters Park?' Fugly suggested. 'It's just round the corner.'

'That's a car park.'

'Aw, stop nit-picking.'

'I know you won't let me go because I'm just a kid.' Norman looked soulfully at his stepbrothers. 'And you don't want me to get injured. But I'd be fine. Honest.'

'Don't be silly, Norman.' Bob patted his shoulder. 'We're not letting you go because we hate you.'

'If we thought you'd really get hurt,' Wiggly added. 'We'd chip in for your cab fare.'

'How about if I go to the Line Dance and don't tell you, eh?' Norman pulled a face. 'What would you do then?'

'Since you've just told us, we'd most probably shoot you.'

'Oh!' Norman fastened his apron more tightly. 'I suddenly remembered. I have to iron the carpet. You three have fun.'

#

Norman was in a very bad mood. He desperately wanted to go to the Line Dance but he didn't have a horse or a shooting iron. All he had was an ironing iron, which was now stuck to the carpet because Wiggly had spilled glue over the floor while applying it to his buttocks.

Norman knew if he could only enter that competition he'd surely win the wooden koala. He'd stay on that mechanical bull so long he'd have to take a packed lunch.

He'd become famous as *the fastest bum in the west.* Then girls would swoon and make kissy faces at him

But what was the use? He had as much chance of going to the Line Dance as a porcupine had of getting into a pair of tights.

While he sat gloomily on the couch, he heard the sound of approaching hoof beats. There was a loud crash outside and a masked man, wearing a gold lame outfit covered in sequins, burst through the door. Norman was temporarily blinded by his clothing.

'Greetings,' the stranger announced. 'My name ees Don Delmonte Los Trios Paranoia Delfuego el Mantovani the Third. I juss move een next door.'

'And you *rode* over to say hello? It's only ten yards.'

'I was een a hurry. I need to borrow a letterbox for mine seems to be meesing.'

'A common occurrence round here,' Norman admitted. 'My brothers can probably fix it, but they'll charge you an arm and a leg.'

'Ah. I had 15 brozzer's of my own, all with deefferent mothers.' The stranger gave a sigh. 'We are a poor family and have donated so many body parts, there are now ony twelve of us combined.'

He hesitated. 'Choo look sad. Ees it because of your face?'

'It's because *my* brozzers won't let me go to the Line Dance. They say I'm too wimpy to be a cowboy.'

'I can see their point.' Don turned to leave and Norman's lip quivered. The brightly clad stranger rolled his eyes. 'Ah... but what the hey! Choo can come wid *me* to the line dance. If choo don't mind riding bare back.'

'Can't I keep my t-shirt on?' Norman asked. 'I don't want to get sunburn.'

'Sure. I'll put an extra saddle on my hores.'

'That's not very PC.'

'Hores! That choo ride. Mine ees called Dobbin.com.au Ees an eco-friendly alternative to Uber.' He slapped Norman on the back. 'You might even ween the wooden koala!'

'I got no chance of weening anything,' Norman sobbed. 'I'm not a real cowboy. The closest I ever got to America was when my stepbrothers pushed me into the sea at Moreton Bay. I don't have a hat or waistcoat or cowboy boots.'

'Poor kid. I see I got here just in time.' The man's accent swiftly changed. 'Son. It takes more than a big water pistol to fill a ten gallon hat, whatever that means.' He drew himself up to his full height of five foot two and thumped his chest. 'A *true* cowboy has something wonderful here.'

'Nipples?'

'A pure heart, Norma.'

'It's Norman.'

'Your stepbrothers?' Don waved his hand dismissively, unleashing a cloud of sequins. 'They can never be true cowboys. Not if they ate so many gophers they felt like inside-out fur coats. Only a true cowboy can win at the rodeo, Normal.'

'My brothers won it last year.' Norman picked glitter out of his eye. 'They beat up the other competitors.'

'Really want the outfit, huh?'

'Couldn't hurt.'

'Something like mine?' Don did a quick pirouette and tripped over the iron.

'Maybe a little more subtle.' Norman picked him up. 'You look like a heavily armed chandelier.'

'O.K. I'll see what I can rustle up.' Don waggled his eyebrows. 'Rustle! Get it?

'Ehm... Yeah.' Norman regarded him suspiciously. 'What's happened to your voice, by the way? Just who are you?'

'Son. I have many names.'

'I know. You strung them all together a minute ago. 'Don' is the only bit I remember.'

'Fine by me.' The stranger shrugged. 'I may look like an exploded diamond mine, but I specialize in saving damsels in distress. They love an exotic accent.'

'In case you hadn't noticed, I'm a bloke.'

'I know. I went to the wrong house.'

'Thank God for that.' Norman clasped his hands together and sank to his knees. 'Please say you'll help me.'

'You can help yourself, son.' Don hauled him up by the hair. 'All you have to do is close your peepers and sing a little song.'

'A little song?'

'A magic song!'

'Oh, God.'

But the stranger was his only hope, so Norman shut his eyes. Don pulled a scrap of paper from his pocket and held it up.

'Sing that.'

'My eyes are closed.'

'Then open one!' Don thrust the paper into his hand. 'Jeez, I can't half pick 'em.'

Norman squinted at the verse and began to croon.

Riding West across the heather

I like guns and I like leather
When at night my horse I tether
If he's cold we sleep together.
Yipee aye yip, yip yippee, yip yippy
Those rattlesnakes are long and slippy.

While Norman mused on this literary gem, Don had time to run out and buy a cowboy outfit from Mr Toys.

Norman had once taken a poetry course at Springfield town hall, though he'd actually gone to do pottery and misread the sign on the door.

'Hmmmmm...Should be "them rattlesnakes",' he said when Don strolled back through the door. 'Gives the verse a more authentic western air than "those rattlesnakes". More "bite" if you like. Pardon the literary pun, but I do feel it fits the metaphor the poet intended.'

He looked down and noticed a pile of clothes on the floor.

'Hey, what a neat trick!' He handed Don back his paper. 'I don't like the meter in this either.'

'Will you forget that and get your kit on!' his companion snapped.

Norman did as he was told. The hat and waistcoat looked a bit small and cheap, but that's because they were made of cardboard. And the footwear was a little odd too.

'These aren't cowboy boots,' the boy objected. 'They're Wellingtons.'

'Son. There ain't any cattle for ten miles,' Don pointed out. 'It *has* started raining though.'

He drew his gun and passed it over. 'Lastly, here is a pistol.'

'But this is yours!' Norman was genuinely touched.

'That's O.K. It doesn't work.' Don put both hands sternly on his hips. 'Remember now. You can only keep this lovely matching hat and holster set if you uphold the first law of the cowpoke.'

'Lose half my teeth and learn to play a banjo?' Norman waved the gun around maniacally.

'Nope. Be loyal, noble and true...and like poking cows.' There was a wistful look in Don's eyes, though it might have been fumes from the superglue. 'Living life in the saddle can be hard and painful, young man. Especially on your bum. My bum is always sore, Normous.'

'Is it as hard and painful as washing my stepbrother's underwear?' Norman asked. 'Underwear they only take off after three months working on the building site?'

'No. Not nearly as hard and painful as that.'

'I guess I'll go for it, then.'

'I'm proud of you, boy. Next, we need a secret identity, so your brothers won't recognise you at the Line Dance.' Don stroked his chin. 'First thing is a proper western name. Y'know, something like Billy the Kid. Got any ideas?

'Rupert the Bear?'

'Try a handle that's a tad more masculine.'

'Techno-Destructor Guy?'

'Not cowboyee enough.' Don tapped his lip thoughtfully. 'How about the Cinderella Kid?'

'Say, *what* now?'

'It's a bit gauche but I think it's you. And for the final part of your disguise?' He searched in his pockets. 'Here we are!'

'It's a pair of glasses.'

'Worked for Superman.' Don plonked the spectacles on Norman's nose. 'Wow! Your own parents wouldn't recognise you.'

'I'm not surprised.' The boy's lip quivered again. 'I lost my mum and dad in a boating accident.'

'What happened?' Don didn't much look like he cared.

'I went to the corner store to buy a packet of Tim Tams. When I came back, they had accidentally gone on a world cruise.'

'Never mind, Normo. They live in the hearts of all righteous cowboys, and in the rocks and trees besides.'

'Actually, they live in Bundaberg. They just won't tell me the address.'

'Whatever.' Don adjusted his mask, which kept slipping down his nose. 'Now follow me! Hi ho, Dobbin.com.au!'

There was a worried neighing sound from outside. Taking several ballet leaps, Don vanished out of the door

'This guy definitely has a few stitches loose on his gun belt.' Norman leaned out of the window and gave a piercing whistle.

'Taxi!'

#

Just before midnight, Norman was back, in a state of panic, closely followed by Don.

'What are you playing at?' Don railed. 'You won the competition! I got so bored watching I went to get us a couple of sherbet dib-dabs. Next thing I know, you and my horse are on the Buzz bus and heading back into town.'

'I saw my stepbrothers taking off in their truck. They'll have a couple of cheese daiquiris at Madam Benbecula's House of Fluff, then be back here, pissed off their faces.'

'They can't hold their drink?'

'No. They got tiny hands like Donald Trump.' Norman sighed. 'Last time I didn't get my chores done before they arrived, they put Lego in my underpants and sat me on top of the spin dryer.'

'Son. That's more information than I needed to know.'

Norman looked down at his feet. 'Hey! I took off in such a hurry, I left one of my Wellingtons stuck in the mud outside Sweaty Benny's Burger Bin.'

'*What*? I borrowed these boots from Chief Break-Um-Knees All Night Camping Barn!' Don gave a groan. 'He can bring down a charging buffalo using his forehead. If I don't get them back he'll be using my scrotum pole as a totem pole.'

'And that's more information than *I* needed to know.'

'Stay here and try not to breathe.' Don ran off to retrieve the missing footwear.

Norman removed his outfit, threw it in the washing machine, grabbed a broom and started sweeping. He could hear his brothers approaching.

'Who was that masked man we passed outside?' Fugly asked. 'He looked like Liberace on a horse.'

'Beats me,' Norman replied innocently. 'How was the Line Dance?'

All three pointed their guns at him.

'Or we could talk about something else entirely....'

'Let's talk about why this place isn't properly cleaned up,' Wiggly snarled.

'And why supper isn't ready.' Fugly peered in the oven. 'There's nothing in here but three hot dogs. I bought em from the pet store yesterday and they still ain't done.'

'I could only get frozen gophers,' Norman explained. 'They're thawing right now. How come you guys are in such a bad mood?'

'We didn't win the prize for staying on the mechanical bull.' Fugly's face was black as thunder, though it was probably soot from the oven. 'Some bespectacled stranger did.'

'When we find him,' Bob warned. 'We'll show him a use for a pair of spurs he *never* considered.'

'Ummmm...' Norman said nervously. 'You don't happen to know who it was?'

'He looked like the Milky Bar kid with acne,' Wiggly replied. 'But he left before we could kill him.'

'I'm so mad I could shoot my own granny.' Fugly wiped his face with a half cooked Daschund. 'If I hadn't done it already.' He patted his stomach. 'I'll eat. I always eat when I'm depressed.' He sighed. 'What it must be doing to my waistline...'

'Sure you wouldn't like a Rice Cracker instead?' Norman rummaged in the bread bin.

'No. Get those gophers now!'

Norman grabbed a handful of thawing rodents from the fridge. They were so rigid, he could hold their tails and call them hairy popsicles.

'I don't think they're quite ready.'

'Right!' Bob drew his pistol. 'I'm gonna to plug him.'

'He hasn't washed the dishes yet,' Wiggly cautioned. 'Just hit him in the arm.'

'OK.' Fugly squinted at Norman. 'You right or left handed?'

'You mean you'd shoot your own brother?' the boy gasped.

'I don't have a problem with that.'

'You don't?' Bob and Wiggly glared at Fugly.

'Not you two!' Fugly stammered. 'I mean him!' He rounded on Norman. 'Oooooooh! Trying to cause trouble between me and my brothers who I love almost as much as gophers on toast! I *am* gonna to kill you!

He pointed the pistol at Norman's head. The boy held the tray in front of his face, three frozen gophers still stuck to the surface. Fugly aimed at his leg instead. Norman moved the tray down.

'Stop moving that around or I'll shoot you!'

'You're trying to shoot me anyway!' Norman tried to climb into the bin. 'You're not thinking this through!'

There was a ring at the door. And if there was one thing Bob hated, it was being interrupted. Before anyone could stop him, he turned and fired.

BANG!

There was a thump from outside.

Wiggly ran to the door and opened it. 'Yikes! You killed the mailman.'

'That's OK. All we ever get is bills.' Bob stared at his gun in puzzlement. 'Besides, I'm a terrible shot.'

'You're right.' Fugly poked at the body. 'Looks like he electrocuted himself on the doorbell.'

'I told you to get a battery for it.' Wiggly threw up his hands. 'But, oh no, you thought it would be cheaper to hook the whole thing up to the mains.'

'I got an idea!' Bob giggled. 'Let's take the body to Woolies supermarket and hide it in one of the freezers. We can lock a little kid in with it!'

'Yeah! One with claustrophobia!'

'We'll tell his mother we saw him go off in a car with two strangers.'

Norman grinned and murmured. 'Those brothers of mine. Scamps. You can't help liking them.'

Suddenly, there was the sound of a siren growing closer. The brothers ran around in panic, then took up karate stances—all being masters at Who-Flung-Dung.

'It's the law!' Fugly looked out of the window. 'We gotta hide the evidence.'

The stepbrothers grabbed the body and pulled it through the house. Wiggly tried to shoot Norman on the way past, but it was hard to do while dragging a dead mailman.

The three brothers rushed back into the room and stood around, trying to appear innocent—which was about as convincing as a drunk ostrich striving to look dainty. The door burst open and in came two policeman.

'Howdy, ya cow-tippin varmints.' The leader was short and wore glasses. 'I'm Sheriff Cornobbler and this is my deputy Slim.'

The stepbrothers gazed at him disbelievingly.

'Those uniforms look like they came from a toy store.' Fugly said. 'And Slim is fat.'

'The correct term is big boned,' Slim sulked.

'Whatever you say.' Bob shrugged. 'Care for a cup of tea while you waste our time?'

'I ain't a drinking man, hombre.' The sheriff plonked himself in an armchair. 'Don't even touch water.'

He grabbed a frozen gopher off the tray next to him, holding it by the tail.

'But I'll take one of these here ice lollies. I'm hotter than a skunk curry after all the chasing around I bin doing.'

Norman wisely stayed silent as the sheriff took a lick and picked a few hairs off his tongue.

'I'm lookin for a boy who left the rodeo without collectin the wooden koala. He was in disguise but left his specs behind. I'm wearin 'em right now, which is why I can't actually see who I'm talking to.'

He stretched his legs out and massaged them. 'I been to every bus stop, bottle shop and vegan restaurant in this town. Me and Slim got saddle sores on our bums the size of grapefruits. Wanna see?'

'Not in the slightest,' Bob muttered. 'Seems a lot of trouble to go to for a wooden koala, though.'

'And $20,000 prize money.'

'Oh.' Bob's jaw dropped. 'Well, I *was* that bespectacled man. Coincidentally.'

'Actually, I think you'll find it was me.' Wiggly pushed him out of the way. 'I just now put my contact lenses in.'

'Sheriff, the only disguises these two ever wore was when they were robbing the local K-Mart.' Fugly elbowed his way forwards. '*I* am that too-modest prize-winner.'

'There's one other way of finding the true identity of our mystery man.' The Sheriff pulled a Wellington boot from inside his trousers

'*That* was a rather disturbing trick.' Wiggly goggled. 'Beats a tube of superglue any day.'

'He left his wellie behind, as well,' the lawman continued. 'Whoever tries this on, an it fits, wins the prize.'

The stepbrothers began yanking off their boots. Norman snapped on a surgical mask. The air filled with a smell like a month old prawn cocktail in an Egyptian boiler room.

'I gotta admit...' The sheriff held his nose. '...that tootsie odour is certainly excessive.'

'S'cuse me.' Slim put a hand over his mouth and ran for the bathroom.

'Boot!' Wiggly held out a hand and the sheriff tossed the Wellington from a reasonably safe distance.

The brothers tugged and pulled but none of them could get the boot to fit.

'Maybe if I took my socks off as well,' Bob suggested.

'I believe that's against the Geneva Convention.' The lawman yanked the Wellington back. 'Looks like you sheep-shimmyin grease weasels is outta luck.'

'Hey!' Norman broke in. 'What about me?'

'You!' The brothers chuckled. 'Don't make us laugh. Oh. Too late.'

'I *am* supposed to try everyone,' the sheriff shrugged. 'Even this obvious loser.'

He threw the boot to Norman, while his stepbrothers hooted and jeered. None of them noticed he had been wearing one identical Wellington the whole time.

Norman pulled it on.

'See? A perfect fit.'

'Well... stick a rattler in my pasta and call it a noisy noodle.' The sheriff scratched his head. 'You win, son.'

'I'll have my money in traveller's cheques, please!' Norman did a little dance. 'You can post my pyjamas to the Bahamas!'

'Now I'm REALLY gonna kill him.' Bob pulled out his gun.

'This boy is now under my protection, lads.' The lawman waved him back. 'The fact that I'd like to step on him then scrape him back off don't affect that.'

'Insult me all you like,' Norman grinned. 'I'm rich.'

'All right, pea brain,' the sheriff shrugged. 'Ready to go, Slim?

'Absolutely.' Slim appeared back in the room. 'I tried to throw up in the toilet but a dead mailman in the bath put me off.'

'Oh, my.' The sheriff folded his arms. 'Unless that's a family heirloom, I'm gonna have to run y'all in.'

'Yeah?' Wiggly leapt to his feet. 'Eat lead, gopher licker!'

The stepbrothers went for their guns, and the air was filled with flying lead. When the smoke had cleared, Norman, Slim and the

Sheriff were completely unhurt.

'Told you I was a rotten shot,' Bob groaned.

'Jeez.' The sheriff patted himself. 'When hunting season rolls round, entire forests must flock to *your* back yard.'

The brothers dropped their weapons and ran out of the door. There was a loud crash outside and a surprised whinnying.

'Aren't you going to go after them?' Norman turned to the sheriff.

'I think you'll find they're embedded in my horse.' He removed his glasses and Norman gave a gasp.

'*Don*?'

'Told you they worked as a disguise.' Don jerked a thumb at Slim. 'This is actually my associate, Fats.'

'I don't mind being called Slim, though.' Fats blushed. 'I think it suits me.'

'Thanks for saving me, guys.' Norman shook their hands warmly. 'I guess I'll just take my £20 000 and be off.'

'I'm shocked, Nomad!' Don's face fell. 'I thought you wanted to be a cowboy? A cowboy's life is supposed be one of self-sacrifice and pain, not flaunting your large assets in front of dusky Mexican beach attendants. You have a hard and windy path to take.'

'I'd rather just take the money.'

'Buddy.' Fats massaged his large butt. 'That money should go to the Bellbowrie Institute for Research into the Treatment of Incurable Anal Sores. After a few years on a horse you'll be glad you used it for that end.'

'Nice use of the double entendre there, partner.' Don nodded.

'You're right!' Norman slapped his knee. 'I don't need the money! From now on it's the open range for me, with the steer as my friend and a cow pat as my pillow.

'That's the spirit.'

'Goodbye masked man. I don't suppose I'll ever remember your name.' Norman gave Don a cowboy salute and disappeared into the sunset.

'Sure you will.' Don pocketed the $20,000. 'It's gonna be on plenty of wanted posters, come morning.'

That's a bit mean.' Fats raised an eyebrow. 'He won the prize fair and square. Leave him half the money.'

'*What?*'

'Do the right thing, buddy.'

'How do you know he'll even come back?' Don complained.

'It's raining and he's only wearing underpants.'

'You're too nice Fats, know that?'

'Call me Slim again. I really like Slim.'

'How about a compromise.' Don grinned. 'Fat Boy Slim?'

'How about I give you a punch in the kisser?'

'I take back what I said about you being nice.' Don counted out half the cash and stuck it on top of the oven. 'Never mind. There are plenty more suckers out there to con.'

Fat's glared at him.

'I mean, plenty more innocent victims who need our help.'

'That's better.'

And off they went, singing their cowboy song.

#

END

About the Authors

The Springfield Writers Group. Established in 2016, the Springfield Writers Group (SWG) is based in Brisbane, Australia. This group of emerging and established writers meet monthly over coffee and too many muffins to support each other's work and efforts toward becoming better writers. There is probably too much time spent laughing and enjoying each other's company, but we do get some work done as well. This anthology represents many months of work, learning, frustration, and joy.

Anyone wishing to contact the SWG can connect through the Queensland Writers Centre, who will forward information.

Our Authors...

Sam Brown writes crime fiction and sci-fi in smoky back-room bars and gin joints, splitting infinitives and spitting tobacco. Her stories are populated with scoundrels, hustlers, whores, and grifters...and those are the goodguys.
Find her online at **www.sirenofbrixton.wordpress.com**

Annie Bucknall is a freelance writer and emerging novelist whose work has featured in some of Australia's best-loved magazines. She loves writing about issues relating to women, parenting, and the environment. She lives with her husband, son, and labradoodles.
Follow her and her gorgeous labradoodles here:
Facebook or Instagram: @AnnieBucknall

Mandy Chandler Former scientist, Mandy has gone rogue and turned her hand to authoring in this, her first published fiction story. When she's not writing, you'll find her wandering the hills of Springfield with her furry sidekick, Hunny (who may be part unicorn)

Website: **https://www.facebook.com/mandychandlerauthor/**

Neen Cohen Neen Cohen is an LGBTQI and spec-fic Aussie author whose heart has always been in making art out of dead trees with squiggles of ink and graphite. Neen loves to roam cemeteries and botanic gardens and can be found writing while sitting against a tree or tombstone.

Blog: **https://wordbubblesite.wordpress.com/**

FB page: **https://www.facebook.com/Neen-Cohen-Author-424700821629629**

Instagram: **https://www.instagram.com/neenauthor/**

Twitter: @CohenNeen

Aiki Flinthart has 16 published novels, including the popular YA fantasy series *80AD,* plus two fantasy/urban fantasy trilogies *(The Kalima Chronicles; Shadows)*. And a non-fiction book *Fight like a Girl—writing fight scenes for female characters.* She has been shortlisted in the Aurealis awards and top-8 listed in the USA Writers of the Future competition. She practices martial arts, archery, knife-throwing, and musical instruments. Occasionally she even sleeps.

Website: **https://www.aikiflinthart.com/**

Twitter: @aikiflinthart

Facebook: **https://www.facebook.com/aiki.flinthart**

Instagram: AikiFlinthart

Lynne Lumsden Green Lynne Lumsden Green is enjoying the ageing process, contrary to all expectations. She writes both fiction and nonfiction, and owns more books than bookshelves. She has stories and articles published by Queensland Writing magazine, DailySF, AntipodeanSF, Aurealis magazine, and in over a dozen anthologies of fiction.

Blog at: **https://cogpunksteamscribe.wordpress.com/**

Jan-Andrew Henderson is the author of 24 teenage, YA and adult fiction and non-fiction books, published in the UK, USA, Germany and the Czech Republic He has been shortlisted for thirteen literary awards and is the winner of the Doncaster Book Prize and Royal Mail Award. He recently moved to Brisbane from Scotland, to see what the sun looked like.

Website: **https://www.janandrewhenderson.com/**

Pamela Jeffs is an Aurealis Award short-listed speculative fiction author from Queensland, Australia. She has numerous short fiction pieces published in national and international anthologies, collections and magazines.

Visit her at **https://www.pamelajeffs.com**

Facebook at @pamelajeffsauthor.

Cassandra Kelly is a writer of steampunk and fantasy and has interests in Australian colonial and ancient history. She has a love of warm weather, gardening, critical theory, and zombie movies, plus has a background in art and photography. Her first novel, *The Green Wave,* was released in 2019

Website: **https://www.cassandrakellyauthor.com**

Facebook: **https://www.facebook.com/CassandraKellyAuthor/**

DA Kelly is a writer and delighter in all things magic. Her stories are relentless, spellbinding mysteries stuffed full of quirky characters, wicked humour and delicious murder. She is writing the first book in her Arabella Black cosy paranormal mystery series, *Brooms Away*. If you like more magic with your murders then watch out for her upcoming novels.

Website:**http://dakellyfantasybooks.com**
Facebook:**https://www.facebook.com/grimsmead/**
Twitter: @dakellyauthor
Instagram:**https://www.instagram.com/dakellyauthor/**

Jem McCusker is a Brisbane based author best known for her Paranormal Romance and Middle Grade Fantasy books. When she's not learning yoga via you tube, she can be found herding small children to various music lessons and sporting activities
Website: **https://www.jemmcusker.com**

Caitlyn McPherson is an emerging author who lives in Brisbane with her feline overlord and pet fish. She could tell you about having studied Creative Writing and Children's Picture Book Writing and such boring stuff, but you just need to know she loves tea, reads a lot and writes YA, Sci-fi, and fantasy. In her spare time she dabbles in art, studies Japanese and is a student of Batojutsu.
Facebook and Instagram under the handle _CaitlynMcPherson_
Website: **https://caitlynmcpherson.wixsite.com/authorartist**

Caroline Molachino is a Brisbane based contemporary romance and women's fiction author. She's been studying the craft of writing for several years and aspires to have a positive impact on people's lives. Her goal is to create worlds in which readers laugh, cry and reflect on the meaning of life.

Instagram: @caroline_ann_writer

Twitter: @caroline_ann_

Monica Schultz is a High-School Mathematics teacher, with a passion for writing urban and historical fantasy. When she isn't writing or teaching, Monica enjoys curling up with her cat and a good book. Follow Monica on social media for upcoming works and updates on life's madness.

Instagram: @monicaschultzauthor

Facebook: @monicaschultzauthor

Twitter: @MonicaSchultz_

Website: **https://monicaschultzauthor.weebly.com/**

Sue Stubbs A dog always appears as a memorable character in Sue's family drama and romance stories. She has two short stories published in anthologies and is a regular web content contributor. In between band rehearsals, she is finishing her first novel unravelling a three generational family drama set in rural Australia.

Find her at **https://www.facebook.com/Sue-Stubbs-Author**

Georgia Willis lives in Sunny Queensland, with her fiancé Jake and their ever growing family of fish. Georgia has a keen interest in both fiction writing and Medical Science, and when she's not writing, or at her job as a scientist, she's down a rabbit hole learning random facts, like; did you know that banana plants can walk up to 40cm in their lifetime!

Keep an eye out for future anthologies from the Springfield Writers Group.
If you enjoyed this one, you can also find two other SWG anthologies at your favourite retailer.

RETURN
ELEMENTAL